COMING HOME

A Mirabelle Harbor Duet featuring
Rocket Man & Someone Like You

marilyn brant

Twelfth Night
Publishing

(Mirabelle Harbor, Book 6)

Coming Home:
A Mirabelle Harbor Duet
featuring Rocket Man & Someone Like You
(Mirabelle Harbor, Book 6)
Copyright © 2017 Marilyn B. Weigel
Twelfth Night Publishing

Cover Design © 2017 E.M. Tippetts Book Designs
Editor - Hamilton Editing
Proofreader - Kimberly Dawn
ISBN-13: 978-0-9983964-3-9

DEDICATION & THANKS

As always, my love and thanks to my family, my good friends, and my amazing readers & early reviewers—I can't express how much I appreciate each of you. An extra thank you to everyone on my personal Facebook page who read through (and tweaked) the Spanish phrases I used in this story. I'm so grateful to you all for your help!

Much love to all the readers/reviewers who've been special friends of this series, in particular: Margie Longoria, Jaleina Canales Aboud, Gina Reba, Kimberly Dawn, Gina Paulus, Stephanie Littlejohn, Brandy Morrison, Sheila Majczan, Vee Stojcevski, the Glenview Book Club, and the members of my FB page - "Marilyn Brant's Mirabelle Harbor Lounge."

And, finally, my deepest thanks to every reader who picked up one of the Mirabelle Harbor stories, took the time to recommend them to others, and/or wrote reviews for the books. COMING HOME is dedicated to YOU.

OTHER BOOKS BY MARILYN BRANT

According to Jane

Friday Mornings at Nine

A Summer in Europe

The Sweet Temptations Collection
~On Any Given Sundae
~Double Dipping
~Holiday Man

The Perfect Pair
~Pride, Prejudice and the Perfect Match
~Pride, Prejudice and the Perfect Bet

The Road to You
The Road and Beyond (expanded edition)

All About Us (novella)

The Mirabelle Harbor Series
~Take a Chance on Me
~The One That I Want
~You Give Love a Bad Name
~Stranger on the Shore
~One Night Love Affair
~Coming Home: A Mirabelle Harbor Duet
~Going for It (bonus crossover novella)

Wanderlust in Suburbia and Other Reflections on
Motherhood (nonfiction essays)

NOTE FROM THE AUTHOR

COMING HOME: A Mirabelle Harbor Duet featuring
ROCKET MAN & SOMEONE LIKE YOU is Book 6 in
Marilyn Brant's Mirabelle Harbor series,
but the two novellas in this collection and all of the
contemporary romances in this series can be enjoyed as
stand-alone stories.

ROCKET MAN

CHAPTER ONE

Sunday, October 22nd

Abby Solinski's flight from Sarasota to Chicago touched down four minutes ahead of schedule and taxied smoothly toward the Arrivals gate. Not that it mattered. Her brother, Allan, was picking her up from O'Hare, and he'd never been on time—let alone early—for anything in his entire, charmingly irresponsible life.

She had a full half hour to meander down to the baggage claim carousels, retrieve her luggage, text her best friends in Florida to let them know she'd landed safely, and eat the second half of a PB&J sandwich she'd packed for the trip, all before she spotted her big brother's dark red truck angling for a space in the pick-up lane.

"Hey, sis!" Allan called out with a wave through his open window.

"Hey, yourself," she called back, motioning for him to stay inside the vehicle. She had no trouble hefting her bags into the bed of the truck by herself, and she figured the sooner they got on the road, the better.

"Are we going home first or directly to the rehab

center?" she asked, slipping into the passenger seat and fastening her seatbelt. Allan had a lead foot.

Her brother grinned at her. "Nice to see you, too, Abby. Missed you."

She laughed. Always late, but always a sweetheart. At least deep down. That was her brother. "Missed you, too. But you know, Mom and Dad have me worried. What's the status today?"

He wrinkled his nose and glanced at the clock on the dashboard. "Dad's rehab session will be over for the afternoon by the time we get to Mirabelle Harbor, so we'd do better to head straight to the house. The doc said he's had a pretty bad knee and ankle injury, especially given his age, but he's hobbling around well enough, all things considered. It's Mom that's the bigger problem."

Allan didn't have to spell out the issues. Abby knew this story—every chapter, every verse, every predictable ending—because she'd lived it. And so had Allan. Their mom was a *hoverer* of the highest order. When one of her loved ones was sick, injured, or in any way indisposed, Jackie Solinski wouldn't leave that person's side. It was simultaneously endearing and suffocating.

"Has Dad announced that he's running away yet?"

Her brother laughed. "Only three times this weekend."

It was an old family joke. Their father was so notoriously frustrated by their mother's helicoptering behavior that he'd periodically claim he was going to pack up his battered army bag and run away like a disgruntled teen. One time, when Abby and Allan were kids, he'd actually gotten as far as the Mirabelle Harbor train station. With a hacking cough. And a fever of nearly 103. It took their mom and the help of two neighbors to collect him in their family's minivan and shuttle him back home and into bed again—where he belonged.

So, last Thursday, when their father tripped over an uncoiled garden hose in the backyard and fell onto the concrete patio, Allan met their parents at the clinic, noted the panicked look on both of their faces when the doc assessed the damage, and called Abby at once.

"We've got a situation up here," he said. "Any chance you can come home and help me run interference with the folks for a week or two?"

Abby spent the next two days rearranging job commitments at Floriday Excursions, the travel agency she worked at in Sarasota, and asking her best friends in town—Joy Canton, Lorelei Beck, and Marianna Gregory— to keep an eye on her condo and her soon-to-be-wilting houseplants.

She also worked part time at Joy's shop, The Beaded Periwinkle, but her friends didn't think twice about covering for her there. Marianna, who was originally from Mirabelle Harbor and who also split her time between Floriday Excursions and The Beaded Periwinkle, offered to work as many extra shifts for Abby as needed.

"Family is the most important thing," Marianna had said with a reassuring shoulder squeeze. "Go take care of your parents first. We'll muddle along here all right for a week or so."

"It just won't be nearly as fun without you," Joy said. "So don't forget to call and text us. We'll be thinking about you. And wondering what fresh mischief your brother is up to."

"Yeah," Lorelei added. "We remember all of those wild stories about Allan and his high school friends. Like a bunch of characters in a *MacGyver* episode."

It was true. Allan had always run with quite the inventively geeky crowd. How could she ever forget the hair-raising science fun of their youth...or his best buddy, "Rocket Rick" Zimmerman?

Abby glanced over at her brother as he navigated the left turn at an intersection, his cool confidence behind the wheel indicative of his command of all things mechanical, chemical, electrical, and combustible. At thirty-one, he was two years older than she, and in and out of more relationships than the lead singer of an alt-rock band. But despite his lack of punctuality and his tendency to cause inexplicable explosions at work, his boss at the chemical engineering lab *loved* him. If anyone could create cutting-edge technology and revolutionize the field, it was her brilliant bro, Allan.

As they passed through the suburbs surrounding lakeside Mirabelle Harbor and then, finally, into their hometown proper, her brother nudged her. "Is it weird to be back?"

"A little. Sure," she admitted. Not that she hadn't seen her parents or her brother in the nearly six years since she'd driven away from Mirabelle Harbor, alongside her ex-boyfriend, Chandler Michaelsen. But it had been a *long* while since she'd seen her family *here*.

An avalanche of memories cascaded through her brain as she and Allan wound their way across town. Rick...Chandler...her younger self... Oh, hell.

Was it good to be back home—or not?

Too early to say.

With their grandparents living just outside of Louisville, most of their big family holiday gatherings were held at their house, a common meeting ground in Kentucky. A few times, her parents had flown down to Sarasota during the winter for a nice warm getaway from the Midwestern chill. And for Abby, living as she did now in the land of towering palm trees and orange groves, seeing the streets of home, lined with sugar maples, made the bittersweet memories rush through her mind even faster.

"The trees are on fire," she observed, stating the obvious and hoping her mixed emotions weren't too apparent to her one and only sibling. "I've missed that burst of color in the fall."

"It's a simple chemical process," Allan said smugly. "But, I grant you, it can be stunning." Then, after a beat, "Don't tell me you got sick of all those tropical plants down in Florida."

"Not a chance." But, while she had no intention of telling her brother this, the truth was that she'd been desperately homesick for a long time. Seeing these familiar old places in Mirabelle Harbor brought back the first two decades of her life with stunning force.

And despite the painful recollections of young love found and then lost, she still felt the stirrings of nostalgia and a weird sort of awakening, just being back here.

"You, um, haven't seen any of the Michaelsens recently, have you?" she asked.

"*Any* of the Michaelsens, or *one* particular member of the family?" Then, not waiting for her to answer, he added, "I've seen his brothers around town. Mostly Blake, since he likes to hang out at Max's Pub. And I heard something about Chance getting married, but I haven't seen his twin. I think the asshat is still in Atlanta."

"Chandler isn't an asshat," she muttered automatically, although she knew he must have appeared that way to those closest to her.

"He acted like one."

"I know, but—" She paused. "Chandler was just haunted, for want of a better word, by some ghost that possessed his spirit and made him restless. He was trying to outrun something. A memory, or maybe a nightmare."

She'd spent the better part of five years trailing around the U.S. with him in search of a place where he could finally settle down. After nine cities, she'd had enough. When he left Sarasota to head northward, she stayed and built up a network of friends who were priceless. Even if Florida wasn't home, precisely. She hadn't been ready to return to Mirabelle Harbor then. Not alone.

As they drove past Sloppy Joe's, where she and

Chandler had eaten countless cheeseburgers, the meaning behind Allan's words finally caught up with her. "Wait— you said his twin brother is engaged? To whom? And when is the wedding?"

"Do I look like the *Mirabelle Harbor Gazette*'s society page? Christ, Abby. I just know Chance's fiancée is Nia Pappayiannis, daughter of the owners of that Greek restaurant and bakery downtown."

"The Gala?"

"That's the one. But I don't know when they're getting hitched." He shrugged.

Olivia would know. Married to Derek, the eldest of the Michaelsen siblings, Olivia had the inside scoop on everything. And though Abby wasn't nearly as close to her as Marianna was (those two had been BFFs since before Marianna moved down to Sarasota, where she was now dating Joy's brother Gil), Abby knew Olivia well enough to ask.

Not that she wanted to call Olivia out of the blue for that reason alone. Fortunately, she had another excuse, thanks to Marianna. Of course if she ran into Sharlene, Chandler's only sister, Shar would tell her, too. In any case, if Chance was getting married, Chandler would surely be coming back to Mirabelle Harbor for *that*. And Abby had to know exactly when that might be, so she could stay the hell away from town.

"Well, maybe if you run into Blake on one of your wild nights of trolling for women at Max's, he'll tell you," she said to her brother.

"Well, Blake's not one for so many nights of wildness anymore," Allan said on a sigh. "His girlfriend is keeping him in line. Women. It's all about control for them."

"Oh, that's such BS." Her brother's inability to keep a good relationship going was legendary, but mostly because he was still so hung up on his grad-school girlfriend, Becca, who'd broken up with him because she'd said he was acting "too jealous, too suspicious, and too possessive." All completely true.

"Maybe," he admitted, pulling into their parents' driveway. "But I'm finally going to go out this Friday night and get some real action, now that I've got my wingman back in town."

An icy shiver crept up her spine. There was only *one* friend he'd ever called his "wingman," but it couldn't be Rick Zimmerman, could it? The guy was off the grid. In Asia. Working on God knew what, but it had to be some intricate physics thing.

"It's gonna be epic," her brother declared. "Rick is back for a big physics convention in Chicago, and he always knows how to make a night a blast." Allan laughed at his own juvenile joke.

"A blast indeed," Abby whispered. How many objects had the two of them blown to smithereens since they became buddies in junior high? Nothing was safe when the pair of them were together. Including, but not limited to, her heart, which was racing as if she were competing in the Chicago Marathon.

Much as she'd had a complicated dating history with Chandler, her crush and intense feelings of attraction for Rick had predated even that relationship.

Suddenly, her stay in Mirabelle Harbor seemed infinitely more dangerous. "You two are, um, going out on Friday?"

"We are," Allan replied, eyeing her curiously.

Whew. At least Rick wouldn't be a factor in her life until then. She might not even see him, if she could convince Allan to just meet him at the bar.

"There's no need to look so worried, Abby," her brother continued, as they hopped out of his truck. "I'm not gonna leave you alone to watch over Mom and Dad for more than a night or two this week. Rick knows about the situation with the folks, and he knows you're in town again, too. He said he was looking forward to catching up with you in person as well."

She almost tripped walking on the smooth asphalt. "Did he?"

"Oh, yeah," Allan said breezily, grabbing her suitcases and striding to the front door. He turned abruptly toward her and added with a grin, "Which is why he's coming over for dinner tonight. Just Mom, Dad, you, me, and Rick. Like old times."

Abby felt the blood from her head race to her feet and her brain flash with a neon slideshow of repressed memories, like a feature presentation entitled "Abby's Most Embarrassing Moments: The Early Years."

Holy High-School Nightmare, Batman.

Rocket Rick was back in town and, soon, he was going to be on her doorstep.

.

CHAPTER TWO

Sunday Night

Rick Zimmerman arrived promptly at the Solinski residence—two piping hot carryout pizza boxes in hand—and feeling every bit the awkward seventeen-year-old kid he once was.

Just a large oak door separated him from the girl he'd always fantasized about, and also from the father figure who'd warned Rick in No Uncertain Terms to keep his teenage mitts off his young daughter.

He checked his watch. Six thirty on the dot. But his finger wavered for a split second before he worked up the nerve to press the doorbell.

Abby Solinski. Back home again.

No longer Sweet Sixteen.

And, at twenty-nine and an independent woman (still single, according to her brother), anything might happen. At least he hoped so.

Mrs. S swung open the door and welcomed him inside.

"Ricky!" She took the pizzas from his hands, set them down, and then hugged him with the fierceness of a den mother. "Look at you. You're a grown man. But I would've recognized that adorable smile of yours anywhere."

Rick felt himself blush. No one had called him "Ricky" in a decade at least.

"Appreciate that, Mrs. S. You look lovely and haven't changed one bit since Allan and I graduated from high school."

She laughed off the compliment, but he could tell she was pleased. Also, he wasn't stretching the truth by much. She'd aged well over the past dozen years. Her husband a little less so, he noticed, when Mr. S hobbled into the room.

"Who have we got here?" Allan and Abby's dad asked with a tired but genuine grin. The man whom Rick had often wished had been his own father throughout his school years seemed to have shrunk slightly in stature, and his face was lined with new wrinkles that deepened whenever he grimaced in pain. This happened with every step the older man took toward him.

Rick worked to minimize the distance between them by taking several long strides over to Warren Solinski. He stuck out his hand. "Hello, sir. Very nice to see you."

"Likewise, Rick. Our son just ran to the store to gather up some decent beverages. Not that I can have any booze while I'm on these damn meds, but that shouldn't stop you young people." He leaned forward to mock whisper, "And I figured some wine might get my wife to loosen her grip on micromanaging me for a night."

Mrs. S rolled her dark eyes. "He's such a high-maintenance drama king when he's injured, Ricky. You have no idea."

Rick laughed and glanced around the room. Allan's absence had been adequately explained, but where was Abby?

He'd obviously not been circumspect enough in his glancing because Mr. S—in physical pain or not—had lost none of his sharpness or observational acuity. "Our daughter is putting the finishing touches on some special fudge brownies she's making. You know how Abby likes her desserts." He raised one thin, knowing, gray eyebrow at Rick, as if the guy had Superman's x-ray vision and could read every single one of Rick's erotic daydreams about Abby.

Oh, shit.

"Er, yeah. She's still got a sweet tooth, then?" he asked. How freakin' lame. But what else could he say? That he'd imagined Mr. S's daughter covered in ribbons of caramel and hot fudge sauce more than once during his adolescence? Uh, no. He'd stick with his stupid-ass conversation.

"She does," her dad replied. "Though we keep encouraging her to go for healthier options. In *all* things."

Rick nodded mutedly. Nothing subtle about that warning, was there?

For a strange instant, it occurred to him that, maybe, he'd been over-expecting when it came to seeing Abby again. After all, it'd been about ten years since they'd spoken in person. Not that he hadn't stalked her a little on social media, just to see what she'd posted. Or if she'd married that A-hole, Chandler Michaelsen. Or anyone else, for that matter.

But keeping tabs on his best buddy's kid sister was one thing. Actually being face to face with his teenage crush was another. That little zing of attraction he'd always felt existed between them might have only been a figment of his imagination. Or it may have faded with the passing years so much as to be irrelevant. How could he assume that either of them would feel even a twinge of—

A stunning, curvaceous blonde strode into the room, wearing a simple pink T-shirt and jeans, and carrying the enticing scent of chocolate on the air current as she entered.

"Hello, Rick," she said, smiling tentatively at him with lips as red as Jupiter's swirling spot, cheeks as pink as her

T-shirt, and eyes as insightful and blue as he remembered.

And he knew, as his mouth ran dry and he struggled to swallow, that he'd gotten it all wrong.

He hadn't anticipated too much. Like an unprepared research assistant, he'd expected far too little from this encounter. The power of his attraction to Abby was going to be a statistically significant force that wouldn't be easily controlled. Not by her protective father or by her chitchatty mother. Not by her fun-loving brother. And not by him, either.

If a collision of their two bodies was going to be averted this week, only Abby would be able to stop it from happening. But Rick fully intended to do everything humanly possible to let nature's pull take its course.

C'mon, gravity. Have at it.

With the briefest apologetic glance at Mr. S, he radiated his most winning grin at the golden-haired goddess standing before him. "Abby," he said. "It's so good to see you again."

Oh, dear gawd. Somebody help her out of this quagmire.

When did Mirabelle Harbor's biggest science nerd turn into Chicagoland's most irresistible charmer?

Abby stared at Rocket Rick. He'd filled out. He'd always been tall, but now he was broad-shouldered and more muscular than his adolescent frame would have suggested possible.

And his lips. They were grinning at her. And moving. Saying things she had yet to comprehend. Or, really, even hear.

"Abby?" Rick looked at her quizzically, and she knew she'd missed something important.

"S-Sorry. What was that?" she managed to ask.

"Sweetie, Ricky just asked if you wanted some help getting things ready in the kitchen," her mother supplied, retrieving the pizzas he'd brought and setting them in the middle of their dining room table.

"I—uh, no. It's all good," Abby said. "Thanks for bringing the main course, Rick. We've got salad and corn on the cob and Mom's green-bean casserole and—"

"And an amazing dessert, from what I can smell," he said with a sensuous licking of his lips that rendered her speechless again.

"And booze," boomed a voice across the room, as her brother burst through the front door with two large brown bags, presumably filled with alcohol. "Dude, you're here!"

"Allan, buddy. It's been an ice age," Rick said, grinning.

"A Pleistocene epoch," Allan replied, a silly geeky greeting that dated back to eighth grade at least, as they man-hugged each other. "How've you been?" Her brother pulled a cold beer out of one of the bags and handed it to his friend. "Take one and start talking. We wanna hear about everything that's going on with you. Right, gang?"

The remaining members of Abby's family professed intense interest in hearing what Rick had been up to since he'd started working for ProtoStratus Labs, but Abby knew she was the *most* interested. Not only in finding out what he'd done and was currently doing, but in what he planned to do. In the near future. Like tomorrow or Tuesday. So she could figure out where *not* to be. The guy made her so darned nervous.

"It's nothing too exciting, really," he told them with an air of either modesty or conversational deflection, Abby couldn't be sure. "And you all already know the big stuff anyway. Finished high school—"

Yeah. With a perfect GPA.

"—got my college degree—"

Degrees, plural. Including a PhD in astrophysics, no less.

"—and started work at the lab—"

A "lab" that required *top-secret government clearance* at the upper levels, where Rick worked, of course.

He shrugged. "I recently finished up a project in Japan—"

A *confidential* project, according to her brother, that somehow involved a particle accelerator. Abby knew better than to ask for specifics.

"—and I'm back here for the convention this week. After that, we'll see what turns up." He directed his incisive gaze at her. "How's Florida been for you, Abby? I heard you were working for a travel agency. That sounds interesting! Are you enjoying it?"

She laughed. Yep. He was definitely trying to deflect attention away from himself. Fine. She'd play along. "You know, it's not particle physics, but it has its highlights."

He grinned at her, took a few steps forward, and leaned close, effectively blocking her vision of the rest of her family and making her feel like she and Rick were the only two people in the room. "What's one of them?"

She considered the things she loved about working at Floriday Excursions and knew her answer right away. "The excitement of the people who book the trips and getaways. There's such a spirit of hopefulness and adventure as they make their plans."

"And what about for you? Do you use your employee discount to sightsee across the state?"

"Not often," she admitted. "I've done enough traveling."

A dark expression crossed his face, one that left Abby in no doubt that Rick knew precisely what she was referring to. Or, rather, *whom.*

Rick and Allan had been high school seniors when she and Chandler were sophomores, and even though she'd had a bigger crush on Rick than on Chandler initially, she still remembered how different the two guys were and how they both had an acute, longstanding distrust of each other. She couldn't count the number of times Chandler had asked her, once they finally started dating as juniors, if she and Rick had ever hooked up.

"No! Not even close," she'd assured her then-boyfriend.

But the bad-boy teen said of the science nerd, "Good. Because I just don't like him. He looks at you funny."

And that feeling of dislike was definitely mutual. She and Chandler had been together for three years when Rick returned to Mirabelle Harbor from college in New York to visit.

"You're *still* going out with that Michaelsen punk? The evil twin?" Rick had said.

"He's not evil," Abby had replied, rolling her eyes as dramatically as she could.

Rick had prodded her with questions about why she hadn't gone off to college out of state, like she'd originally planned, and he learned that it was largely because Chandler insisted on staying in the Chicago suburbs. When Abby said she lived at home and went to school nearby, Rick's jaw tensed. Then he'd crossed his arms, which were much scrawnier back then. And he'd also scowled. "Maybe he's not *evil*...but he's just bad for *you*."

Unfortunately, it took Abby several years before she finally came to that same conclusion for herself.

"Yo," her brother interjected, pulling Abby back to the present. "Can we take this work discussion to the table? I'm starved."

Abby quickly stepped back from Rick and surveyed the room. Allan was busying himself unloading beverages, but their mother was staring at her with a curious smile, and their dad shot her a look that was simultaneously baffled and distressed.

Rick, however, had his attention riveted on her and, from the speculative look in his eyes, his big brainiac mind was whirling. That always spelled trouble.

Abby wasn't sure how she made it through dinner. Her stomach roiled relentlessly, and she barely managed to finish half her plate. Every time Rick's gaze caught hers, something happened inside of her, but she couldn't quite identify it. Honestly, it was less like the fluttery excitement of flirting, and more like flu symptoms.

On top of it all, her father was acting strangely. She attributed this to his feelings of frustration with his recent injury and the difficulty he had moving so much as a muscle without pain, as well as his obvious exasperation with Mom's hovering.

He stood up and reached for a slice of pepperoni pizza, lost his balance, and fell back into his chair. Mom got too solicitous for his liking, and Dad's irritation spiked.

Allan spent much of the meal jabbering about his post-Becca dating woes. "Can't wait for our night on the town," he said to Rick. "Are you sure you're not free until Friday?"

"Unfortunately, no," Rick replied. "The convention gets going early tomorrow morning, and they keep us pretty busy throughout the week. But Friday night will be fun." And, again, he gazed at Abby with an expression so thoughtful, serious, and contemplative, it would have been almost calculating, had he been a different man.

But he wasn't.

He was *Rick*, she reminded herself. And he'd rebuffed her timid teen-girl advances years ago. He wasn't going to be interested in her now.

The conversation at the table swerved around to her

father's knee and ankle trauma, and Rick dutifully asked questions about his rehab schedule. But none of those distractions quelled the queasiness of sexual tension Abby was feeling in her gut, however pointless.

She thought of her string of post-Chandler flirtations. There'd only been a few, and most weren't even relationships, just brief crushes. Like on the pool boy at her condo complex in Florida or her favorite pizza delivery guy. The handful of actual dates she'd gone on were unremarkable, lackluster, and short-lived.

She found herself wondering about Rick, who played his dating history very close to the vest, despite Allan's attempts to loosen his lips with alcohol and questions during the evening. Even the Mirabelle Harbor gossip mill never had much dirt on Rick. Although, she supposed it had to be easier to keep a low profile when a person lived on another continent and was accustomed to doing classified projects for NASA or something.

"And how are your parents?" Mom asked Rick.

His response was careful, Abby couldn't help but notice. "Same as ever," he said with a quick, brittle smile, and Abby knew his relationship with his stepfather was probably just as distant as it'd ever been. Rick's real dad had died when he was two, and his mom remarried when he was in the sixth grade. It was what had brought his family to Mirabelle Harbor originally.

When Rick admitted that he wasn't staying at the conference hotel in the city, but here in town—somewhat reluctantly—just because his mother had insisted, Abby knew that none of Rick's feelings about his mom and stepfather had changed in the past decade.

And it made her sad.

He'd always seemed so happy to hang out with her family, even if there was a persistent undercurrent of awkwardness between the two of them.

"So, tell us about this convention of yours," Dad asked,

rather formally, Abby thought. "What's the schedule like?"

"Tomorrow it'll be the opening lecture in Chicago, followed by a long day of workshops and seminars. In the evening, there'll be the Physics Slam at the conference center, and—"

"What's a Physics Slam?" Mom demanded to know. "Sounds a bit rowdy."

Abby, Allan, and Rick all laughed. Dad just looked suspicious.

Rick launched into an account of the event, looking relieved to finally get to stop talking about his parents. "It's kind of like a talent show, where everyone uses something cool and familiar to explain a complicated physics concept. Like writing a poem or a song about one of Abby's incredible brownies as a way of describing the science behind the cooking process." He sent her one of his sexy grins as he mimed doing a dance number around her pan of fudge brownies. "It's stuff like that, only the concepts discussed are significantly less delicious. But the researchers try to be creative, using weird analogies, raps, and audience interactive performances to get tough topics across to lay people."

"Sounds like an exciting and active week," Abby told him a few minutes later, when he helped her carry a load of dishes to the sink.

It was just the two of them in the kitchen, and she tried to bury herself in the cleaning up, fully expecting him to leave and join Allan and her parents in the living room.

He didn't.

Instead, he moved closer to her until little more than a few inches separated them. "I wasn't entirely forthcoming with your brother," he whispered, and the tiny hairs on her skin started dancing around on her forearms. "Tomorrow will definitely be a hectic day, and there's nothing I can do about that. But I'm willing to skip out on all of Tuesday night's sessions—if you're willing to spend the evening with me. Just the two of us." He paused and waited until she stopped futzing with the dishes in the sink. "Abby, what do you say?"

"Um," she replied, ever so eloquently, and finally met his gaze. "*This* Tuesday?"

He laughed, soft and low, and the butterflies that'd been in her belly since he arrived started flapping their wings and causing that vaguely ill sensation again.

"I'm only in town for a week. So, yes. *This* Tuesday."

"Oh, I'm sure you have other things you want to do, now that you're back in the area—"

"No, I don't," he said, cutting her off and shaking his head for emphasis. "Let me pick you up and take you out on the town. It'll give me something to look forward to after a couple of days of endless workshops. Say yes. Please."

Well, if he was going to insist. "Yes," she murmured.

"Good. Maybe don't mention it to your family, though." He eyed the entrance to the living room with an edge of apprehension. "At least not yet." Then he squeezed her hand, and it singed all five of her fingers with blistering desire.

Before she could say anything else, he pulled his hand away like she'd burned him, flashed her a brilliant grin, and bolted out of the room.

CHAPTER THREE

Monday Night, October 23rd

The Physics Slam was in full swing.

Rick glanced around the auditorium and saw a sea of intrigued faces, young and old, lit with delight at the creative way major topics in the field were being explained to the audience. It could be a heady experience. He remembered the first time he'd come to one. It'd been like the science equivalent of a rock concert.

But, while this was usually his favorite event at the International Physicists Convention, tonight he was having a devil of a time concentrating.

Some university guy was rapping about quarks and neutrons with a few members of his department, but all Rick could think about was particle collision in the form of human physical attraction or, basically, what it would be like to finally kiss Abby.

When she mentioned that she'd traveled "enough" last night, he'd had to compute factorials mentally to keep from swearing aloud. He'd *hated* Chandler Michaselsen with every nerdy fiber of his being during high school and college. That guy was *so* cool. *So* popular. *So* able to quickly and easily capture Abby's attention and, for whatever reason, not set off warning bells in her father's head.

Which was still a sore spot for Rick. How the hell had Mr. S preferred Chandler as a boyfriend for Abby over him? The Michaelsen family was a decent one— admittedly, they had to be less screwed up than his own— but Chandler himself had been such an ass. Rick still wanted to knock him out cold for winning Abby's heart and, then, hurting her. No way could he relax until he knew for sure that she was truly over the prick.

A new rap began with the same University of Chicago team. They were good. This time entertaining the crowd with some double entendre sexiness in the form of molecules pumping and grinding. At least that was what Rick saw when he watched them rap and dance onstage. And the audience was loving it.

See? Geeky science guys had *skillz*. His peers knew all about action and reaction, cause and effect, the scientific method of observation, and hypothesis testing. Most men liked to think they were good in bed. Rick wasn't prone to bragging, but he *knew* he was in the upper ten percent on that particular bell curve. He'd never been satisfied with hypotheticals. He preferred hard data—emphasis on hard— gleaned from hours of trial and error. He was very observant and knew exactly what to do based on years of prior "experiments" with his subjects. He refused to accept any outcome that didn't result in his ex-lovers' exceptional levels of satisfaction. It had always been a point of some pride.

Rick had been waiting a long time for this chance with Abby. He wasn't going to fiddle with a process that worked. Once he had her in his arms, he knew what to do. She would be the recipient of one hundred percent of his attention and experience. All he needed was to get her alone for one night and watch for her unique signals—the ones that would tell him how she liked to be touched and when he could begin doing it. And that opportunity was less than twenty-four hours away.

Rick wasn't someone who'd make reckless bets, but he intended to be so good that she wouldn't be able to think about any other man on the planet but him. That, and her absolute pleasure, were the only outcomes he would accept.

He pushed his notebook and pen away, leaned back in his chair, and studied the dancing molecules with renewed interest.

Tuesday Night, October 24th

Abby felt the nagging sensation of nervous energy—building and circling throughout her body—with each passing hour of the day. By twilight, she was nearly pulsing with anticipation.

True to her word, she hadn't mentioned tonight's planned get together with Rick to her family yet, but she was going to have to come up with some explanation for her evening disappearance soon. Allan had promised she wouldn't be the only one at home with their folks this week, but he'd been at work during the weekdays and, last night, he told her he was only going to be gone an hour and was, instead, away for nearly four. Her brother was here tonight, though, and he owed her a little break.

Especially since Rocket Rick didn't seem inclined to just hang out at their house, watching *Wheel of Fortune* and the usual Tuesday night TV lineup with her and her parents all evening.

She got an after-dinner text from him saying, "Leaving the conference center now. I'll be at the end of your parents' driveway in 26 minutes."

"That's very precise," she replied.

"Loretta never lies."

Abby's heart jumped. Was he with a woman? One he apparently trusted implicitly with directions? "Who's Loretta?" she typed.

"My GPS system," came his fast reply, and she laughed. This was a bad sign when the mere mention of another female's name made her immediately and irrationally jealous. She needed to take a step back and seriously chill. She and Rick were just friends. Very old friends. Period.

"I'll be ready," she texted. "Would you like to come in when you get here or shall I meet you outside?"

"Meet me outside, if you can. I really just want to spend tonight with you."

Well, that was direct. And not entirely friend-ish. Huh.

The TV contestant was solving the final word puzzle when Abby pulled her brother aside and said she was going out for a few hours.

"Really?" Allan said, squinting at her. "Meeting friends?"

"Something like that," she told him.

"Who?" he asked.

She grabbed her purse and pretended not to hear him. "I'll be back in a bit," she said loudly to her parents, who were staring with rapt attention at the lady guessing letters on the screen. Abby waved to all three of them and slipped out of the house before Allan could repeat his question.

Thankful for the cover of darkness, Rick's rental car wasn't easily spotted idling just past the driveway. She hopped in, he grinned at her, and they sped away.

"Allan's going to be ticked when he finds out that we spent the evening together and didn't include him," Abby said, trying to get used to seeing Rick again for only the second time in a decade. She still was a little thrown by being so close to this...this *man* he'd become.

Rick shrugged. "He wasn't planning on including you when he and I go out this Friday. So, I say turnabout is fair play."

She smiled. "All right. Be sure to tell him that when he complains. Where would you like to go tonight?"

"I was planning on Max's Pub, but then I remembered that the Blackhawks are playing against the Maple Leafs tonight. It's their first matchup of the regular season, so the place will probably be crawling with hockey fans."

"Would you like to try the new wine bar next door to Max's? I haven't been there, but my mom mentioned it was getting pretty popular."

"Sure," he said, driving toward Harbor Square.

The Lounge, Abby realized, wasn't exactly new to the year-round residents of Mirabelle Harbor. From the looks of it, as they stood outside and waited for a group to leave so they could enter, the place had become rather well established during the past few years. But, of course, neither she nor Rick had been around to experience it before tonight.

This made her feel two oddly conflicting emotions. She was like a stranger visiting here for the first time while, simultaneously, feeling like she'd been rocketed back to her teen years in her hometown and all was unchanged, just because she and Rick were standing side by side.

"Hey, if you don't like the look of it, Abby, we can ditch. Plenty of other places to grab a drink."

"Oh, it's not that. Here is fine." She glanced at him, studying his handsome face for a moment.

"What then?"

"It's just weird, you know? Being back in town, but not everything's the same as when we left. I'm sleeping in my old room at my parents' house. I'm almost thirty, but just being there takes me back to high school."

He laughed. "Tell me about it."

The entry into The Lounge cleared. He led her inside and they found seats at a tiny table in the corner. Out of the way. Almost quiet.

"My mom and stepdad still treat me like I'm seventeen," he told her. "Just walking into their house made me want to race down to the basement to play videogames on my old Atari."

"Do they still make those?"

"Hell, no. I might be able to find a few on eBay, but Franken-Father threw out my entire system as soon as I stopped coming home for regular holiday visits. He always hated it when I stayed up late to play games."

She hadn't been sure whether to broach the subject of Frank, Rick's stepfather, but since he'd brought him up and used the old nickname, maybe Rick wanted to talk. Or vent. Or something.

"So, your relationship with him is still pretty tense, huh?"

He shrugged. "Not tense so much as nonexistent. Frank has a tendency to want to erase me from the house and from my mom's life as much as possible. Mom just barely stopped him from turning my old bedroom into a ten-by-ten display case for his fishing trophies. He's removed most traces of me from the other rooms, though. Mom still has a photo of the two of us on the mantle, and she managed to keep a couple of postcards I'd sent her from Japan taped to the refrigerator. Aside from those tiny clues, I'm pretty sure no one who walked in their home would guess she had a son."

That Rick spoke those words without overt bitterness surprised Abby. And she couldn't help but wonder how he could express anything other than resentment and frustration toward his stepfather. She felt both of those, along with a flash of anger, on his behalf.

"That really sucks," she murmured.

"Yeah, well, what can you do? We don't pick our

26

families."

She nodded, but she realized that—in her case—that wasn't entirely true. Once she'd made the decision to stay in Sarasota, she'd chosen a surrogate family. Friends like Joy, Lorelei, and Marianna were women she'd come to love like sisters. Not that she didn't still feel close to her brother and her parents, but just because she'd never had a biological sister, it didn't mean a relationship like that was closed off to her forever. Her BFFs were living proof.

"So, um, what about friends?" she asked him. "I mean, at your job and where you live. Are there any, um...special people in your life?"

He looked amused. "*Special* people? What are you asking, Abby? If I have a girlfriend—or, perhaps, several?"

She could feel herself blushing.

Okay. So subtlety wasn't exactly her forte but, given the vibe she'd been getting from him, she had to know his relationship status. Unless she'd been completely hallucinating, Rick seemed to be giving out signals that indicated some sort of interest in her. Abby had to know if it was a completely platonic thing—the joy of reconnecting with an old friend—or, maybe, if it might mean something more.

They'd each ordered a glass of red wine when they came in, and Abby downed about half of hers before replying. "Yeah, I guess that's what I'm asking. About girlfriends, singular or plural."

He gulped some of his wine, too, before he replied. "Nope. Neither. There've been a few short-term romances. I mean, I haven't been a monk during the past decade. But nothing especially serious. Not like your relationship record."

She stiffened at this reference to Chandler. "Well, that one is long over."

"Is it?" He looked into her eyes so earnestly that she was riveted to her chair. His blue irises pierced her with a gaze of both intensity and something else. It almost looked like longing.

"Yes," she whispered. And even though her response was a soft one, the definitive ring of certainty in her tone was unmistakable. Even she could hear it in her voice. When she and Chandler parted ways in Florida, it had been a permanent decision.

Rick didn't say anything more about that, he just finished his drink and motioned for her to do the same. Then he pulled out some cash for the waitress, pushed himself to standing, and held out his hand to her. "Let's take a walk, Abby."

She placed her palm in his large one and was instantly reminded of the only other time she'd held his hand. It was her freshman year in high school and his junior year. Her grandma had just passed away, and they'd been close. She was crying by herself in the backyard, and Rick had stopped by with flowers—a condolence gift from his mother to her family. He spoke briefly to Allan, but then he'd found Abby, reached to take her hand, and pulled her into an awkward but comfortingly warm hug. She'd sobbed all over his shirt, but he just kept holding her for what felt like ten minutes. He kept his fingers laced with hers, even after they broke apart. In fact, he didn't let go until he heard the screen door to the patio slide open. Her dad came out to find her and take her to the funeral. Only then did Rick spring away.

Funny. She hadn't thought about that moment in ages.

Rick's mind seemed to be a thousand light-years away, too, but he held her hand firmly as they left The Lounge. Who knew what he was remembering?

She got a sense of what he was thinking a few minutes later, though, when they were strolling across Harbor Square, a new chill in the autumn air and the distinctive sounds of high schoolers with their car windows rolled down, calling out to each other on Cherry Avenue. They were honking their horns and laughing and making a general nuisance of themselves.

"I hated almost every second of high school," he murmured, tugging her closer. "Except when I was with you and your family. Or when I was riding my motorcycle."

Abby remembered the beat-up, secondhand Kawasaki he'd fixed up and driven around town. "Still got it somewhere?"

"Nope. Another casualty of Franken-Father's spring cleaning session one year. But, in all fairness, by the time I graduated from high school, it was mostly held together only by rust and hope. Loved it, though."

He had. She half suspected that he'd gotten so good at physics as a byproduct of his love of that motorcycle. She could see now what an escape it must have been for him.

They ambled around the Square for a long while—holding hands, window shopping, and chatting casually about things they remembered from years ago. It was a strangely easy to talk with him, despite all of the time that had gone by, although she couldn't quite pull her mind away from the way their fingers were entwined. And when he rubbed the back of her hand with his thumb, the sheer sensuality of this small movement made her pulse quicken and her skin tingle. Whether it was intentional or not, he was making her want him. And that was hazardous to her heart.

So, when her cell phone beeped with an incoming text, she pulled away—half reluctant, half relieved.

Allan.

"Hey, just letting you know Mom and Dad are going to bed, and I'm headed back to my place to crash for the night. They seem fine, so you can stay out later, if you'd like. Just be quiet coming in."

"Thanks!" she replied to her brother. "I appreciate the heads up. See you tomorrow after you're done with work."

Allan sent her a thumbs-up emoji and she put her phone away.

"Everything okay?" Rick asked.

"Yeah. All is well at home." She shivered as the wind gusted through the open space between the trees, the chill seeping beneath the light fabric of her sweater. Clearly, she'd gotten too accustomed to the Floridian climate in the last couple of years. Her blood was thinning.

Rick pulled her close to him—almost instinctively, it seemed—and wrapped his arm around her shoulders. This, she realized, was both better and worse than holding hands. She wasn't remotely cold anymore but, surrounded as she was by his body heat, her desire for him spiked even higher than before. She knew she was treading on extremely dangerous ground.

But this desire only grew with each minute in Rick's company. And she could blame her heightened emotions for many things: Her continually flushed skin. Her erratic heartbeat. Her very inappropriate fantasies, featuring Rick and his hot motorcycle. And, also, her improved memory, which kept uncovering little nuggets from their youth and offering them up to her for examination.

"Allan still has his," she murmured.

"His what?"

"His copycat motorcycle," she told Rick. "Because, of course, he had to be *just* like you back then, remember? Monkey see, monkey d—"

"Where?" He stopped abruptly in the middle of the sidewalk and turned to face her.

"Where what?"

"Where's his bike?"

"Oh. I spotted it in the back of my parents' garage when I threw out the trash yesterday. But it's a wreck, Rick. It's been broken for at least five years. It's probably beyond repair."

Rick raised his eyebrows and the corners of his lips shot

upward. "C'mon. You know I love this stuff, and the night's still young. Take me to this hunk of junk and let me see it for myself."

His buddy's old bike was a dented-up, tin can, piece of shit that deserved to get crushed at the yard, but Rick's heart filled with pure lust the instant he laid eyes on it. A degree of lust that was second only to what he was feeling for the beautiful woman who'd brought him here.

He'd spent the first half of the night attempting to calm his worries that she could actually hear his pounding heart when he was next to her and the other half trying to engineer just the right moment to kiss her breathless.

Truth be told, he was still working on both, but the motorcycle had given him a good idea, and he'd take the gifts offered to him without complaint.

He glanced at Abby's disbelieving facial expression and almost laughed aloud. She was adorable.

"You can't be serious," she said, when he pulled her dad's toolbox from the garage shelf and flipped it open. "This thing isn't fixable."

"I'm a physicist, remember? I build rockets. This isn't even much of a challenge."

She looked flustered. "But, Rick, even if you get it to run, it'll be too dangerous to ride."

"Not true."

"It sure as heck is! What's the deal with you men and your hot wheels? Allan almost got himself killed half a dozen times on that thing. Chandler had some kind of Harley fetish, and he finally bought one in Florida when we broke up. I got to keep the car." She crossed her arms and glared at him. "And you—you still miss that death trap on two wheels that you used to ride. It's crazy. I don't know how any of you can feel safe on one of these things."

Rick, kneeling by the back tire, had already assessed the damage to the bike and knew the fix was surprisingly simple. Allan hadn't been as heavy into motorcycle maintenance as he'd been, so there was a common engine part that needed to be replaced—he knew where he could get it tonight—and a few bolts that could use a bit of tightening. One quick stop at the hardware store. Plus, a little muscle. Whole thing shouldn't take more than an hour total. But hearing Chandler's name got his hackles up.

"A sense of security and safety on a motorcycle has everything to do with who's driving, Abby. Trust me."

"Why should I?"

He glanced at his precision watch and tapped the shatterproof glass with his index finger. "Because by ten o'clock tonight, we're going to take this baby out for a spin."

She actually snorted. "You're delusional. I am *not* riding on that heap of rusted metal with you or with anyone else."

He stood up and crossed the space between them with three long strides, until he was near enough to feel her uneven breaths on his skin. It was all he could do not to crush her mouth with his right then and there. But he was a strategist, and he knew how to be patient.

Evoking the one ace he knew he had up his sleeve, he leaned in close and whispered, "Oh, yes, you will, Abby Solinski. And you know why? Because you bet me one favor—no questions asked—that I couldn't catch that baseball senior year. And I *did.* I've been waiting over a dozen years to collect on that. Now, it's pay-up time."

She shook her head, wavy blond strands swaying enticingly against her shoulders in a frenzy of movement. Like string theory in action. "You can't hold me to that bet! I wasn't even sixteen then. It was just a stupid high school thing. You should've forgotten about it—I did."

He grinned at her panicky justification attempts, but he wasn't letting her off the hook. "I most certainly did *not* forget, and I don't recall there being a time limit on the wager we made," he informed her. "And it'd been *your* idea after all. So, no. You're not wiggling your way out of this, sweetheart. You owe me one favor, and I'm getting it tonight."

Little did she know that this hadn't been his first choice for collecting on that sweet victory. He'd been biding his time as a teenager, waiting for just the right moment to claim his prize, which would have been that long kiss he'd been daydreaming about for eons. But then her dad had warned him off, and that was that.

Well, it was the end of his fantasy back then. Now, it was a whole new ballgame.

He grabbed the wrench from the toolbox and winked at her. "When I fix this machine, we're going for a ride."

Abby was shaking from the top of her helmet right down to the toes cushioned inside of her brown suede boots. Fear of riding her brother's hunk-o-junk motorcycle was only a small part of her anxiety.

The larger, more worrisome reason was that she was straddled on the leather seat behind Rick, her jean-clad legs spread open, her thighs touching his thighs, her chest pressed tight against his back, and her arms wrapped around his torso.

His extremely broad and hard torso.

If it weren't for the cool autumn breeze blowing mercilessly on her body, she might have already spontaneously combusted.

"Ready?" Rick asked, jangling the ignition key from its chain, which Allan had kept stashed in the motorcycle tail box, and grinning wickedly at her.

"No," she answered truthfully. "Not even close."

He rested his other hand against hers, sandwiching her fingers between his palm and his firm chest. "Don't worry," he said in a voice that would have been reassuring in almost any other circumstance. "This'll be fun. Wanna bet on it?"

She elbowed him—or tried to. "I'm never making another bet with you in my life."

He just laughed, turned the key, and kicked the bike into gear.

Abby squeezed her eyes shut and held her breath, bracing herself against an agonizing crash and certain death.

But there wasn't any pain.

Only peace and, after a few moments, a rare sense of flight.

Cautiously, she opened one eye and then the other. The soft rumble of the motorcycle's engine was white noise in the dark night.

She noticed Rick had chosen to take smaller roads— King Street, Western Way, Spring—to get to Main Street, but riding through the center of town proved to be nothing short of beautiful. Mirabelle Harbor glittered at night. And as they crossed the intersection at Cherry and wound down the road to Mirabelle Parkway, Rick picked up speed.

He turned north, zipping by Eastman Field and taking smaller roads yet again—this time by the lake. They went past the private homes along Lake Michigan, including the stately Michaelsen mansion, where Chandler grew up and where Olivia and Derek still lived. Abby didn't know if this route had been chosen intentionally, but Rick's whole body tensed as they drove by.

Still, he kept going. Further and further northward, until there was only the road, the lake, and them. And it was stunning. Almost magical. Like Aladdin taking Jasmine on a magic carpet ride. Like seeing with new eyes something—or someplace or someone—she'd always loved.

Everywhere they rode was at once familiar and different. And not just because she hadn't been home in so long. Mostly, it was because she felt she'd rediscovered a treasure she hadn't realized she'd been missing.

Oh, Rick Zimmerman. Where have you been for the last ten years of my life?

He didn't speak for the entirety of their journey. He just pointed every once in a while to an especially lovely view and, a few times, he squeezed her fingers to make sure she was doing all right.

She was.

And then, because all good things had to come to an end—or so she'd been told since childhood—it was over.

Rick cut the engine on the street in front of her parents' house and walked the bike up to the garage. A thoughtful gesture, she thought, to keep the noise to a minimum. It wasn't even eleven p.m., but her parents went to bed much earlier these days. They could be light sleepers, and her dad in particular had had some restless nights since his accident.

After Rick wrestled the motorcycle back into its space and closed the garage door, he finally spoke—in a whisper, though, as if to keep from breaking the enchantment. "So, did you like it?"

His half smile told her he already knew the answer, but she'd indulge him. He'd earned it.

She shook her head with mock gravity. "No." Then after a beat, "I loved it, which you darn well know. My apologies for ever doubting you."

"Ah. Then I should've insisted on you taking that second bet. Lost opportunity."

She chuckled. "I never would've agreed."

He took a few steps toward her on the dimly lit

driveway, his car just a few yards away. She didn't want to see him leave.

"You always did have a stubborn streak, Abby."

"Well, you were hardly the perfect teen. You had a tendency to explode things."

He grinned, teeth flashing. "True. And I'm about to do something right now that could blow up in my face. Big time." He swallowed and inched even closer to her, her heart rate skyrocketing when he brought the pad of his thumb to her cheek, stroked down to her jaw, and then pulled her face up toward his.

He paused for an infinity—waiting for something. Several seconds later, she realized it must be for *her*. To break away from him, if she'd wanted.

But she wanted no such thing. She didn't want any distance between them. None at all.

Somehow, she telegraphed this desire to Rick. Maybe he read it in her eyes. Or maybe it was her lips, when she licked them and strained upward to get closer to his.

Abby didn't bother analyzing whose mouth touched whose first, just that they finally did.

After all of these years, after wanting him for so long, after an unrequited crush that spanned most of her young-adult life and had been frozen in a time and place they no longer inhabited, everything thawed and came alive in an instant.

He took her, breathed her into him, possessed her.

She'd always laughed when she heard such aggressive descriptions of a kiss. Scoffed at the dramatic nonsense of it.

But nothing short of *possession* could explain the sensation she experienced. She and Rick embodied each other, until the blackness was illuminated and the world surrounding them flooded with light.

"Abby? Is that you out there?" her father's gruff voice called from the doorway. "And who's that out with you?

Rick?"

The bright light was from the front porch lamp that he'd turned on, ostensibly to check for intruders. Or wayward daughters.

"Oh, shit," Rick murmured. "We're busted."

"Uh, yeah, Dad. It's just me and Rick," she called back. "I'll be right in, okay?"

Her father uttered something unintelligible, and Abby could hear her mother saying, "For heaven's sake, Warren, get inside! You'll catch a chill."

Abby met Rick's gaze and they broke into soft laughter.

"Would you like to come in the house? I could make us some coffee or something," she said.

"With both of your parents up, staring at me like a naughty teen? Not a chance." He kissed her forehead lightly. "But I'd love to see you again. Soon. Like tomorrow. And the next day."

The open and seemingly endless ride they'd shared tonight had lulled her into a false sense of timelessness. She was suddenly reminded that their evenings together were strictly limited. They had, what? Less than a week before he was finished with his conference and relocated to somewhere new... A few days longer and she'd have to return to Florida. It would go by faster than the streetlights on their nighttime motorcycle ride.

"Okay, but it'll need to be later tomorrow night. I came here specifically to help my parents, and I promised Mom we'd paint their master bathroom tomorrow. So, maybe, ten p.m.?"

"Fine. Let's see if we can keep those plans from Allan again, though. Much as I love your brother, I don't want him horning in on these next two nights. He's already claimed Friday. I'd like Wednesday and Thursday to be just for you and me. Alone."

She wouldn't argue with that. The things she wanted to do with Rick—alone—were multiplying by the minute.

"Are we going to go for another bike ride?"

He shook his head. "I have a different kind of wild ride in mind." And with a mischievous and incredibly sexy twinkle in his eye, he hopped in his car and sped away.

CHAPTER FOUR

Wednesday, October 25th

Rick couldn't concentrate on the Plasticity of Nucleotides.

Or on the Anatomy of a Proton.

He napped for a full ninety-three minutes during the morning seminar on Quarks & Leptons, and he actually doodled all through the Red Dwarfs lecture.

Worst of all, he found himself rapping a modified version of the Physic Slam winners' "Precision Collision" during unguarded moments, which, embarrassingly, coincided with him coming face to face in the men's restroom with one of the convention's most distinguished organizers.

Dr. Byron Prescott, an MIT (1978) and Stanford (1984) grad, currently a big wig on staff at the University of Chicago, raised an amused grayish eyebrow. "Catchy tune, wasn't it?"

"Uh, yeah," Rick admitted. "Can't get it out of my head." He washed his hands and splashed some water on his face. "You did an excellent job selecting the participants this year."

Dr. Prescott grinned. "They were good, yes. But, now that I know you like a bit of rap music, maybe you'd be interested in being in on it next year, eh? We can always find a spot on our team for a physicist with a great mind and a little rhythm."

"Well, I don't think—"

"Ah, just keep your options open, Dr. Zimmerman. We know you've recently finished up in Japan. If you ever want to swing over to the academic dark side, just give me a call at the university."

"Thanks," Rick said, and then beat a hasty retreat out of there.

But that was only the beginning of the afternoon pressure fest.

Dr. Yuri Sarenslov, his boss at ProtoStratus Labs, was waiting to ambush him during the hour-long lunch break. "Have you given any further thought to the New Zealand opportunity, Rick? Just found out that Dr. Masters from Columbia is heading the new rocketry program there, and I know you enjoyed working with her."

That was an understatement of the highest order. Dr. Alexandra Masters and Rick had shared a passion for Two-Stage Orbital Rocket Launchers, SpaceX technology, and semisweet Pinot Grigio when they'd both been working on assignment in SoCal. Then she got transferred to Auckland, and he flew to Tokyo and, well, long-distance relationships had a way of fizzling out. Especially when two people were both more committed to their work than to their love lives.

He and Alexa had more or less parted as friends, but Rick knew the invitation—and the temptation—to pick up where they'd left off would be a near certainty if they were working together again.

Long days in the lab. Late nights. Shared workspace and state secrets. It would be so easy. And so damned convenient.

Everything real love probably wasn't.

He exhaled slowly and turned to his boss. "When would you need to know?"

"Early next week. At the latest." He waved his phone like a prop. "They've got you on the shortlist of candidates, but they'll need to open it up to everyone soon. So, if you're even remotely interested, you'd better speak up quick."

"Got it. Thanks, Yuri."

The older man squinted at him. "You're a young guy, Rick. The time to make your mark on the physics world is *now*. No wife. No kids. No house you have to maintain. You've got nothing holding you back."

"I know," he said, smothering a sigh. And maybe that was exactly the problem. Why he'd been feeling so restless in Japan these last few months. Maybe he wanted something—or someone—to be there, holding him back. Or just holding him.

Like Abby.

Merely thinking about her made him as hard as the chrome on Allan's bike. And Rick still had to wait another nine hours before he even saw her again. *Damn.*

When Allan first told him in that email that his sister would be in Mirabelle Harbor this week, he knew in a second that he would've moved heaven, earth, and any number of celestial bodies to cross paths with her again. The excuse of having this conference to attend felt like divine intervention.

But he'd thought it would be a simple reality check. A chance to face his past in person and gauge his personal growth from then to the present moment. An opportunity to let Abby and all of those youthful fantasies go, once and for all.

Instead, a whole new set of desires had materialized within seconds of seeing her, vanquishing his former fantasies to the realm of adolescent silliness. Replacing them with something decidedly adult and much more urgent.

"Just don't wait too long to make up your mind," Yuri warned. "Some opportunities are once in a lifetime."

That was precisely what Rick had been mentally debating. Just not in relation to his job.

"What do you think of the Precious Petunia or the Fading Violet?" Abby's mother asked her, holding up paint swatches of each at the cavernous home store.

Abby winced. Both colors looked to her like variations of nausea, if that sensation could be made visible.

"Or there's Blue Bayou," her mom continued. "Burnt Umber Sunset. Or even Fuchsia Fields Forever. Too bright?"

Considering some of the more depressing color options her mom had been contemplating—from Back in Black to Guantanamo Gray—the Blue Bayou was definitely in the lead, and Abby told her so.

"Great! Let me ask the nice man over there how many canisters he thinks we'll need. Maybe I'll do an accent wall in Sierra Silver Chrome."

Abby nodded encouragingly at her mother, but the thought of any kind of chrome only made her think of Allan's motorcycle—and Rick. Again. It'd been impossible to get him off her mind last night. Or this morning. Or this afternoon, for that matter. She'd checked the time on her phone countless times already today, and did it once more.

Only 2:06.

How many hours before she got to see him again?

Almost eight.

She leaned against a long shelf in an aisle filled with varnishes and stains, crossed her arms, and moaned.

"Well, that doesn't sound good, Abby," a familiar

woman's voice said with a chuckle. "Need a doctor?"

Abby straightened up and swiveled around, recognizing the lady at once. "Olivia?"

The other woman squealed and raced over to Abby, hugging her tightly.

Abby hugged back just as hard. It'd been years, but Chandler's sister-in-law was still as lovely as ever, despite having married into that challenging Michaelsen family and being the mother of three boys. Their mutual friend in Sarasota, Marianna Gregory, who'd moved to Florida after getting divorced and then losing her job in Mirabelle Harbor, still spoke weekly with Olivia. And the woman standing before her in the aisle had always been very kind to Abby, too. Despite what had happened between her and Chandler.

Still, as they pulled apart and started chatting, it was a shock to be in her presence again. Last time Abby and Olivia were together in person was at a Michaelsen family gathering a few weeks after Chandler's mom's funeral, and a few days before he and Abby began their U.S. driving adventure. One that went on for years and resulted in her living twelve hundred miles away from Mirabelle Harbor.

"It's been too long," Olivia said sweetly, and Abby knew she was being utterly genuine. The two of them had exchanged Christmas cards every year and had even spoken on the phone several times, but it was very different being face to face. Something Abby had recently learned, especially after finally seeing Rick again.

"It has," she said. "How are you and Derek and the boys?"

"We're fine, but you know I'm disappointed. Still..."

Abby shrugged. "We tried to make it work."

"I know. Not your fault for Chandler's restless ways, but his sister and I were looking forward to making you a part of the family officially. Unofficially, of course, you'll always be one of us, you know."

She felt her throat tighten with emotion. "Thanks, Olivia. That means a lot, considering...everything."

One of the hardest parts of breaking up with Chandler was not getting to be a regular member of the Michaelsen clan. As difficult as some of them could be sometimes (Blake came immediately to mind), she'd loved them all. Especially Olivia and Sharlene. But it was just too painful to keep in touch frequently after Chandler left. Too many memories and dashed hopes.

"My brother tells me that Chance is engaged now. Is that right?" Abby asked.

Olivia nodded.

"Congrats to him and his fiancée!"

"Thanks. I'll pass your good wishes along to the happy couple. They're planning on a small Christmas wedding."

Then: a long moment of silence. She and her old friend were both probably wondering the same thing. What this meant for Chandler. If his twin brother's wedding would finally bring him back to Mirabelle Harbor—and soon. Christmas was less than two months away. He wouldn't miss something so important, would he?

Finally, Olivia said, "Well, you know it's a good thing I still have *some* friends in Florida who keep in touch regularly. Marianna mentioned you were going to be in town this week, so I've been keeping an eye out for you. Glad we ran into each other or I would've had to hunt you down."

Abby laughed. "It's been a bit of a whirlwind." She filled Olivia in on the situation with her dad. "But I would've had to hunt you down before I returned to Sarasota, in any case. I'm sure you know why."

Olivia's brow winkled up in confusion. "Should I?"

"Marianna gave me orders to deliver some fudge to you."

"From Fudge Fantasia?"

"You guessed it."

Olivia clapped her hands and bubbled with giddiness at the prospect. "Oh, my goodness! I'm *addicted* to that stuff. It's like chocolate crack, Abby! Seriously, I've been planning a trip to Florida just to buy a case of it. And, okay, to see Marianna and finally meet Gil." She laughed. "I was looking forward to surprising you down there, too, and getting introduced to your jewelry-making partners in crime, Joy and Lorelei."

"Oh, you've gotta come down. They'd all love to see you! The white-sand beaches are gorgeous, and you'll appreciate them even more in winter when Lake Michigan is a skating rink. Plus, it's been so fun to watch Marianna and Gil's relationship develop over the past year. Joy's brother is a wonderful guy, and the two of them seem really happy together."

Olivia agreed. "I'm thrilled for Marianna. I couldn't believe it when she told me this summer that they were buying a house together. If things at home hadn't been so busy with the boys and, now, with the wedding to prepare for, I would've gone down sooner. So, maybe I'll plan for this spring."

"Keep me posted."

"I will. And you let me know if there's anything I can do for you or your parents while you're here. If you can think of something that might brighten your dad's spirits, I'd love to help out."

"Oh, Olivia, thanks. Mom and Dad are okay, though, and Allan and I have most everything covered. It's just that my father is pretty cranky when he's in pain, and my mother is always worried about him." Abby didn't mention her dad's odd, overprotective streak, which seemed to intensify ever since she'd been back home, and especially after her late night with Rick yesterday. Dad had asked her upwards of *three million questions* about where they were last night and what they were doing, etc., etc. It was like she was sixteen all over again, instead of nearly thirty.

"Just know I'm here if you need me." She patted Abby's arm and grinned. "And our home phone number and my cell are both unchanged. So, anytime you want to drop off that fudge, I'll make myself available."

Abby laughed. "I'll definitely get it over to you this week. I promise."

"Good. Because I fully intend to bribe you with a piece of fudge or two so you'll stay and have coffee with me. And with Shar, as well, if she can sneak away from her students and that boyfriend of hers."

"Boyfriend?" Last Abby heard, Sharlene had sworn off men for good after her divorce. "Who's the lucky man?"

"Declan Night."

"The hockey player?"

"Yep. Former hockey player, current owner of the sports shop, The Penalty Box, on Main. They've been together a few months now, which, in Shar and Dec's world, is like a decade in normal-couple time. I know she'd love to catch up with you, too."

"That'd be fun," Abby murmured, feeling a pang of envy that just about everyone on the planet seemed to have found a happily ever after in love, except for her.

Of course there was Rick. And that kiss they'd shared. But how long could a relationship between them last? A few more days, at most. Right?

If Olivia noticed Abby's mood shift, she gave no sign of it. Instead, with a warm parting hug, Chandler's sweet sister-in-law dashed off, and Abby was left to contemplate what might have been. If her ex had more staying power. If whatever really drew him away from her—maybe a compulsion, maybe another woman—hadn't been so strong. If keeping a relationship going wasn't so darn hard.

She watched her mom still talking with the store associate, while overseeing the mixing of the paint. There were rolls of painter's tape on the end cap of the aisle, and Abby grabbed one to add to their list of purchases. They needed to protect the trim, and there was no way to know if Mom had enough tape at home.

She thought about the people and places in Mirabelle Harbor that she'd missed. Ones that, unlike Rick, were constants. Lake Michigan, for instance. Max's Pub and Harbor Square. Her parents and brother. The high school. Olivia, Shar, and the Michaelsens.

It was a funny thing, though. When she'd first gotten back into town, memories of Chandler had made her melancholy. But the feeling faded considerably after seeing Rick again. There was almost no space left in her brain for anyone else.

And his kiss. *Oh, boy.* So many sparks. Incendiary, like the blazing October trees aflame with color. Just thinking about him made her burn up.

He had such talent—and she knew the skills he'd shown her were just the tip of the iceberg. Like the way he fixed Allan's bike or his modest explanation of what he did professionally.

Yet, when he kissed her last night, it'd been so much more than her being impressed by her high school crush. He'd dazed and dazzled her. Blinded her with science. Most of all, he'd made her rethink her own life and choices.

Not that he'd still be here if, say, she decided to move back to the Midwest. But he'd reminded her—vividly—of the many things she still loved and missed about home, even with such wonderful friends in Sarasota and the fairly contented life she'd created for herself there.

Abby found her mind running through scenarios and possibilities for her future. Thoughts that, until this week, hadn't even occurred to her. Potential options that, until this very moment, had seemed as distant as some faraway galaxy.

"Hop in, Abby," Rick whispered through the open window of his rental car, after she'd snuck out of the house at ten o'clock on the dot, her parents safely asleep. "I've got somewhere special to take you."

She slid into the passenger seat and buckled up. "It's a little cooler tonight. Am I dressed warmly enough for what we're doing?"

He nodded. "Yep, and I promised you another wild ride, remember?"

Oh, yeah. She remembered.

He sent her a look so heated that she almost unzipped the jacket she'd put on to ward off the chill.

"I intend to make sure you get that," Rick added.

The sensuality of his smile was going to be her undoing. Abby stole a glance at the backseat of the sporty Kia he was driving. Energy efficient, it was, but she'd known more spacious vehicles... "What, um, did you have in mind?" *And where?*

Clearly, he must have guessed the direction of her thoughts because he laughed. Loudly. "You'll see. We should get there in about twenty minutes." Then, abruptly, he reached for her hand. "I couldn't stop thinking about you today, Abby. You were on my mind every damn moment."

"Same here," she admitted. "I was counting the hours until now, actually."

He squeezed her fingers but didn't let go. "I was counting the hours, the minutes and, during an especially monotonous workshop on New Discoveries in Quantum Theory, the seconds."

She smiled. "For what it's worth, that sounds more fascinating than the endless hours my mom and I spent painting the master bath Blue Bayou."

Rick snorted. "You'd be surprised."

It wasn't until they crossed into the suburb of Glen

Forest, home to the Four Corners Amusement Park, that she had an inkling of what he was up to.

"Is 'Freaky Fright Fest' going on? I didn't think the park was open on weeknights in October."

"It's not," he informed her. "At least not to the public. But some of the rocketry engineers are members of the North Lakes Physics Consortium, and they worked out an arrangement. A special event open only to convention attendees tonight. Some of the roller coasters are running just for us and for our guests." He pulled out two tickets and handed them to her. "Hope you still like corkscrew coasters, 'cuz we're going on one in about ten minutes."

"Ha!" she burst out. "Don't tell me. You're going to narrate the entire ride with explanations of the velocity, the acceleration, and the aerodynamics of motion, right?"

"Nope. I'll be too busy screaming."

"What about when the coaster stops moving?"

"Then," he said with a sly grin, "I'll be too busy kissing you."

She blushed. "Oh."

As if to prove his point, he pulled into the first available parking spot, turned off the car engine, and drew her to him. "I saw you eyeing the backseat," he whispered before kissing her. "Just letting you know, I'd be open to a change of plans." More kissing. "Though, given the non-tinted windows and the cramped space, there's a good chance we'd get caught." Even more kissing. "But I'd risk it."

If his kisses could singe her from the inside out, she was almost afraid to imagine what making love with Rick would be like. It was enough to override her mental circuits and render her motionless for a minute.

He inched away from her, gazing into her eyes with a depth and intent that was, at once, unplumbed and inscrutable. "I'm only half joking, you know. Between your parents' house and my mom and stepdad's house, we don't have many options for being truly alone. Not unless we check into a motel, and that would have to be outside of Mirabelle Harbor or we'd be recognized. It's almost worse now than during high school. At least, as teens, we could hide out in the janitor's closet or behind the bleachers."

She couldn't help but laugh. "I know. Anywhere else in the world, it'd be easy to be alone. I've got my own condo in Sarasota."

"And I've got a company apartment in Pasadena and a flat I just vacated in Kagoshima. I could've had a spacious hotel room at the conference center in Chicago, too, if my mother hadn't insisted I stay with them."

"Family," Abby said, grinning. "They're going to make us crazy this week."

He agreed.

They got out of the car and walked, hand in hand, into the amusement park. A few seconds after they were locked into the first coaster, Rick suddenly burst out laughing. "Your brother!" he exclaimed.

"What?" Abby glanced around in panic. "Is he here?"

"No, no."

The large metal roller coaster began its rickety ascent, slinking and clanking all the way up. It was taking her higher than she'd been in a long time. The world around them glittered magnificently at night. She could see for miles and miles and miles. Then all movement lurched to a stop at the apex and suspended them in anticipation.

She gulped the cool night air, and turned to Rick. "What about my brother?"

"Allan's got his own place," he replied. "I just realized that, maybe, we could borrow it."

She gasped, even before the coaster began its downward plunge, and together they screamed with pent-up energy and elation into the expansive atmosphere of the autumn night. Thrilling cries that seemed to reverberate out from them and echo to the edge of the day and to the reaches of the solar system.

CHAPTER FIVE

Thursday, October 26th

Abby downed three large mugs of coffee, but she still almost fell asleep in her apple-cinnamon oatmeal Thursday morning.

Despite the fact that the amusement park had closed at midnight, Rick hadn't dropped her off at her parents' house until well after two a.m., and it took her another hour to finally fall asleep.

They'd gone parking down by Barrett's Pier. Making out like they were seventeen-year-olds or something. It should've been embarrassing. Instead, it was nothing short of euphoric.

Her phone beeped and jolted her awake.

Rick.

"Pretty sure I just snoozed through 56 minutes of Dr. Hayward's 60-minute lecture on Advancements in Particle Acceleration. Who needs to know every possible update, though, right?"

She grinned and texted him back. "Um, YOU. Isn't that a big part of your job?"

"Smart mouth," he wrote. Then, "I'm a little fixated on your mouth, actually, and I can't think of any quick comebacks anyway. I'm exhausted."

"Same here. You wore me out and kept me up way past my bedtime."

"Oh, darlin', I haven't even begun to wear you out."

She blushed, glad he couldn't see her face. It was true, they hadn't gotten all the way to home base, but they'd run *way* past first and second and ventured into third. She still felt tingly from all the places he'd touched her during the wee hours of the morning. And she wanted more. A lot more.

Before she could compose herself enough to type anything, he texted, "We're still on for tonight, right? 8ish?"

"Yes. Mom and Dad are going to their friends' house—the Pattersons—at 7:30 for bridge."

"Good. Counting the minutes."

"Me, too," she typed.

"No, Abby. I'm REALLY counting. 614."

She grinned.

Five minutes later, her phone buzzed with a new text.

"609 now."

She laughed, waited sixty seconds, and then texted him. "608..."

He sent her a smiley emoji and, periodically throughout the day, a numerical update, which never failed to make her grin like a giddy school girl.

"What's *that* look mean?" Olivia Michaelsen demanded that afternoon when Abby stopped by her house to hand-deliver the fudge Marianna sent from Sarasota.

Abby quickly slid her phone back into her pocket and tried to play it cool. "Uh, nothing. Just a message from a friend."

Sharlene, Olivia's sister-in-law and Chandler's big sister, who'd come to the house right after work so she could see Abby, too, regarded her dubiously. "Girlfriend, that look wasn't caused by some ordinary 'friend.' Who is he? Do we know him?"

Abby blushed.

It wasn't outside the realm of possibility that Chandler's nearest and dearest female relations knew Rick Zimmerman. Between the two of them, Shar and Olivia knew just about everyone in Mirabelle Harbor. Their hometown, while it was a large northern Chicago suburb, had the heartbeat of a small town.

And the wildfire gossip of one.

Abby wasn't willing to take chances.

"He doesn't live here," Abby said, crossing her fingers behind her back. *At least not anymore.* "But he kisses like the apocalypse is coming," she admitted.

"That good, huh?" said Shar.

Olivia fanned herself and popped another square of fudge into her mouth.

"Chandler was a total bonehead to let you go," Shar added, ever the snappish big sister. She crossed her arms and studied Abby speculatively.

Olivia finished chewing and shook her head. "He made the wrong decision, that's for sure. He was just too young. But he'll regret leaving you. He probably already does."

"I hope not," Abby said honestly. "It took me a long time not to feel so sad about our breakup—and I still have a down moment every now and then. But I think it actually *did* work out for the best. Chandler and I had a lot going for us, but we were both too inexperienced in relationships to know that what we shared might not be enough. He probably sensed it before I did." She paused. "He's a good guy. Just not, as it turns out, the right one for me."

The two other women exchanged a glance.

Then Shar said, "But you think the Apocalypse Kisser might be?"

Abby blushed again and sort of chuckled. "I don't

know. Maybe. I've just—I've never, ever felt like this."
She decided it was high time to turn the tables on the two
of them. "I suspect you both know what I mean."

Olivia, married to Derek for thirteen years, grinned.
And Shar, who'd clearly been reveling in her newish
relationship with Declan, the hockey guy, turned an
interesting shade of pink.

"Yeah, I thought so," Abby said, which made all three
of them burst out laughing.

They ate some more fudge, talked and laughed for a
while longer. Before they parted ways, both Shar and
Olivia hugged Abby so tight, it reminded her that they were
really and truly still her friends, no matter what had
transpired between her and Chandler.

It was a good visit in a healing, cathartic way, and it
helped her put the final sealant on a relationship that long
needed to be closed.

The better for her to be open to something new, right?

Abby was pretty sure her father wasn't playing bridge
so much as some other game.

He'd been flashing his "invalid" card all evening, like
an ace in his pocket. And, in a surprise move that had
completely blindsided her, he insisted that the Pattersons,
the Anthonys, and the Blasicks come over to the Solinski
house tonight, rather than all of them going to the
Pattersons' place, because Dad's supposedly "aching
ankle" made it—quote—"too difficult to travel across
town"—unquote.

What a bunch of baloney.

Mom took the change of plans in stride, though, and
began whipping up appetizers for their guests. Abby,
however, was *highly* suspicious of his behavior.

Had her father engineered this game of musical houses to keep her from slipping away with Rick? Had he somehow guessed that she'd had plans tonight and they didn't include binge-watching old episodes of *Outlander*, like she'd said?

"Abby, your mom is sitting out this hand," Dad observed. "Why don't you sit in for her?"

It was nearly eight, and she'd sent Rick a warning text about the situation, but he hadn't responded with a plan, just a "Hmm. We'll think of some way to spring you out of detention."

That was all fine and good—she liked his sense of humor and his spontaneity—but not if she had to play cards for an indefinite amount of time before her mom even returned to the table.

"I'm not really in the mood for—" she began.

"Oh, c'mon, Abby. The night's young, and you have hours and hours left to watch that Scottish time travel show you like so much." Her dad raised a mischievous eyebrow, all but daring her to contradict him.

"Do join us," Mrs. Anthony encouraged.

Abby felt herself giving in, and she even took a step toward their card table when the doorbell rang.

"Who could that be?" Mr. Blasick asked, confused. He glanced around the room as if counting heads to check which players were missing. "I thought we were all here."

"I'll get that," Abby said, leaping for the door.

Rocket Rick. Thank God.

He looked devilishly handsome, emphasis on devil, with a grin on his lips and a large platter of baklava in his hands.

"Heard there was a bridge party in progress," he said to everyone, stepping into the room. "Anybody here want a fresh Greek pastry from The Gala?"

Ooohs and *ahhhs* followed, and Abby's mother said, "You shouldn't have, Ricky, but I'm so glad you did!"

"Not above bribery, are you, *Ricky*," Abby said in her best murmur of mockery.

He winked at her and whispered. "Nope. Give me ten minutes and we'll make a break for it."

Everyone in the room knew the Pappayiannis family, who owned the Greek restaurant and bakery in the middle of Mirabelle Harbor, and they all loved their rich desserts.

Abby couldn't think of them without thinking of Nia, though, the daughter of the owners and the soon-to-be bride of Chandler's twin brother. Did Rick know about their upcoming nuptials, too?

She couldn't help but wonder.

As far as she knew, Rick had never had anything against Chance Michaelsen. Just Chandler. Always Chandler.

All the couples in the room knew Rick and, of course, they'd heard from Abby's parents that he was back in town. Upon seeing him, they began shooting questions his way, from the benign and simple —"How long did you spend over in Japan?" Mrs. Blasick inquired—to the profound and highly complex, such as Mr. Patterson's entreaty to Rick that he "should explain once and for all that Theory of Relativity."

"Better make it thirty minutes," Rick mouthed to Abby, before sitting down beside Mr. Patterson and launching into a layman's explanation of Einstein's most well-known brainstorm.

Meanwhile, across the room at her father's table, Abby had no choice but to play what felt like an eternity of bridge, all while sneaking frequent glances at Rick.

Her father, whose knee and ankle miraculously didn't appear to bother him in the least when he jumped up to grab one of Mom's crab cake hors d'oeuvres, alternated between glaring at his hand of cards and surreptitiously studying her every movement. He was in an odd, frenetic sort of mood that night, and Abby didn't know what to make of it.

But one thing was certain—if he was well enough to be manipulative, she didn't need to worry quite so much about him at this point.

At the earliest opportunity, she turned the seat back over to her mother. "Please let me fix the mini pizzas, Mom. It's your turn to play. Really."

"Well, if you insist, sweetie."

Oh, yes. Abby most definitely insisted.

She escaped to the relative safety of the kitchen and busied herself with the appetizer prep, hoping it would be only a few minutes until she and Rick could slip away.

Unfortunately, that wasn't how it played out.

Not by a long shot.

The back door swung open and in came her brother. "Ah, there you are, sis."

"Hey, Allan, how are—"

"So, where have you been sneaking off to late at night, hmm? I've been hearing alarmed reports from the folks."

"What?" she said, dropping the spoon she was holding and splattering pizza sauce on her shirt. "Mom and Dad have been complaining about me?" Their father had been acting strange enough, yes, but he hadn't said a word to her directly, and their mother seemed her usual self.

"Not Mom. However, Dad is—and I quote— 'concerned' about you. He peeked in your room last night at midnight and you weren't there. Although, apparently, you returned eventually." Allan raised his brows.

"He's checking up on me now?" Abby was indignant. "I'm not in high school anymore."

Her brother smirked, but didn't comment on that. Instead he said, "And then there's the mysterious case of my newly repaired crotch rocket."

"Mom hates it when you use that expression."

Allan glanced around the otherwise empty kitchen and crossed his arms. "Well, she's not in here, is she? And don't change the subject. Tell me how, exactly, did it get fixed?"

"Uh, well...Rick and I—" she began.

"Did I hear my name?" Rick said, peeking his head into the room. He waved at Allan. "Hey, what's up, man?"

"You tell me," her brother said with a sly grin. "I've heard you and my sister have been out on the town, and Abby here was just about to explain how my motorcycle returned to working order again."

"Oh, that's on me," Rick said gallantly. "I'd been craving a good bike ride, and when Abby mentioned you still had yours, I couldn't resist. Sorry if I overstepped—"

"Hell, no, buddy. I'm grateful," Allan interrupted. "I can't wait to go for a ride again myself. It's just, um..." He motioned between Abby and Rick. "What's going on with you two?"

"Nothing much," she insisted.

"Mostly talking," Rick replied at the same time.

"We've just been catching up," she added, but she could feel her face heating up and Rick's gaze trained on her.

"*Mostly* talking," Allan repeated, snagging one of the leftover crab cakes from the counter. "I can only guess what's going on the *rest* of the time." He took a big bite, somehow managing to chew and grin simultaneously.

"Your sister and I are friends," Rick said.

"Yep. And I'm Betty Crocker," her brother retorted, grabbing another appetizer. "C'mon, you two. I don't care what you've been doing behind my parents' backs, but I'd be more inclined to believe you were planning a bank heist than just 'catching up' like old high school friends." He chuckled. "Anyway," he turned to Rick, "you're not doing anything now, are you, man?" He didn't wait for a response. "Because I need some serious relationship advice, and *you're* who I need to talk to." Allan began to steer him toward the backyard patio.

Rick glanced over his shoulder at her and was about to protest, but Abby shook her head and waved him outside to talk to her brother. "It's okay," she mouthed.

He grimaced, which made her smile, but he followed Allan. The last thing she heard before the screen door swung shut was her brother saying in a pained voice, "It's about Becca. I heard she was seeing someone else, and I—dammit, I just want her back..."

The bridge couples seemed intent on staying at the house extra late. Abby cooked snacks and the older people munched on them. Allan returned to the kitchen a few times for beers, but he wouldn't relinquish his hold on his best buddy.

Rick came into the kitchen a couple of times, too, rubbing his eyes and looking weary. As the clock ticked toward eleven o'clock, he snuck in again, pulled her into the attached laundry room, and kissed her.

"I've been sitting just a few yards away from you, missing you like crazy, Abby." He sighed. "Tonight didn't go as I'd planned. At all."

She couldn't pretend not to be disappointed, too, but she understood the situation. "My brother needed you."

"Perhaps. But *I* needed *you*." He brought his lips to hers again—a warm, toe-curling, delectable kiss. "Just keep part of your evening free tomorrow, okay?"

"Tomorrow's Friday. Aren't you and Allan going to Max's Pub?"

"We are," Rick said. "But only because I'd promised. I've already informed him that, even though I'm starting the night out as his wingman, I plan to end it with you."

CHAPTER SIX

Friday Night, October 27th

Rick had laid out for her "the plan," as he envisioned it.

"Allan and I will be at Max's—discussing Becca ad nauseam, no doubt—but then you'll meet us there at nine thirty. He can either stay and chat with us for awhile, leave to go hang out with your parents, or head home. But I was supposed to fly back to Pasadena on Saturday, and I'm changing my flight to Monday morning. I know you've got a Sunday evening flight back to Sarasota, but, if you're willing, I'd like to spend the weekend with you."

Abby let him know without hesitation that, yes, she was willing. Friday night, Saturday, and half of Sunday. It was hardly as much time as she would've liked, but she'd take what she could get. Neither of them voiced any plans *beyond* the weekend, however, which was telling. After all, what could they say? *Yeah, you're cute, but you live across the country. So, chances of making out with you more than a few times per year are unlikely...*

Then again, that was still more promising than any of Abby's other romantic interests had been recently. A totally pathetic realization, in her book.

After another full day of helping her parents with household tasks, setting things up so it would be easier for them when she wasn't there the following week, and making sure her dad went to physical therapy and completed all of his exercises, Abby fixed her parents a hot pot of coffee and sat down to enjoy a cup herself.

Her mother, as usual, couldn't sit still. So, while Mom puttered around the kitchen, throwing together some sort of chicken-and-veggie casserole thing for dinner, Abby and her dad were alone in the living room.

He eyed her warily over his green "#1 Dad" mug, and the space between was filled with words left unsaid.

"What?" she finally asked.

He sighed. "I worry about you, sweetheart."

"Well, you don't need to. I'm fine."

"You're living in a tiny condo, halfway across the United States—"

"Yes, but I have work there, even if it's not what I majored in. And friends. *Good* friends."

He nodded his acknowledgment of that. "But are you happy?"

Was she happy? Huh. She squinted at her dad. How, exactly, could she answer that?

"I suppose," she said, but that sounded lame and unconvincing, even to her own ears.

"What about since you've been home?"

"This week?" She could feel herself brightening. "Yeah, it's been great. Seeing you and Mom. Allan, too. Reconnecting with Rick."

He raised his eyebrows. "Nice to see you smile like that, Abby." He paused. "You've spent some extra time with him, haven't you?"

"With Rick? Yes," she admitted. "But, you know, he's leaving after the weekend, and so am I. It's just been really, really nice to, uh, talk with him again."

Her dad made no immediate reply, but he seemed deep in thought. It gave her a chance to slightly change the subject and to put into words an idea she'd been pondering ever since she'd been back in Mirabelle Harbor. Or, truth be told, for quite a few months before this.

"You know, being home again has been wonderful. I love my friends in Sarasota, but I've been missing life in the Midwest and all of you here for a while." She took a long sip of coffee and just let that thought percolate in her dad's active brain.

It didn't take long for him to react. "Oh, sweetheart, we'd *love* to have you living near us again. Or even with us, if you needed a place to stay up here for a while."

"Thanks, Dad. If I decided to move back, I'd get my own place. But it's really good to know I have options. Thank you. There are a lot of career opportunities in Chicago, of course. Maybe it's not the worst idea to move into the city. See if I can finally get a job in my field."

Although she'd been working at Joy's jewelry shop making various beaded bracelets and necklaces, as well as at the travel agency booking local excursions for tourists, her actual bachelor's degree had been in graphic design. There was something extremely appealing and exciting about the possibility of doing real work related to her professional passion.

"A very promising idea," her dad said, nodding. "Sounds like you're finally ready."

"To move, you mean?"

"To stop waiting for Chandler Michaelsen to return to Florida for you. To start living your life, Abby."

She tried to swallow back the lump that had formed in her throat and the hard truth of what her father had just said to her.

Had she been waiting for Chandler?

Much as she'd known it was best for them to break up, perhaps a little piece of her heart hadn't let go of the hope that they'd be together again. She may have sent him on his way and let him continue his impetuous trekking around the country to whatever, wherever, or whomever he was looking for, but until she'd been back home this week, she hadn't entirely given up on Chandler's return. And until she'd spent time in Rick's company, she hadn't wanted to consider seriously any other relationship.

But Rocket Rick had changed that, hadn't he?

She kissed her dad on the cheek and raced into her childhood bedroom, where she'd left her laptop and her cell phone. Grabbing her phone, she texted her friends in Florida. "Ladies, do you have a few minutes to Skype tonight?"

Her phone pinged with an almost instantaneous response from Joy. "For you? Name your time."

Marianna replied next. "We're all together, Abby. I'm at The Beaded Periwinkle with Joy and Lorelei."

And then Lorelei texted, "No time like the present, sweetie. Whatcha doing now?"

Abby laughed. She *loved* her friends. "I'm getting online and Skyping with the three of you!"

As soon as their computers connected and she could see her friends' faces, Abby almost started crying. "Oh, you guys, I miss you so much."

"We miss you, too," Joy said. "Like crimson clouds on pancakes." This made Abby and her other friends burst out laughing. Only Joy could come up with unusual descriptions like that. She had a condition called synesthesia, which made her senses a little scrambled compared to the rest of their group. Joy could taste colors and touch numbers and see auras. Her vision of the world was uniquely beautiful.

"What's going on up in Mirabelle Harbor?" Marianna asked. "I know you've seen Olivia. I got a wildly enthusiastic thank-you voicemail from her yesterday for the fudge."

"Oh, yes," Abby said. "She loved it. Devoured half the package while we were together."

"Good," Marianna said. "But that's not why you wanted to talk."

"Is everything okay with your parents?" Lorelei asked. "You look unsettled."

"They're doing fine. My dad, though—he just said something, and I think it might be true." Abby told them about her conversation with her father, about the possibility of moving back to Illinois, and especially about seeing Rick this week, and how it'd been helping her to let go of the past. Namely, her long-dissolved relationship with Chandler.

"None of us want to see you leave, but getting over Chandler is a good thing," Marianna said.

"Although, I remember some of the stories you told us about your brother and his friends," Lorelei said, somewhat suspiciously. "Wasn't Rick one of the ones who was always blowing things up?"

Abby nodded. "He's grown up a bit since then." At least she hoped Rick was no longer inclined to detonate random objects.

"Has he been kind to you?" Marianna asked. "Honest and respectful?" These were big qualities in Marianna's book, especially given the nastiness of her ex-husband. Joy's brother, Gil Canton, was a total sweetheart and a perfect boyfriend for Marianna, but Abby remembered hearing about her dreadful ex and his issues.

"Yes, to all of the above," Abby answered truthfully.

Joy, who'd been listening intently, crossed her wiry arms. "I'm not at all pleased that you're considering leaving Sarasota," she said, "but I know there's no place like home." She paused, a pained look flashing across her face. "If you decide to move back there, I can't tell you how much we'll miss you." She huffed a little, her nostrils flaring like a baby dragon, and Abby knew she'd miss her terribly.

"Nothing's for certain yet," Abby said. "It's just that, with my parents getting older, and in light of the fact that I've been putting my career and romantic life on hold for so long, coming back to Chicago now doesn't seem like a bad idea."

"And this Rick guy? Tell us more about him, Abby," Joy demanded.

She tried to explain what it felt like to be around him again. How many memories it brought back. The attraction she'd always felt...and still did. "But he no longer lives in Mirabelle Harbor. I'm only going to get to spend this weekend with him before he flies back to California and, possibly, on another assignment out of the country soon."

"Sounds really pointy and opaque to me," Joy said. "I don't trust him." Neither of these responses were entirely surprising, coming from Joy. There'd been a man she'd liked quite a lot, and he'd lied to her. Even though he hadn't intended to hurt her, Joy didn't take well to being hoodwinked. By anyone. "So, here's what I think. Y'all need to come down here together so we can inspect him." She glanced between Marianna and Lorelei. "Right?"

"Not a bad idea," Lorelei said. "I could get Jamison to rough him up a little, if he isn't good to you. Bet he's got a tool or two he could use."

Abby grinned. Lorelei and Jamison had recently celebrated their twentieth wedding anniversary. Her friend's husband was a near genius with carpentry. He had *lots* of tools. "I'm not sure Rick is prepared to put his life at risk just yet."

"Should I put Olivia and Derek on the case?" Marianna asked. "They know everybody in town. If they checked up on Rick and found—"

"No!" Abby said quickly. "I don't want *any* of the Michaelsens involved in this. Not yet."

"You're not trying to protect Chandler's feelings, are

you?" asked Joy, perceptive as always.

Abby thought about it. "No. At least not entirely. I'm not ready for him to find out that the first guy I've felt anything for in ages is Rick Zimmerman, though. The two of them hated each other."

Joy arched her eyebrows. "It gets curiouser and curiouser."

"And I'm just trying to protect my heart. Even letting someone like Rick back into my life is a big leap, especially when it'll probably be over before it even has a chance to begin."

"How is he in bed?" Lorelei asked bluntly. "Any good?"

She felt herself blush a color that must've looked like pure scarlet to her friends. "I don't know. It's only been a week, so we haven't—"

"But you *want* to," Lorelei said.

Boy, did she ever.

Abby nodded. "If he makes love anything like the way he kisses, I'm a goner."

"Hmm," Joy murmured, still not looking like she was going to be easily won over.

Lorelei, however, winked approvingly, and Marianna smiled at Abby through the screen. "Something to keep in mind," Marianna said. "Second chances in love *are* possible. Don't let your fears about how one relationship ended affect your hope for a future one. From everything you've told us, Chandler and Rick seem like very different men."

"They are," Abby had to agree. "For good or bad, they really are."

Allan raised his shot glass in Rick's general direction,

ostensibly to clink "Cheers," but Abby's brother was distracted tonight. He was glancing wildly around Max's Pub—for what or for whom, Rick couldn't be certain—but, clearly, his old buddy was taking this Guys' Night Out thing very seriously.

Rick reached across the table with his beer bottle and made contact with Allan's glass. The other man downed his Kamikazi in one gulp, then turned toward him and grinned.

"Isn't this *great?*" Allan said for probably the third time in the past hour and a half. "You and me, out on the town again. No girlfriends to have to go home to or to hear complaints from later. Just me and my wingman."

"Uh, yeah." Rick drank a few swigs of his beer, but this was only his second bottle and he was already easing up, especially with Abby meeting them soon. Allan, however, had just swallowed his fourth shot of vodka, triple sec, and lime—and it looked like he had plans for more. "You might want to slow down, man, or you'll have one helluva hangover tomorrow."

"I'll deal with tomorrow when it gets here," Allan informed him. Then he pointed at a stacked blonde, two tables to their left. "Her. I wanna talk to *her.* C'mon!" He rose unsteadily out of his seat.

Rick had elicited a promise from Allan not to drunk-dial Becca tonight, but nothing was going to stop the guy from flirting with every pretty woman in the busy bar. "Why don't you just stay put for a few minutes, and see if you can catch her eye?"

Allan plopped back down in his chair, eyes blinking and his skin slightly flushed. "Maybe just for a coupla minutes," he slurred, motioning to their server that he wanted another shot. "Damn! I haven't felt this good in a long time. Why don't you move back to the Midwest, Rick? Be awesome to get to see you more than once every five or six years."

"Well, the nature of my work requires access to rocket

launching stations in—" he began, but he quickly realized his friend wasn't listening. The blonde had, in fact, glanced their way, and she smiled enticingly at them.

Rick sighed. But then his phone buzzed.

Text from Abby.

"Still want me to crash your party?" she typed.

"Hell, yeah," he wrote back. "Don't wait 'til 9:30. Come now."

"On my way," she replied. And for the first time in nearly two hours, Rick smiled.

By the time Abby reached the bar, her loquacious brother was buying drinks for the blonde and her BFF, and he was practically sprawled across their table.

Abby observed him for a moment and winced. "Has he been acting like this all night?"

"It's gotten worse just in the past half hour," Rick admitted. "He seems to be on a mission to erase Becca's existence from his memory by chasing most of the single women in the room, trying to charm one or more of them to go home with him, and soaking his brain in alcohol. Not always in that order."

She considered this. "Fortunately, it looks like there isn't a woman here who's inebriated enough to take him up on his offer. But we might need to drag him back to his place."

Rick nodded. "Yeah. And sooner rather than later."

The bartender, Gina-somebody, hastened their decision to leave.

"You guys might want to take Allan home," she told them. "He's usually a real decent guy, if a little quirky, even when buzzed. But he's verging on out-of-control tonight, and I'd prefer not to see him dancing on any tables, okay?"

Rick shot a look over at his buddy, who was, in fact, seated in a semi-upright position and squirming on top of the blonde's table. He appeared to be performing an unlikely rendition of Jay Sean's "Down," more or less in time with the bar music.

"Sorry," Abby said to Gina, as the bartender backed away from them. Abby then stared at her brother, just as he began rapping along with Lil Wayne's guest solo in the song. "I'll never be able to un-see this, will I?"

He laughed. "Probably not."

So, despite Allan pleading to stay at Max's a while longer, Rick and Abby escorted him out—and none too gently, in Rick's case—and deposited his drunken ass at his apartment.

But, after even that short ride in the car, Allan's complexion had gone from flushed to oddly ashen. He expressed a desire to be left alone in the bathroom so he could be well situated for the puking to come.

Abby rolled her eyes, but she was too kindhearted to leave her brother in his apartment by himself when he was sick. And Rick, grudgingly, agreed that they'd better stay with him, at least until they knew he was out of any serious danger.

Unfortunately, that kicked a huge dent in Rick's romantic plans for the evening. He muttered several curses under his breath as he eased Allan onto the bathroom floor and hunted down a clean towel for the cockblocker.

"Two nights in a row," Rick hissed, shaking his head at Allan.

"S-Sorry, man," his drunk pal said.

"You should be."

"So, you really like her, then?" Allan asked, pointing toward the front room, where Abby was busy digging in her purse for aspirin and getting him a fresh glass of water.

Rick nodded.

"That's wild," Allan said with a half laugh, half hiccup. "You and my sister. Who'da thought?"

Abby entered, bearing medicinals.

Allan took them gratefully, but he still looked

69

miserable.

"Are you going to be okay?" Abby asked.

Her brother shook his head. "I miss Becca. *Really* miss her." He glanced apologetically at Rick. "I know I said I wasn't gonna text her tonight, but I texted her anyway." Allan started sniffling.

Rick groaned. Abby crossed her arms and sighed.

"And I think I'm gonna be sick now—"

Oh, hell. It was going to be a long night. And not in a fun way.

Sometime after midnight, once Allan was cleaned up, breathing normally, and safely tucked in bed, Rick finally had the chance to have Abby all to himself.

"This wasn't exactly how I imagined the evening," he admitted.

She chuckled. "Well, no. Me, either."

"Your big bro is going to be in bad shape tomorrow— and not just from the hangover. Whatever he texted to his ex-girlfriend will most likely bite him in the butt."

"I don't doubt it. Becca had some good reasons for breaking up with him, and I don't think his behavior tonight will reverse her opinion. She probably wants to smack him upside the head."

He reached for her hand. "Yeah. *I* want to smack him upside the head. Can't believe he messed up tonight as well as last night for us."

"I'm disappointed, too," she said with a shrug. Then, after a lengthy and awkward pause, she added, "But let's be real, Rick. We've had fun this week, but it's not like this thing between us could last much longer anyway, you know?"

He hated this kind of defeatist talk. Ending something

before it even had the chance to begin. He was in no way prepared to give up this quickly. "Why does it have to end, Abby?" He leaned in to kiss her, but she pulled away.

"We live thousands of miles apart, even when you're not working on some top-secret project overseas. And—" She drew a deep, shaky breath. "And I'm not going to trail after you or anyone else anymore, like a lovesick puppy. I did that once already, and it got me nowhere, except abandoned half a dozen states away from home."

Damn that Chandler.

Rick was seeing the full gamut of reds on the color spectrum. Before he could compose himself enough to speak, though, Abby added, "I know you're in a period of transition, and I am as well. I've really loved being with you again these last few days, but I'm considering moving back permanently to the Midwest, and I know you probably need to live somewhere else to further your career." She squeezed his fingers. "So, much as I wish we could keep exploring this, um, sort of relationship, I know it's a short-term thing, and that's all."

He was considered a mild-mannered guy in most circumstances. His temper had a long, long fuse. But not with this. Not now. Not after all this time and all those years of waiting.

"No, Abby, that's *not* all. Stop setting limits on us. On me. And especially on yourself. I get that our connection is surprising and that it's been quick. So the hell what?" He swallowed hard and tried to rein in his growing ire—not with Abby, of course, but with that bastard ex-boyfriend who made her give up on the hope of long-lasting love. "It's not like we just met five days ago. We've known each other since we were kids. The two of us finding each other again has been incredible. And sure, I realize that us staying together as a couple isn't a foregone conclusion or that it'll necessarily be easy, but it isn't something insane either. It's not *inevitable* that it'll fall apart. We just need to give ourselves a chance. Let this play out."

She shook her head slowly, sadly. "But why me, Rick? And why now? Had we not accidentally both been in town this week, none of this would've happ—"

"It was no damn accident."

Her jaw dropped open. "What do you mean?"

His heart was hammering so fast and furiously that he'd have bet money she could hear it pounding this time. But he inhaled and answered her. "Do you honestly think I would have chosen to come to this conference or consented to stay in Mirabelle Harbor with my folks for *this long* if Allan hadn't told me you were coming home? Shit, Abby. I would've *made up* a physics convention to have a reason to come back here to see you. I was just lucky a legitimate one was scheduled, but my boss didn't require me to be at it. I asked him—as a personal favor—to let me tag along."

She looked utterly confused. "You came back—on purpose? For *me?*"

"Yes! That's what I'm trying to tell you. My feelings for you aren't a recent thing, okay? I've been half in love with you since we were teenagers, Abby Solinski."

"But—but wait. Back when we were in high school, I had a major crush on *you*. I practically threw myself at you when I was sixteen, and you blew me off."

"Only because your dad made it clear that I'd better not set foot in your family's house if I messed with you. Hell, you have *no idea* how hard it was to pull away from you when you leaned into me that night after we all watched that movie. I wanted to kiss you so bad. But your family was practically *my* family when we were in school. Your brother was my closest friend. Your mom fussed over me in a way my own didn't. And your dad was my mentor. The man I looked up to most, far more than my Franken-Father. I was head over heels crazy about you, but I couldn't take the chance that I'd be banned from your family, no matter how I felt."

"What about later, though? That time after you'd graduated, you came home from New York and we talked. You looked so irritated—"

"Yeah, exactly. I thought, once we were both away and in college, maybe I could make things happen between us. But you were still living here and still dating Chandler then..." He let the thought trail off and tried to shrug away the pain that always accompanied the memory of Abby with that A-hole.

She was squinting at him, as if trying to calculate some complicated algebraic equation. "You liked me for all of those years?" She shook her head. "I just—I don't believe that, Rick. I mean, I know why I fell for *you* back then. You were cute, super smart, an upperclassman. Someone we all knew would be going places. Your sense of humor was usually over my head when we were in school, and you always acted like I was your best friend's pesky little sister. Nothing more. I think you're revising history in your head. Or getting sentimental in your old age." She smiled weakly at him. "Why on earth would you have liked *me?*"

He actually rolled his eyes in sheer exasperation. "Listen to me. I don't know what kind of crap that Michaelsen prick pulled on you to make you doubt your worth, but despite having a less-than-fantastic home life when I was growing up, I'm not some damaged, tormented, manipulative punk like him. I'm not broken or dark or anything so dangerous and dramatic. I'm just a regular guy—"

"You're a rocket scientist, Rick. You're not a *regular* guy."

"Fine. I'm a *regular* rocket scientist, who's in love with you, and you're not going to get me to claim otherwise. I mean it. Your brother's a good friend and all—well, maybe not tonight." They both laughed at that. Then he continued. "But half the time I was at your house, I was there because of *you.*"

"That's a lie," she said, but she was grinning a little.

Slowly, surely, he'd get her to believe the truth. "Yes," he admitted. "That's a lie. It was actually significantly more than fifty percent. More like eighty-two percent of the time."

She snorted, and he knew he was pulling her around, however reluctantly.

"Hey, remember the bottle bombs that Allan and I made that day at the beach?"

"How could I forget. You two almost got yourselves killed, and Mom was fit to be tied."

He nodded. "I was trying so damn hard to impress you. Your brother thought it was all about the physics for me, but that day, it was all about you. You were as much my passion back then as the science experiments that filled my life." He paused, met her gaze, and held it. "So, all in all, nothing's really changed in the past thirteen years."

Rick leaned in to kiss her again and, this time, she didn't pull away. Not for a long while.

"I'm still having a hard time wrapping my head around all of this and what it means," she whispered eventually.

"I know. But I've got a plan. A new and improved one." He pointed toward Allan's bedroom, where they could hear her brother's soft snores drifting through the apartment. "He owes us. Majorly. And tomorrow, he's gonna pay up. I know just how." He held her close and, man, he didn't want to let her go. Not ever again.

"What have you got in mind?"

"The details will come, but tomorrow is all ours. You and I are going on a formal date, Abby, and this time we're not hiding it from *anyone*."

CHAPTER SEVEN

Saturday Late-Morning, October 28th

The next day, after checking in on Allan and making sure he was all right, Rick began putting his strategic plan into motion.

First, he had a *long* talk with his buddy, delineating the specific ways Allan could help him out. Abby's brother, despite his headache from hell and his chagrin over his behavior from the night before ("I was actually dancing to 'Down' at the bar and, um, singing along? Shit, man. Why didn't you stop me sooner?"), promised his assistance in every way possible.

Next, Rick had reservations to make and advanced tickets to buy.

And, finally, he needed to go grocery shopping.

He told Abby to expect him to pick her up at noon, and he showed up at the Solinski house right on time.

Mr. S greeted him coolly and ushered him inside. "Hello, Rick."

"Hello, sir. You seem to be walking smoothly today. I hope that means your injuries are improving."

"They are," the older man said. "Thank you." He paused. "Abby's still getting ready. She'll be out in a few minutes."

"Great." Rick nodded and exhaled. From the expression on Warren Solinski's face, the guy wasn't going to make this easy on him. But Rick wasn't a teenager anymore. Much as he respected Abby's father, he wouldn't be dissuaded from his mission so easily. And that mission was nothing short of winning Abby's heart and her confidence and convincing her to give their relationship a decent chance.

"So, what are your plans for my daughter today?" her father said stiffly.

"Well, a lot of that depends on Abby," he replied. "I have lunch reservations at a couple of places downtown—I thought I'd let her choose—and tickets for us to go to the Art Institute in Chicago this afternoon. Beyond that, I've got a few movie or theater options for the evening, a drive or motorcycle ride along the lake, and ingredients for a homemade dinner, if she's willing to risk my cooking." There. He'd told Mr. S the salient points. Except, of course, for the post-cooking plans, which involved a whole lot of kissing and touching and possibly more...

"Huh," her dad said. Then, to Rick's surprise, he added, "She's been much happier this week, seeing you again. I'm grateful for that."

Rick swallowed. Maybe he was getting bolder now that he was over thirty, or maybe he was just more mature, but he didn't want to tiptoe around something so important. "I'm glad to hear that, sir. It makes me very happy to be around her, too." Then, after a beat, "I know how much you love your daughter, but you were wrong about me all those years ago."

Mr. S shook his head. "No, Rick. I was right. Exactly right." He paused and it was nothing short of interminable before he spoke again. Then, finally, "Back when Abby was in high school, I thought Chandler Michaelsen was the safer choice for her. He was closer to her age and in the same grade. He came from a good family, but he was so squirrely. So restless. I thought she'd give up on him *years* sooner. But I underestimated her degree of commitment and loyalty." He sighed, his voice weary. "If she'd dated *you* back then, I knew for sure she'd stick with you. You're a forever guy. And, honestly, I thought you were both too young for that. Joke was on me, though, because she stuck with Chandler instead, and for far too long. Left Mirabelle Harbor because of him and didn't even consider coming home again—until now."

He met Rick's eye and looked worried. "I don't want anything to change her mind about that. We miss her here. But interfering in her life was clearly a mistake I made, Rick." He shrugged and sunk into an armchair. "I was right about you. I was wrong about *her*."

Rick almost had to sit down himself after hearing this. Her father's words illuminated everything. Changed everything he thought he'd known about Abby and her family...and Rick's place in it.

"Really?" he whispered.

A whole conversation—left unspoken because, in many ways, it was now unnecessary—passed between the two men.

"Really," Mr. S replied. "Just be good to her, okay?"

"I will," he promised.

"Ricky!" Mrs. S exclaimed, coming out of the kitchen and embracing him. "Would you like a little snack before you and Abby go on your date?" She grinned at him like an eager schoolgirl and started chattering excitedly about these crisp apple turnovers she'd just pulled out of the oven. Rick wasn't remotely hungry after her husband's revelation, but how could he possibly refuse Abby's mom anything?

"They sound delicious," he said, and he managed to eat about half of one before Abby finally emerged from her bedroom.

She was stunning.

He set the plate down and had to instruct his mouth to stop gaping at her and say something instead. "Wow" was all he managed to mutter.

This lack of eloquence on his part didn't seem to derail her. She smiled shyly at him and said, "Sorry it took me so long, but I'm ready to go whenever you are."

"I'm ready," he replied immediately. "Right now."

They said goodbye to her parents and headed toward the door.

"I'll call if we decide to stay out late," she said to them, waving.

"Oh," Rick said, addressing Mr. and Mrs. S. "I meant to tell you both to expect Allan in a few hours. He's coming over to see you and has something fun planned for the three of you this afternoon and evening."

"He is?" Mr. S asked, squinting at Rick.

"He does?" said Mrs. S, sounding surprised.

"He's awake and coherent?" Abby whispered to him.

"Yep," Rick replied loudly, in answer to them all. Then he shot Abby his most charming grin and, in front of her parents, reached for her hand, kissed the back of it, and tugged her out of their house and into his car.

Abby couldn't have dreamt up a better day.

A cheese and steak fondue lunch at The Melted Cauldron in the city, complete with a chocolate fountain for dessert, which was accompanied by cut fruit, cake wedges, and a hilarious explanation from Rick on the physics behind the fountain mechanism. She couldn't stop laughing.

Then a few hours at one of her favorite museums in the

country. With her love of art and design, there was no place better to stroll around and take in the stunning visuals and the masterpieces on display. It was inspiring and fun and an absolutely perfect way to spend a Saturday afternoon.

When she told Rick this, he winked and said, "Good. My plan's working then."

"What's your plan?"

"To make today as memorable for you, Abby, as every moment with you is for me."

Ohhhhh, Rick!

What woman's heart wouldn't melt into a puddle of creamy dark chocolate if someone said that to her?

He had a list of movies they could see or stage plays they could attend and other restaurant options in the city, but when he offered her a motorcycle ride at twilight and then a dinner he intended to cook for her himself, she jumped at the chance for both.

"All right," he said, kissing her lightly. "We'll head back to Mirabelle Harbor."

Apparently, Rick not only had Allan's extra key to his place, but he'd also extracted a lengthy list of promises from her brother, including—but not limited to— transferring Allan's now-working motorcycle from their parents' garage to his complex's parking lot and leaving the bike's keys on the kitchen counter in his now-cleaned one-bedroom apartment.

Abby inhaled deeply, a sweet floral scent surrounding her. "Did he actually use air freshener in here?"

Rick nodded. "The groceries for dinner tonight are in his fridge, as are the bottles of wine. And the sheets on the sofa bed are brand new."

She cut him a sharp look. "The sofa bed?"

He shrugged and lifted the corner of his lips mischievously. "Just sayin'. We have options, Abby. *Lots* of options."

She felt herself flush. "Good to know," she murmured.

Although, it occurred to her as they were riding Allan's bike along the lakefront and taking in the beauty of their hometown as the sun sank to the west, if Rick could be so prepared when it came to meal provisions and activity arrangements, he probably was *very* detail oriented in other ways. Hmm. The mere thought had her mind whirling and her skin tingling in anticipation.

Dinner at Allan's proved to be a wondrous thing. She hadn't thought much could top the feasting fun of their fondue lunch, but his homemade penne Bolognese, fresh garden salad, warm garlic breadsticks, and red, red wine (like the reggae song) made for a mouthwatering meal.

"I'll confess to not having made dessert," he said, pulling a round, dense, rum-soaked tiramisu from the fridge. "But I figured, why not let the experts handle this one?"

It was from a well-known Italian bakery, Bellissima Blanca, in a neighboring suburb, and every bite was pure heaven.

Much as she didn't want the evening to end, she checked the clock and glanced at Rick. "It's after eight p.m. How long do we have until Allan comes back?"

"Until tomorrow morning. Part of the deal he and I made—well, let's face it, that I forced him to make"—they laughed—"was for him to step it up tonight and spend time with your parents, so they wouldn't be alone and would worry less about you. He's got DVDs to watch with them, microwave popcorn, sodas, and more. And he's also got his overnight bag, so he can crash at their place. Unless there's an emergency, his orders are not to disturb us until at least noon tomorrow."

"I'm impressed," she said. "You're good."

"If you think so, Abby, that's all that matters."

He rummaged through her brother's collection of CDs, scrolled through the selections on his iPod, sitting in its dock, and then winced. "I think the radio is our best option."

Abby laughed as Rick flicked on the stereo and tuned it in to Mirabelle Harbor's only radio station, 102.5 "LOVE" FM. Blake Michaelsen was one of the regular DJs, but some other guy was in the studio that night, spinning romantic tunes.

When Michael Bublé's "Save the Last Dance for Me" came on, Rick held out his hand and they began to dance in the middle of her brother's living room. Her body hummed along with his touch, as one song turned into two, three, and four: Chase Bryant's "Little Bit of You," MKTO's "Classic," and an Old Dominion hit called "Song for Another Time," which had Abby reminiscing about songs she knew and loved from past years, similar to what the lead singer of that band was doing.

For her, though, it was music like "You and Me" by Lifehouse, "Lonely No More" by Rob Thomas, and 3 Doors Down's "Let Me Go"—all of which reminded her of Chandler in some way. Thankfully, the pain of those memories had faded considerably. She could almost, almost enjoy listening to those great songs again.

She pulled away and stared at Rick. Oh, she *wanted* him. But, despite their proximity to the sofa bed as they danced, he didn't seem to be making moves in that direction. Why?

It took her a handful of songs and another glass of wine before she managed to work up the nerve to ask. "What's going on, Rick? We're finally alone and, well, the clock is ticking on our time together this weekend. Why, exactly, aren't you making a move on me?"

He broke into a grin that was like the first flash of sunlight at dawn. "I'm a strategist, Abby. I *am* making a move, but I'm playing a long game here. I know you're focused on this idea that we only have until tomorrow evening together, but I don't want this to be a one-night or even a one-week thing. I want you to feel cherished by me and certain about us. And I'll know it when it happens. What I've been setting up is something a lot bigger than just getting laid tonight. Although, I'm not opposed to that either." His grin broadened.

"A long game," she repeated. "Cherished...and certain?"

"Yes. I can explain it another way, too. You've watched space shuttles take off before, right? On TV?"

She nodded.

"Okay, all that most people see and hear is what goes on in the last few hours, minutes, and seconds before the blast. But, of course, there's a whole lot that needs to happen before that final 3-2-1 countdown. There are 'holds' built into each event. Pauses during the countdown that allow a cushion for the launch team, so they can ensure there's enough time for all of the necessary tasks and procedures to get done safely and completely. For instance, at T-43 hours and counting, the test navigational systems are activated. Or at T-27 hours and holding, which typically lasts for approximately four hours, the launch pad is cleared of all non-essential personnel and the cryogenic propellants start to be loaded into the orbiter's PRSD system."

"The PR what?"

"The power reactant storage and distribution system," he explained. "At T-11 hours and counting, the orbiter's fuel cells are activated and there's a switchover from the orbiter's purge air to gaseous nitrogen."

Abby squinted at him. "I literally have no idea what just came out of your mouth."

"That's okay. My point is that for *lots* of time before the actual launch occurs, critical things are being set up. Preflight calibration needs to be performed. The flight crew needs to be briefed on the weather. There are comm checks and inspections of the cockpit switch configurations. At T-9 minutes the flight recorders are activated and there's a final 'go' or 'no-go' decision on the launch polls, conducted by the test and launch directors and the mission management team. It's better to delay than to push forward and risk disaster. But, if it's a go, at T-31 seconds the auto sequence starts. At T-10 seconds the main engine hydrogen burnoff system is activated. And at T-0, we've finally got solid rocket booster ignition and liftoff but, again, only if *everything else* passed inspection beforehand. Only if we're safely cleared for the takeoff."

"And you're saying—what? That our kinda/sorta relationship has to be set up as carefully as a NASA mission? That you'd planned a perfect day for me, created a beautifully romantic night, right down to the new bed sheets, but that if I don't say or do the right thing now, at T minus-something, you won't let us sleep together?" Seriously, she was going to combust soon if he didn't touch her, and that had nothing to do with booster ignition or whatever. Why didn't he get it? They only had this *one* night left.

But Rick just laughed. "That's not exactly what I'm saying, no. I'll try it one more way." He took her hands in his and drew her closer to him. "Abby, I *want* to sleep with you. Believe me, there's almost nothing on Planet Earth I want more, but until I've managed to convince you that my feelings for you are strong and go back years and years, then it's better for us to wait. When we launch this rocket— and we *will*—I want it to shoot straight up, safely, and on course for the moon. Nothing less."

Ah. Maybe she was the one who hadn't been getting it. "Make no small plans, eh?" she murmured.

"Exactly," he said, and then he kissed her. A tender, sensuous, slow, and deeply inquisitive kiss.

And they spent the rest of the night swaying together on their makeshift dance floor, whispering to each other, kissing some more and, eventually, collapsing side by side onto the opened sofa bed—limbs entwined, but clothes still on—where they didn't stir until morning.

CHAPTER EIGHT

Sunday, October 29th

Abby awakened from their daydream-like but fairly chaste night to glimpse the sunrise through her brother's window. But that wasn't the only light she saw.

She also saw a man—Rick Zimmerman—sleeping next to her. A man who'd proven by both word and deed that he cared for her. Truly cared. His loving spirit filled her with a rare sense of hope and, on the wings of that feeling, she decided to initiate her own countdown.

She reached for him across the mattress and ran her fingertips up his jean-clad thigh. Even through the roughness of his clothing, she could find the hardness of his erection. Mmm. That was a good sign.

At the intimacy of her touch, he propped open one sleepy eye and smiled radiantly at her. "Good morning to you, too."

She smiled back and continued to blatantly feel him up.

His breathing quickened and he arched a bit toward her hand. "I'm, uh, guessing you're trying to tell me something, right?"

"Yeah, T-2 minutes," she said, tugging at the waistband of his jeans and flipping open the top button. "Until ignition."

"Oh, you sexy science girl, you're speaking my language."

She laughed. "You know that's not true."

"Maybe not so much a science girl, but sexy? Yes, that's true, Abby." He stilled her hand against his body. "You sure this is how you want to spend this morning?"

"I'm sure."

"What about after today? Is it over, or are you willing to give us a shot?"

"The distance, Rick—"

"Stop thinking about the distance. Just tell me what your heart feels about *us*."

What did her heart feel about being with Rick? God, what *didn't* her heart feel? She'd wanted him in her life since the day Allan had brought him home from school and introduced him to the family. She'd had a deep crush on him for almost as long. And, this week, he'd given her the gift of being singled out, her thoughts and passions respected, her affection treasured and reciprocated.

"I want us to be together," she admitted. "I don't know how it's going to work, and whenever I think about the logistics, I get confused and scared. But if you're asking about how my *heart* feels, that's clear, Rick. Every bit of it wants you."

"That's all I needed to know." He kissed her and, because he was apparently very capable and a master of high-level multitasking, he also tugged off all of his clothes and most of hers without any help. Impressive. Then he said, "Crosscheck," scanned her naked body, winked at her, and retrieved a condom from the crumpled pile of denim on the floor.

"Yeah, I figured you'd be as prepared for this as you've been for everything else that came up this weekend," she observed, as he slipped it on and her heart beat like crazy with the certainty that he'd be against her, inside of her, in moments.

"See how well you know me?" he murmured. Then, "T-15 seconds." He brought his hips flush with hers. His skin caressing her skin. His fingers reaching between them and making her wetter. His breath mingling with hers. His gaze connecting with her own and not looking away.

And though she didn't say this aloud, she tried to convey it to him in the way she looked back at him. That the anticipation and joy of making love with him was far stronger than the fear and pain of what tomorrow might bring.

A split second before Rick's lips touched hers and their bodies connected fully, she heard him whisper, "And we have liftoff."

The physics convention had ended on Friday, and Rick knew he needed to give his boss, Yuri, an answer about New Zealand by tomorrow or Tuesday.

Here were the pros of that job offer: It was a beautiful country, and he'd always liked the southern hemisphere's night sky. His department head would have great legs, a clever mind, and a good sense of humor, and she would appreciate several qualities of his, too. The work would be satisfyingly challenging, and he'd be well-compensated for his time and skills. Yuri and his colleagues would be united in praising him for his excellent professional decision.

Here were the cons: Abby wouldn't be there.

So, obviously, the cons had it.

He'd break the news to Yuri later today. For now, he had to suck it up and let Abby go, hoping against hope that it wouldn't be too long before he saw her again. He had a few ideas for how they could make this relationship work, but he needed to think through all of the specifics and contingencies and have some serious conversations about his career goals with other people, not just with Abby.

He reluctantly dropped her off at her parents' house so she could spend the afternoon with them before her early-evening flight, and he tried to kiss her farewell so passionately that he hoped it'd make their parting very difficult to forget. Making love with her this morning would be an experience burned on his brain until the day he died. He hoped it proved to be half as beautiful and memorable for her.

Allan was going to drive Abby to O'Hare, so Rick had nothing else to do but head back to his mom and stepdad's house, attempt to gather his thoughts about how to reorganize his career and, if he were being honest, mope around because he missed her already.

He just couldn't get that damn particle rap song from the Physics Slam out of his head. "Precision Collision" was haunting him, and the lyrics seemed so unnervingly applicable to his love life that he was both fascinated and annoyed.

No sooner had he'd determined that he needed to blast some classic Pearl Jam to try to disrupt the earworm from burrowing further into his brain, he got a call from Allan.

"Just dropped my sister off at the airport," he said. "There's still time before her flight takes off. Are you sure you don't want to meet her here? Try to stop her from leaving?"

"No," Rick replied. "I've made a few big moves already. I don't want her to feel rushed or pressured. She's got to see this situation clearly by herself and make a choice in the next few weeks or months. Not doing anything, though, is also a choice. And if she goes that route, it'll be telling, too." He hoped to God she wouldn't just return to Sarasota and let this fade away. "Don't try to corner her, Allan."

"I won't. But she really likes you, man." There was a pause. "And I'm pulling for you both."

Rick swallowed. "Thanks, buddy."

Not more than twenty minutes later, his phone buzzed with a text. Abby. He eagerly clicked open her message. "My flight to Florida starts boarding soon. Miss you already. What are you thinking about?"

A new sliver of hopefulness returned to Rick's chest, infusing it with something happy and unexpected. He wasn't wrong. They *could* do this.

He texted her exactly what was on his mind.

"I'm thinking about this rap:

'I'm a charged neutron with a positive pack.
You've altered me, and I can't change back.
We're bound together in this particle dance.
It was an inside job, I didn't stand a chance.
But I know the strength of a bond that's true.
It's why you're with me and I'm with you...'

Or something like that."

There was a long pause, and he could almost hear her laughing at the lyrics.

"Catchy," she texted, along with a smiley face.

"Truthful," he replied, with a pair of heart emojis.

There was an even longer pause.

When her next text came, though, it was worth the wait. "I'm falling in love with you, Rick. I don't want us to be apart."

"Me, either."

Really long pause.

"They're boarding now. Calling my row."

He grimaced but forced himself to reply immediately. "I'll be thinking of you every minute. Text me when you get home, okay?"

"I will," she wrote. And then, complete radio silence.

Less than an hour later, his phone buzzed.

"I'm home," Abby's text said.

How was that possible? He stared stupidly at the screen. He knew the math, and her trip had to take longer than that. Between boarding time, flight time, travel time from the Tampa/St. Pete airport to Sarasota...there were several hours that were unaccounted for.

"How did you get there so fast?" he typed.

"Cab," came her speedy reply.

Cab?

And then he heard a car honking in his parents' driveway. He raced to the window and looked outside.

There she was.

Standing next to a yellow cab, cell phone in hand, shivering even with her jacket on in the autumn chill.

He ran outside. "Abby!" he called out. "You're *here*."

She grinned when she saw him and slipped her phone into her pocket. "You said for me to text you when I got home."

He reached her as fast as he could, wrapped his arms around her, and held her tight. "Yeah, but I thought—"

She relaxed into his embrace and sighed, her head resting against his chest and his madly beating heart.

"Now I am," she said.

EPILOGUE

About Six Weeks Later, Downtown Chicago

Abby had the radio blasting pop/rock hits and was thigh-deep in half-emptied packing boxes. It might take her the rest of December but, eventually, she'd get all this stuff put away.

It'd been a whirlwind since she'd made the decision to delay her flight back to Florida and talk seriously with Rick—face to face—about their future, but it had undoubtedly been the right choice.

After he'd greeted her at the door of his parents' home, they came up with a basic action plan that involved working through career and living-arrangement options and what their timeframe was for putting everything important into place. Then they drove over to her mom and dad's house and they explained to them what she and Rick knew thus far.

"I need to sell my condo in Sarasota, move back to Illinois, and get a new job," she told them.

"I need to cancel my lease on my apartment in Pasadena," Rick told them, "and move back to Illinois.

Specifically Chicago. I've got a lead on a job opportunity downtown."

Mom and Dad exchanged a glance, but neither of them looked displeased with this news.

"If everything goes as I hope," Rick added, "I'll be here permanently in a couple of weeks, with a job lined up for January and a place to live in the city."

"And if everything goes the way I'd like, the condo will be on the market in the next week or two, and I'll be back home before the holidays to begin job hunting, hopefully for something in my field," she said.

"You'll be moving back to Mirabelle Harbor?" her mother asked, her eyes bright with happiness.

Abby and Rick looked at each other. "That's still to be determined," Abby said. "Rick and I need to see how things go, but I might be living in Chicago, too. With him."

Her father frowned slightly at the possibility that his daughter was considering moving in with a man she'd been dating all of one week, but that was the extent of his disapproval and, ultimately, it was fleeting. It wasn't as though her family didn't know Rick well. And once both of her parents realized that Abby was determined to come home to stay and that Rick was willing to move mountains (or, at least, his entire career trajectory) to make that happen, her mom and dad couldn't have been more pleased.

So, here she was. Back in the Windy City. No graphic design job yet, but her Florida condo had sold within a month, and she had money from that coming in to tide her over. Plus, she had the most amazing friends in the world, who Skyped with her almost daily, sent her funny texts and emails, and were planning visits to come up and see her.

In fact, Marianna and Gil were flying up for Chance and Nia's wedding this coming weekend and, not only would she and Rick see them at the ceremony, the four of them were sitting together at the reception. It was, primarily for that reason, that Rick had consented to go to this Michaelsen wedding at all. He knew how supportive of Abby her friend Marianna had been from the beginning, how sweet Olivia and Sharlene continued to be as well, and how much Abby was determined to put her past with Chandler behind her.

"For the record, though," Rick had said when Abby showed him the wedding invitation, "just know that I'd rather take your friends out for pizza and a beer than do the 'Hokey Pokey' with them."

She'd laughed at that. "Don't worry. We don't have to stay late at the reception. And we'll see Marianna and Gil under more relaxed circumstances a few days afterward. They want to get together with Allan and my parents, too."

At this, he smiled. "That'll be fun. Maybe we can rope Becca into joining us."

Ever since the week following that night at Max's Pub when her brother had drunk-texted his undying love to Becca, the former couple had actually been on more cordial terms. Allan apologized sincerely to her for his behavior—both for recent events and going back to the time when they were together—and she, likewise, admitted that she'd missed him and was sorry their relationship had ended so messily. Cautiously, they were giving casual dating a try.

As for Abby and Rick, there was nothing casual about their dating relationship. The several weeks they'd spent on opposite coasts, collecting their belongings and preparing to move, had been the longest of Abby's life. To quote her nerdy lover, there was "a chain reaction" when their paths collided in Mirabelle Harbor that fall, and "it fundamentally changed" them both.

She knew it was true, too.

So, when she finally got back to Illinois, they didn't bother with the pretense of finding separate apartments. They just moved in together. Which was why she was faced with unpacking all of these darned boxes.

Rick, who would've been helping her under normal circumstances, had left hours ago for a meeting in the city. It was with Dr. Byron Prescott, a big physics honcho at the University of Chicago, who'd hired him almost immediately once Rick made his intentions clear that he wanted to move back to the Midwest. The two men were fleshing out details for second-semester classes at the college, where Rick would be teaching a few upper-level graduate courses, doing extensive research in the department, as well as working in affiliation with nearby Fermilab. He'd be heading a project involving high-energy particle physics and something called "neutrinos," which Abby didn't understand to save her life. But Rick was excited, so she was excited, too.

She pulled out a framed photograph, taken in Sarasota at Joy's shop, The Beaded Periwinkle. It was a picture of Joy, Marianna, Lorelei, and herself—laughing over something while making their popular endangered species bracelets—and Gil had snapped the shot. Her friends had given it to her before she'd left Florida, a loving reminder that she would always be part of their tribe, even if she was living over a thousand miles away.

After dusting it off, she placed it in a prominent location on her nightstand in the bedroom and grinned. She should take a picture of it and text it to the ladies. "I'm thinking of you," she'd type as the caption. They'd like that.

She wandered into the front room to grab her cell phone but was startled by a knock at the door.

"Just a minute," she called out, wondering who might be there. A friendly neighbor from across the hall? The UPS guy? Someone delivering someone else's lunch order by mistake? She wasn't expecting anybody.

But when she peered through the peephole, her jaw dropped and her brain froze. Even though she had no idea what she'd say when she faced the visitor, she unlocked the door and swung it open.

The man who stood in front of her looked disheveled, rough, and wary in his dark leather jacket, white shirt, and black jeans. This wasn't unusual for him, though. What was unusual was that, since very few people knew where she lived, he must have come seeking her out specifically. His appearance at her door was no accident.

"Hey, Abby," he said. "I—um, I missed you."

She took a deep breath and exhaled slowly. "Chandler," she whispered. "It's been a while."

~End~

Turn the page for Chandler's story and the exciting conclusion to the Mirabelle Harbor series!

SOMEONE LIKE YOU

CHAPTER ONE

Chandler, Tuesday, December 12th

I pulled into a parking space just before the Cherry Avenue and Main Street intersection, got off my Harley, flipped up my helmet visor, and looked around for the first time in nearly six years.

Home Sweet Fucking Home.

I hadn't planned to return to Mirabelle Harbor for a few more long years and definitely not in ass-freezing December, but the only way I could've gotten out of this trip was if I were dead. And while weddings were a kind of torture I wouldn't inflict on my worst enemy, they did manage to rank marginally higher than funerals.

Unfortunately, it was no enemy who'd called me back home to be in his wedding party. It was my twin brother, Chance. So, basically, I was screwed.

I zipped my leather jacket up as high as it would go and rubbed my hands together for warmth. Even inside my gloves, my fingers were icicles. Having been born a Midwesterner, I knew these temps were considered mild for the area, but it was gonna take an hour in a hothouse for me to completely thaw.

Aside from the cold, the sad memories of being here again chilled me to the bone. Dad had died. Mom had died. The part of me that used to love living in this town had died with them.

Our sister, Shar, however, was adamant that I drive myself back to Mirabelle Harbor and start acting like the kind of best man my twin deserved.

"This means a *lot* to him," she informed me with the scolding, big-sister tone in her voice that was always so damn irritating. She wasn't *that* much older than us. But being a teacher probably went to her head. All that disciplinarian shit that went on in the educational world. Always made me wanna break into the chorus of Pink Floyd's "Another Brick in the Wall."

But I let her give me the lecture she'd called to deliver. And, when Chance called me himself to let me know the date and the final details, I listened as attentively as I could—considering my level of drunkenness at the time.

It'd been a Friday night, for fuck's sake, and he was such a sober little boy scout. Healthy eater. Fitness guru. Moderate drinker. Helpful to old ladies who needed a hand carrying groceries. Unrelentingly responsible. And insanely excited about his wedding to Nia Pappayiannis, this Greek-American chick he fell in love with a couple of years ago.

It was amazing he and I were identical twins. I'm not sure two people who looked so much alike had ever been so different on the inside.

"You'll be here for my wedding, right?" Chance had asked me.

"Yeah, I'll be there."

"For *sure*, Chandler?" he'd said, confirming.

For a guy who didn't talk much, my brother could be damned persistent. "Yessss," I'd said. "For sure." Which was why I was now all the way up in Illinois freezing my balls off instead of in the heart of Georgia.

My bike and I were about ten yards away from Harbor Fitness, Chance's workplace, and I briefly considered making that my first stop in town. Plus, truth be told, I'd missed my twin. But I didn't want to disturb him on the job—he took all that fitness-training shit with his clients so seriously—and, besides, our sister-in-law, Olivia, was expecting me soon.

Didn't stop me from inhaling a few more lungfuls of the icy air and checking to see what was new and what was familiar in good ol' Mirabelle Harbor.

The downtown was bustling with holiday shoppers. The coffee shop just to my right, Not the Same Old Grind, was doing brisk business on account of their hot beverages.

The Gala across the street was the Greek restaurant and bakery owned by Nia's family, and they looked to be gearing up for the lunch crowd.

I'd just driven by The Penalty Box, that sportswear store belonging Shar's hockey-player boyfriend, and it looked overrun by customers buying bags of athletic wear.

Couldn't help but wonder about the bookstore, Between the Pages, though. I knew from my last Internet search that it was still in business and still located just around the corner on Cherry, but I wasn't able to see it from here. I'd have to actually drive down the street, and I couldn't bring myself to do that. Not yet. I didn't even know for certain if Jaleina still owned it and worked there, but I had a hard time imagining the place without her.

Finally, I kicked my bike back into action and drove to my childhood home—what we lovingly called Michaelsen Manor—on Lake Michigan. Now the house belonged to my eldest brother, Derek, his wife, Olivia, and their three boys, James, Riley, and Peter, but it was where I'd be camping out for the next week until this damn wedding was over.

Olivia welcomed me with a huge hug—it always amazed me how tight she could squeeze for a petite woman—and ushered me inside. Weird to be in here again, though. It was like I emotionally regressed a decade just by walking into the foyer. I was almost thirty, but I felt like a teenager again.

"Chandler, your hands are frozen!" my sister-in-law exclaimed, after her fingers brushed mine. "You need warmer gloves."

"Nah," I said, shoving my thin riding gloves into the pockets of my jacket. "I won't be staying here long enough. I'll be back in the land of sunshine and peanuts in no time. These'll do."

Olivia frowned. "Still. Derek probably has a pair you can borrow while you're here. I'll ask him when he gets home."

My eldest brother was at work in downtown Chicago doing some kind of investment thing. I could never quite wrap my head around that stock-trading crap, but he liked it and was good at it. And the rugrats were in school. I glanced around the hallway, catching sight of a few framed family photos on the wall. Yeah, it'd be wild to see my nephews again. The older two would barely remember me. And Peter—last time I saw him he was a baby. Now he was in first grade.

"The kids have school this whole week?" I asked.

"Yes, thank God. I've got seventeen million things left to do before the wedding, so I took this week off and half of next. But their vacation starts on Friday afternoon."

"When do they get back today?"

"The bus drops them down the block at three thirty. You'll hear them before you see them." She grinned. "They're so excited to see you, Chandler."

"Likewise."

She pulled me into the kitchen, poured me a hot cup of coffee, and set about making me lunch while we caught up on shit. She mostly asked me questions about my life, and I answered. I lived a simple existence down South. Atlanta was a big city, so I got to satisfy my wanderlust, moving around three times to different parts of town. I'd worked for four different tech companies in the past couple of years and left when I got bored. I was feeling the edges of restlessness again and getting ready to move on, but I didn't know where. Maybe North Carolina this time. Maybe Virginia.

"Any chance it might be Illinois?" she asked me.

"With this cold weather? Hell, no. There's not even snow on the ground right now and it's like the Arctic around here."

This made her laugh as she put the finishing touches on the sandwich she was creating for me. It'd been a helluva long time since anybody'd fixed me a meal that wasn't some hastily thrown together morning-after breakfast or a late-night frozen pizza with a beer chaser. I watched her, fascinated by this whole domestic routine. My big brother was a lucky guy. He'd struck gold, not once, but twice.

But thinking about *that*—about the other woman in Derek's life before Olivia—was strictly verboten. My taboo crush on my brother's ex-fiancée was no smarter these days than it'd been in high school, some fourteen years ago. But holy hell. Jaleina Longoria had been *hot*. That one time I spied her through the crack in Derek's bedroom door, half naked, when our parents were out and he thought Chance and I were at the movies—that was forever seared in my memory. What I wouldn't give to know what she looked like now...

"Everything okay?" my sister-in-law asked, catching me staring into space, remembering.

I nodded and took a big bite out of the fancy grilled panini she set in front of me. "Just a little tired," I admitted around a mouthful of chicken sandwich, all smothered in pesto sauce and some sort of artisan cheese. "This is good, thanks."

She put a bowl of chips on the table and a platter of cut fruit, too. "It was a long ride home, wasn't it?"

Longest fucking ride of my life. But I just said, "Yeah."

"Well, after you finish, you can rest up. We fixed your old bedroom for you to stay in this week, so if you need a nap, you can take one. And you'll probably need to replenish your energy before my sons get home and pounce on you."

I laughed. "Which one of them am I displacing?"

"Riley. But don't feel bad. He's beside himself with excitement to get to bunk with James. Peter's actually jealous and wanted you to sleep in his room instead."

"Whose room does Peter have?"

Olivia squinted up at the ceiling. "Pretty sure it was Blake's."

"Just to the right of the linen closet?"

"Exactly."

"I won't tell my nephews this, but Blake always claimed his room was haunted. Told us about weird noises at night and furniture that had been moved when he was asleep."

"What?" She looked worried.

"No, no. It's not true. Blake was just making shit up to keep Chance and Shar and me out of his room. He admitted it, under some duress, years later."

"What kind of duress?"

"He was wasted, and Chance and I were sitting on him."

She burst out laughing. "Okay. I believe that. Shar didn't join in?"

"Nope. She wasn't there, but Abby was with us. She even took a few incriminating photos." I grinned at the memory, and then winced a little, thinking about Abby Solinski, my ex-girlfriend. The longest and best relationship I'd ever had by far. She was a sweetheart, and I'd screwed things up big time between us. The guilt still sucker-punched me whenever I thought about it.

My sister-in-law's expression had turned odd.

"What?" I asked her.

"Just, um—you mentioned Abby. She...she was in town a couple of months ago. Did you know about that?"

I shook my head. Last I'd seen her had been in Sarasota a couple of years ago when we broke up. She'd watched me with tears in her eyes as I rode away on my bike. She'd even tried to keep in touch at first, but I was a shithead, and she wisely gave up on me. Not her fault what happened but—hell. She'd wanted something I couldn't give.

"Actually, Chandler," Olivia said, speaking gently. *Too* gently. "She just moved back."

"Abby's living in Mirabelle Harbor?" This wasn't a huge surprise, I supposed. She hadn't hated her life here the way I had. Then again, she didn't have a pair of dead parents haunting her at every turn.

"No." There was an awkward pause. "She's living nearby, though. In Chicago. And, uh, she's living with somebody now."

This, I had to admit, did surprise me. "Anyone I know?"

"You might, yes. Rick Zimmerman—do you remember him? He was a couple of years ahead of you guys in school."

That asshole? Shit.

I forced myself to take another bite of my sandwich and tried to make my face look indifferent to this news. "Hmm, yeah," I mumbled.

My shrewd sister-in-law could probably see right through me, though. She continued on in that annoyingly gentle tone about how it was so *nice* to see Abby again and that she seemed *happy*, which was a *good* thing, right?

Maybe. But with fucking "Rocket Rick"? That science nerd had been after Abby since we were all in high school together. I wanted to be happy for her—she *deserved* to finally get all that romance crap she loved—but, damn, I wished she'd chosen anyone other than that show-off brainiac who'd almost burned down the chem lab and half of our school.

"You've seen her? Recently?" I managed to ask.

Olivia nodded. "Shar and I met her for lunch in the city this past weekend. She sold her condo in Sarasota and the moving van hadn't yet made its way up here, so she was enjoying a little downtime with us before unpacking. She's planning on finally getting a job in graphic design."

"That's good. She always liked art and creative stuff."

"Yes, it'll be great for her," she said enthusiastically. "And Rick's going to be teaching a couple of grad courses at the University of Chicago next semester. He's also involved with some physics thing at Fermilab that's impossible for normal people to understand."

Of course he was. "Where in the city do they live?"

Olivia narrowed her eyes at me. "Why?"

"Oh, stop looking at me like I'm gonna cause trouble. I'm just curious."

She crossed her arms, clearly not believing me. "I haven't been to their place yet, but Abby told us it was an apartment on Lake Shore Drive."

"Ah, high-class digs." And just vague enough of a description that I'd never be able to figure out where, specifically, it was. "Well, she's a beautiful person. She's kind and loyal and...and I wish her well." All true about Abby. Couldn't necessarily say the same about Rick.

My sister-in-law studied me carefully. "Just so you know, Abby and Rick are going to be at the wedding this weekend."

"Really?"

It was going to be so fucking awkward if the first time I saw her since I left Sarasota was at my twin's wedding. Maybe I should talk to her first. Somehow.

"Yeah," Olivia said. "A lot of people in town will be there. Nia's family is huge, and they know tons of people. And, honestly, so do we."

That was the understatement of the millennium. Just between Olivia, Sharlene, and Blake, most of the residents of Mirabelle Harbor were covered, and it wasn't as though Derek and Chance were hermits in town. Which, of course, made me wonder if Jaleina had somehow gotten an invitation as well. Talk about awkward. Of course, even if she did, I couldn't imagine she'd accept it.

"You got a copy of the guest list?" I half joked. "Maybe I should check to make sure I know what I'm getting myself into on Saturday."

"Ha. I do, but I'm not going to show you, Chandler."

"Why not?"

"Because you need to be there no matter what," she said firmly. "Now, c'mon. Eat the rest of your lunch, and then I'll let you unpack. Not that it'll take long." She eyed my small leather sack that I'd brought inside. It'd been attached to the back of my motorcycle and held enough clothes for a few days, which was all I'd need.

I laughed, but I did as she said, and soon I was staring at the walls of my childhood bedroom. A place where my fantasies came to life again, as if I'd never left. And where the grief of losing Mom and Dad wrapped itself around me like a freakin' fog. I wouldn't be able to take a nap. To sleep here, I'd have to be exhausted, not merely tired.

Plus, I knew Olivia was a creature of habit, and I had a sneaking suspicion that I could get some classified information out of her without her knowing it.

As soon as she went down to the basement to do laundry, I waited five minutes and then called out to her that I was going to run an errand or two. Reacquaint myself with the town. "Be back in a few hours, okay?"

"Okay!" she called up. "But don't forget, the boys want to spend time with you after school, and Derek can't wait to see you. He's going to try to come home a little early tonight."

I checked the display on my phone. It wasn't even one

o'clock. I had plenty of time. "No problem. I'll be back soon." I inched over to the desk in the living room, just to the left of the foyer, where Olivia had always kept her letters, stamps, and...address book. She was traditional that way.

I flipped to the "S" page of the book—Solinski. Saw the listing for Abby's parents' house in Mirabelle Harbor, a Sarasota address that had been crossed out in a different color of ink, and a new addition for Chicago. Lake Shore Drive.

Bingo.

I memorized the specific building and apartment numbers, slipped on my jacket, helmet, and gloves, and took off for the city.

Abby's building was a beaut. An older one, but well-maintained, with character and charm. Obviously expensive to live in, especially with a view of the lake like that, but I'd bet it was well worth it.

Unlike my family, Abby hadn't grown up with much money—and neither had her main squeeze, though the guy probably made a bundle now. But I knew Abby had solid middle-class values, that she was a good saver and a hard worker. She'd do all right.

I was working up the nerve to ring the buzzer when a mom with three children left the building. Gawd, poor lady! Lugging a stroller with a baby in it and two kids hanging off her on the side. I held the door for them and smiled super politely. She was probably too preoccupied to even notice me slipping inside.

I took the flight of steps up to the second floor, checked for Abby's apartment number, and listened. I could hear music playing. Was that Imagine Dragons? She'd liked that group and so many others. Didn't hear any other voices, though, so I raised my fist to knock.

But I didn't make contact with the door. I pulled my hand away, fidgeted like an anxious seventh grader, and waited some more.

Damn. Why was I so nervous all of a sudden? It was just Abby, me, and—oh, hell—about half a truckload of guilt.

Before I could weenie my way out of it, I made myself knock.

"Just a minute," she called out.

Man, it'd been so long since I'd even heard her voice. A deep pang of longing and regret hit me in the gut. I'd just driven down here on impulse, without really thinking about what I needed to say to her. I should've written a few phrases out on a note card or something. My sincerest apology in ten words or less.

The door swung open, and there she was, staring at me with a look of utter shock.

My mind blanked for a sec when I first saw her. Lovely as ever, but not mine anymore. Maybe she never was.

"Hey, Abby," I finally managed to blurt. "I—um, I missed you."

I couldn't read anything on her face beyond her stunned expression. Physically, she'd hardly changed in the last two years. Still beautiful with that softness around her eyes and lips that reminded me of how kind and sensitive she was. A gentle spirit that I'd crushed, just by being myself.

"Chandler," she said, her voice barely above a whisper. "It's been awhile."

I nodded. "It has. And I'm sorry about that. I know it's my fault."

"Uh—" She squinted at me then glanced down the hall. "Are y-you here with anyone? How d-did you know where I lived? I mean, I literally *just* moved in."

"I got back to Mirabelle Harbor today, and Olivia

mentioned that you were in Chicago."

"Olivia *gave you* my address?" Her surprised expression flashed with anger.

"No, not exactly. Please don't be mad at her. She had no idea I'd stoop to riffling through her address book to find your place, and she doesn't know I'm here now. If she did, she'd throttle me. She only told me you were in the city, and that you were living with, eh, someone. And—" I paused, willing her to invite me inside. But she didn't. Hesitation was written all over her face. So the next thing I needed to say came out like a gush of water from a hose that'd been turned on full blast. "Look, Abby, I'd understand if you don't want to let me in or talk to me at all. But I'm not sure if you'll be comfortable with your neighbors overhearing my confessions, and I owe you a few." I gave her my most winning grin and, thankfully, scored a small smile.

It made my heart flutter a little with remembrance, especially when she cracked the door open a bit wider and I knew she was about to cave. But I also knew that this fluttering-heart feeling was sentimental, not carnal. I missed Abby like hell—but as a longtime friend, not as a lover.

She motioned for me to come inside as she wove through an obstacle course of cardboard boxes to get to the radio. She switched it off with one hard click, then turned to face me. Less stunned now, more curious.

"Sorry about the mess," she said. "The moving van just came yesterday."

"Yeah, I can see that." I forced myself to look away from her and take in the room. "Looks like a great place."

"It'll be nice soon. Once I can get everything put away." She paused. "So, did Olivia tell you who I'm living with?"

"Yes," I admitted. "Rick Zimmerman." I fought the bile that rose up just saying his name aloud and tried to keep the sarcasm out of my tone. From Abby's slight frown, I didn't quite manage that. I gave up and crossed my arms. "He always *did* have a thing for you."

"So everyone keeps telling me. I hadn't thought so at the time, but—"

"Oh, c'mon. Of course he was crazy about you, Abby. You're beautiful, smart, creative, sweet, so damned easy to love—"

"And why, exactly, wasn't that enough for *you*, Chandler?" she interrupted, all the hurt still there, just under the surface. It slayed me.

"'Cuz I'm a fucking fool," I whispered. What else could I say? It was the truth. But I took a deep breath and said the rest, too. "And because I want what I want. To come and go as I please. To not be tied down to any one place."

"Or any one person?"

"I *never* cheated on you, Abby. You have to know that. And I didn't leave Sarasota so I could be with someone else. I just needed to leave."

"So, there's no one, um, special in Atlanta?"

"Is that what you thought?"

She shrugged. "I didn't know what to think."

There'd been a lot of late-night bar hookups but, no, I could answer honestly that there was no one remotely special to me in Atlanta. And I told her this.

Of course, she'd asked the wrong question. She hadn't asked about Mirabelle Harbor.

Abby shifted uncomfortably on the plush carpet, wearing these cute Santa socks. Perfect for the season. "So, why did you come down here to see me, Chandler? What confessions do you have that my new neighbors shouldn't overhear?"

I took a deep breath and slowly released it. "Just that I knew when we were together, especially during our last year, that I was dragging you around the country when I should've let you go, and for that I'm sorry. Sorry I couldn't stay in one place with you. Sorry I couldn't go back to Florida to get you once I'd left. Sorry I couldn't be the man you needed." I sighed, opening up and telling her what she ought to finally hear from my lips. "For what it's worth, both my sister and my sister-in-law will never forgive me for our breakup, so the Michaelsen family punishment will be eternal and unpleasant."

At this, she sort of chuckled. "Oh, get real. Shar and Olivia love you. And they know I'm doing fine now. Rick and I are right for each other. And we're happy."

"I'm glad to hear that. Truly. You deserve good things."

"Thanks. I wish the same for you, too. Sooner, I hope, rather than later."

"Appreciate the wish, sweetheart, however unlikely it is to come true." I moved in to hug her—she was so soft, warm, familiar, even after having not seen her for a couple of years—and she let me do it. All those years of memories rushed back in a heartbeat.

Damn. It would've been so much easier if I could've just stayed with her and loved her like she deserved. If being with her could've been enough to keep me from pushing onward. But it wasn't, and it was better for Abby that our ties were severed. That she'd gotten some closure, and I'd finally manned up and apologized. I smiled into her hair, remembering the way we used to—

A door slammed shut behind me, and Abby and I sprung apart as an infuriated male voice said, "What the hell are *you* doing here?"

Aw, shit.

I swiveled around to face that pain-in-the-ass physics genius, who looked like he was about to go fucking ballistic. "Hey, Rick. Long time, no see," I said lightly.

The guy looked from me to Abby and then back to me again. "I could've waited longer, Chandler."

"Rick!" Abby cried.

The nerd, who'd beefed up considerably in the past decade, took several purposeful steps in my direction. I knew enough about pissed off boyfriends of women I'd hit on in bars to know that he wanted to rip my head off with his bare hands.

Rick actually said something to that effect, which surprised me and nearly kept me standing in the same dangerous spot.

Abby reached out and pushed me away before her brainiac boyfriend could throw the first punch. "Rick, stop. Please. Chandler just came by—briefly—to apologize for how things ended in Sarasota. And—" She shot me a significant look. "He wanted to wish us well. Right, Chandler?"

Rick didn't utter a sound, but he stared at me. Hard.

"Right," I agreed before "Rocket Rick" could jettison me out of their apartment and halfway on an unplanned mission to Mars. "Abby, great seeing you again. And Rick, uh—" I got myself over to the door. "It's been, well, you look—very fit."

He crossed his arms and continued glaring.

"Yeah," I said. "So, I'll keep an eye out for you both at my brother's wedding, but it's gonna be crazy that day. If we don't have a chance to chat much—"

"We won't be offended," Rick interjected, his expression icy.

Abby rolled her eyes. "*I'll* look forward to seeing you on Saturday, even for a few minutes, Chandler. Thanks for the visit. And please say hi to all of your family from me, okay?"

"I will." Then, with a quick wave, I strode out of their apartment and into the Midwestern chill, which was downright balmy compared to Rick's gaze.

Riding back to Derek and Olivia's house on my bike left me feeling light, though, like I'd left a heavy load on the side of the highway and could now fly freer, even if I still wasn't quite ready to go "home."

This time, as I motored through the middle of Mirabelle Harbor, I turned right on Cherry Avenue and drove past the bookstore.

Yep, there it was. Between the Pages. Still looking the same and especially busy on this late afternoon. Customers poured in and out of the place. Well, there were only thirteen shopping days 'til Christmas, after all.

I turned a few blocks down from the store and drove back—slower this time. I spotted just a flash of her, but she was standing there for real and in the flesh.

Hell. I would've recognized that gorgeous silhouette anywhere in the world: Jaleina Longoria. Eight and a half years older than me. My brother's former fiancée. And the untouchable woman who'd been my Ultimate Fantasy since I was sixteen.

Only good thing about Chance's flippin' wedding was that the one person in the world who could make me as tongue tied as a preteen—and, simultaneously, as hard as granite—wouldn't be there. No way would she come to a Michaelsen event after everything that went down between her and Derek.

And that was a relief. Because I had toasts to give and best man duties and crap to perform, and I wouldn't be able to concentrate for shit if Jaleina was sitting there, staring at me, and reminding me of all the reasons why it was still unrealistic for me to desire her so damn much.

CHAPTER TWO

Blake, Tuesday Night

It was obvious to Blake that his kid brother was squirrelly as hell tonight. The question was *why*. Chandler had been back in Mirabelle Harbor for what? Six hours? Seven? And already he looked like he wanted to bolt.

Couldn't blame the guy—at least not entirely. With prying Michaelsens swarming around like gnats, big family dinners had never been Blake's favorite form of inquisition either, and the clan had been even worse when he was a single man. In ways too numerous to count, Vicky had saved him.

So Blake sympathized. He knew it had to be hard for his little bro, especially with his twin getting hitched, his ex moving on without him, and the entire family watching his every move.

But he also sensed that there was something *else* up with Chandler. Something weird. Though it'd better not be about him taking drugs, or Blake would beat the shit out of his ass.

"Blake," Vicky said, sidling up to him. "You got quiet

all of a sudden. What's up?"

Just looking at her sweet face made him happy. It was the craziest damn thing. "Nothin' on my end, babe. Just keeping an eye on my brother. The dude's a fucking mess, and I don't know the reason."

She turned her gaze to Chandler and studied him in silence for a moment. "He does look...weathered, for want of a better word. Beaten down a bit by life. At least compared to Chance. But then, he drove a long way to be here. And there's a difference between being the groom and being the best man. He probably doesn't want to take the attention away from his twin."

He grinned at this. Vicky had never met Chandler before tonight, and she didn't know the brother of Blake's youth. Chandler was free-spirited, fun-loving, as talkative as his twin was quiet. Blake doubted it'd ever crossed Chandler's mind not to monopolize a conversation, no matter who else was in the room. But something had changed in the guy after their parents had died. He'd seemed hell bent on running away and, let's face it, he'd succeeded.

But Blake's girlfriend was right. The Chandler that had returned to Mirabelle Harbor was worn. Drained from the great effort of fighting a battle with the road. He looked tired out from the race.

"Yeah. I'm a little worried about him," he admitted.

This worry was further justified during dessert when Nia said brightly, "Oh! My mom and I finished the seating arrangements for my side—our family's friends and all of the Pappayiannis relatives."

"Good," Olivia declared, waving her fingers. "Hand it here," she added as Nia rummaged through her purse for the list. "Chance, do you want to help decide who sits at which reception table for our side?"

The groom-to-be looked at her in mystification and said with utter solemnity, "No, thank you."

Everyone gathered around the large dining room table burst out laughing—Nia loudest of all.

"I think you and Shar are probably going to have to make the final decisions on your own for that," the future bride told Olivia, pulling out her list. "We've got some friends in common, so please feel free to play around with the tables if you think of a better arrangement."

Nia pointed to the sheet of paper. "I've got my Wisconsin relatives—Aunt Helen, Uncle Theo, my cousins Jason and Nick and their plus ones—all together, and I added a couple of my single friends at their table because I know my family is chatty. Margie from the coffee shop is coming, and Jaleina will be there. So will—"

Blake saw Chandler's jaw drop halfway to his chest. "Jaleina Longoria?" he interrupted. "She's coming to the wedding?" He glanced wildly around the dining room, first at Nia and Chance, then at Olivia and Derek. No one but Chandler appeared surprised by this revelation.

"She's a good friend of mine," Nia said softly. "I love visiting her at the bookstore. And, um..." She looked to Olivia and Derek for guidance.

"And Olivia and I were delighted Jaleina could come," Derek said to Chandler, despite the latter's clear astonishment.

"I know you probably think it'll be a little awkward for us," Olivia added. "And it will." Everyone laughed. "But Mirabelle Harbor is a small suburb, and it would've been silly to leave her off the guest list just because she and your brother had...history."

Chandler took in this news, but if the guy was acting strange before, it was even more apparent now.

"I'm just surprised," he told them.

Sharlene shot Blake one of her "What the hell?" looks.

Chance studied his twin thoughtfully.

And Declan, Vicky, and Nia—the not-quite-Michaelsens (yet)—just watched this interaction with interest.

Vicky leaned in toward Blake a few minutes later and whispered, "Was it just me, or did Chandler's reaction to Jaleina coming to the wedding seem unusually strong?"

"It wasn't just you. Pretty sure you called it right."

"Did he not like Jaleina when she and Derek were engaged?"

He shook his head then shrugged. "You know, I don't know. Maybe that's it. I hadn't noticed any animosity between them, but I was away at college. Only Chance and Chandler were living in the house back then because they were still in high school. Shar was at the university, too. Although Derek had been living at home for a semester around then because he was doing an internship. It was before Dad got sick..." He let that melancholy thought trail off and just tried to remember back to that time. It'd been a happy period in his family's history—at least, he'd always believed so.

But if some weird shit had gone on back then that he didn't know about, he'd figure it out. No way would Blake willingly overlook something important that was happening with the people he loved. He'd just have to keep an extra close eye on his squirrelly little brother.

~Chandler~

Oh, FUCK!

Jaleina was going to be at my brother's effing wedding after all. Shit. Shit. Shit.

Now I'd have to see her, too, and try to fake my way into sounding polite and charming, when all I'd want to do was—well, images of raking my fingers down her back and ravishing every single inch of her body flooded my mind.

When I could finally get away from the probing gazes of my relatives and their significant others, I crashed on my bed upstairs and replayed in my head that semester when

Chance and I were sophomores and Derek was home for his grad-school internship. When Mom and Dad—God rest their souls—were out with their friends, and our clever big brother would sneak Jaleina into the house. They'd be laughing softly in his bedroom and doing other things that made me irrationally jealous, wishing it were *me* in there instead of him.

She was so damned far out of my league back then. Twenty-four years old and stunning when I was sixteen and gawky. And I was still as horny right now as I was back then, just thinking about caressing her smooth skin, kissing those full dark-pink lips, running my hands through her long light-brown hair that was streaked with rays of gold.

Worst of all, I'd *liked* her. I'd enjoyed every second of our conversations, no matter how brief. Jaleina didn't talk down to me or treat me like a kid. She was well-read even then, and witty and kind and thoughtful. When I showed off and taught her how to do some easy computer thing that she claimed not to know, she acted believably impressed.

Looking back, she must've been pretending, but I loved that she made the effort to make me feel a little more like a man, back at a time when I knew I wasn't even close.

No way out of it now. If I was going to have to see her on Saturday anyway and suffer through every fucking embarrassing emotion, why bother to avoid her this week? Her bookshop opened at ten o'clock tomorrow morning. Guess where I'd be at 10:05?

CHAPTER THREE

Jaleina, Wednesday, December 13th

I yawned. Clearly, I was getting too old for this routine.

As I unlocked the door to my bookshop, I figured I'd better start acting my age and getting a few extra hours of sleep. I should really push my workouts to eight thirty in the morning, rather than go to the gym at the crack of dawn. I'd been up since six a.m.—only because it allowed me to zip into Harbor Fitness for the earliest exercise class and then zip out again before Chance even arrived on the scene. Seriously, I needed to get over my aversion to running into members of the Michaelsen family.

Chance was a good guy and I'd always liked both him and his twin, Chandler, but I still didn't relish spending a ton of time with their family. Didn't matter how pleasant they all were to me. Thankfully, the big wedding was this weekend. I was happy to attend for Nia's sake, but I knew I'd be relieved when Saturday was over.

I rubbed my eyes and went to plug in the coffee maker. C'mon, little stainless-steel machine. Start perking. Please.

The coffee had just begun to brew when I heard the

bells chime and an early customer enter the store.

I turned to look at the door and—oh, hell!—speak of the devil.

Chandler Michaelsen.

After several years away, the guy still had a noticeable presence when he entered a room. A trait he shared with his brothers, although he was a slightly torn and tarnished version of his twin and tended to sport a little more facial hair than his clean-shaven mirror image.

But, wow.

While he'd only shot up another inch or two in height, he definitely looked grown up. Manly. Intense.

"Jaleina," he said, breathing out my name in a way that was uniquely his. Even if I hadn't been able to tell him apart from his twin visually, which I always could, I would've been able to do it aurally. Chance and Chandler had dissimilar speaking patterns and gave off distinctly different vibes. Like "Good Neighbor" versus "Danger Boy."

"I heard these crazy rumors that you were coming back to town," I told him lightly. "Guess you couldn't miss your brother's wedding, huh?"

He grinned and bowed his head with a rueful nod. "My family insisted my attendance was required. You'll be there, too?" he asked me, although I got the feeling he already knew the answer.

"I will, yes."

"Good." Then he said something that completely blindsided me. "I hope you'll save me a dance at the reception."

I laughed this off. "Very gallant of you, Chandler, but I'm sure you'll be too busy with the young ladies to hang out with an old one."

His eyebrows shot up. "You're not old and, no, I won't be." He crossed his arms and gazed at me in a way that was almost...*assessing.*

I felt a sudden flush of warmth, which was totally inappropriate. He was practically a kid compared to me. Well, an almost thirty-year-old kid. But, anyway, I knew he couldn't be serious.

Regardless, the subject desperately needed to be changed. "So, what are you doing with yourself these days?" I asked. "Still living out East?"

"Kinda. I've lived a few places. Doing tech work at IT firms, mostly. Troubleshooting computer problems. That kind of shit."

"Well, those are desirable skills," I said, meaning it. "My computer has been giving me fits lately whenever—"

"Maybe I can diagnose it," he interrupted, glancing around the bookstore, as a few new customers entered. "Is it here?"

"No, it's my home computer. And I wouldn't want you to trouble yourself with—"

"It's no trouble, Jaleina. Just let me know when I can stop by and I'll take a look. Need to keep my *desirable* skills sharp during my northern sabbatical or they could get rusty." He grinned again in that manner that made me certain he wasn't merely talking about computer competence.

The guy was undoubtedly used to getting his way with women. He'd been brimming with sexual intensity even as a teenager, but *now*—jeez. Chandler was a potent force to be reckoned with, and I wasn't as immune to it as I should have been. Not by a long shot. He was Derek's baby brother, for God's sake. It was practically cradle robbing even just flirting with him. This had to stop.

But it didn't.

He spent half the morning with me at the bookstore, keeping me company when I wasn't helping other customers, asking me questions to prolong our conversation, and getting me to laugh aloud in spite of myself. Best—or worst—of all, he made it clear that he wanted to see me while he was in town and not just in passing at the wedding.

Loneliness could make a woman weak, and it'd been far too long since I'd had a significant other in my life. Just showed what could happen when a woman was thirty-eight and hadn't gotten laid in over a year. Having a guy paying attention to me was seductive, even if he was too young for me and couldn't possibly be sincere in his interest.

In my defense, though, no one who hadn't known Chandler for nearly a decade and a half, the way I had, would have thought he was anything like the scrawny teen of years' past. His twin hadn't left town and had grown into a sexy and confident man, too, but Chance was wholesome, for want of a better word. Absolutely perfect for Nia and an all-around sweetheart to the residents of Mirabelle Harbor, if somewhat serious.

Chandler was many things, but wholesome and sweet weren't two of them. A person could read the difference in the expression in his eyes. The firm brackets around his lips. The posture he used when he strode into a room. He had a way of claiming every step he took, like a predator.

And heaven help me, while in his company, it was strangely difficult to think of myself as a lecherous older woman out to corrupt him. Not when he was staring at me like a wolf.

As Chandler and I continued to chat, one customer came up to the front register, arms full of books. She wanted to buy a six-volume set of Jane Austen novels, along with a pair of bookmarks with literary quotes.

"I hope you'll enjoy these," I told her as I bagged her purchases.

"Oh, I already love Austen," the older woman gushed. "These novels are for my granddaughter. I want to get her hooked while she's still easy to influence."

"How old is she?" I asked, expecting her to say a teenager or, maybe, a young woman in her twenties.

"Just turned four," the woman replied. "Can't start too early introducing her to Jane." Then she winked and all but waltzed out the door.

Chandler and I laughed.

"A super fan," he noted.

I agreed. "Then again, it's really romantic that Chance and Nia are getting married on Jane Austen's birthday, December sixteenth. From what Nia told me, that was her first choice for the wedding date."

"I'm not surprised. Nia, Shar, Vicky, and Olivia are all period drama freaks."

I crossed my arms and mock-glared at him.

"Not that there's anything wrong with that," he added quickly, raising his palms in a sign of surrender. "But Blake and Declan were complaining about all the Regency costumes and literary shit their girlfriends are into. Chance and Derek know better than to say anything. But there's some *Pride and Prejudice* marathon on PBS this week, and the ladies have been going crazy over it. Blake starts to gag every time the subject comes up."

This made me grin just thinking about it. I knew what an extensive reader Blake Michaelsen was, despite his tough-guy image. He'd been an outstanding customer of mine for years. So I also knew he had to be putting on an act for his family. The guy had read nearly all of the classics, including several novels by Austen, and not a single soul had made him do it.

"*Persuasion* is my favorite of the stories, but I've been watching the *Pride and Prejudice* marathon on TV, too," I informed Chandler. "It's excellent."

"Well, you'd fit right in with the rest of my family then," he said, stopped abruptly, and then grimaced at the awkwardness that followed. "Sorry, Jaleina. I didn't mean—"

"It's okay," I tried to reassure him. "That's water under the bridge. Really."

He muttered something I couldn't catch. Something about "Derek" and "fool." I might have been flattered if I'd heard the whole thing, but it didn't matter in any case. I wasn't a Michaelsen woman, and I never would be. Derek had made sure of that.

Honestly, after seeing him and Olivia together, it was all for the best. There was something that hadn't fully meshed with Derek and me. At the time, I'd blamed our differences in ethnicity, which was easier than thinking we just weren't soul mates. The Michaelsens had always been a tight-knit bunch, and though I would have loved to have been a part of that camaraderie, it might have been worse if I'd married into the family and never quite fit in.

As my Mexican grandparents used to say, *"No podemos escapar de nuestra herencia."* We cannot escape our heritage.

And, anyway, I didn't want to.

But it was likely my family's cultural background or my more modest upbringing would never have been an issue. After all, Nia was a first-generation Greek-American, and she'd slid right in with the Michaelsens, in spite of their old money and their WASPishness. Maybe I would've been marginalized for no other reason than because I was *me*.

Chandler seemed to be reading something in my expression that I thought I'd done better at hiding. He immediately asked me about my family. About my parents and my brother, who lived in Southern California. About my *abuela*, Clarita, who'd immigrated to Texas when she was fourteen and married my grandfather, Lorenzo Longoria. They'd moved to California, too, where he'd passed away a few years ago.

"Must've been hard to lose your *abuelo*," he said. "I remember that you were really close to your grandparents."

I nodded. I'd come to Illinois on a college scholarship and stayed, but Chandler knew I flew back often to see my family and talked with them frequently on the phone. "Every so often, I'll make *sopapillas* in his honor. Or, when I'm too lazy to actually fix his favorite pastry by hand, I go out to La Vida Feliz and order it."

"Oh, man, that sounds good." He licked his lips in a way that shouldn't have been nearly as sensual as it was. "Is this a new restaurant?"

"Not so new. It's been around for about five years, but it must have opened after you left town. It's about fifteen or twenty minutes away. In Glen Forest."

"Spent a few months in San Antonio a few years back, and I ate like a king. *Soy como un rey*," he said with a self-deprecating laugh, pointing to his chest as if he really were royalty.

I laughed, too. It always thrilled me to hear someone speak Spanish, even if it was just a few words. I wondered if he still spoke the language sometimes. *"Sigues usando el español?"*

"Nah, not really. I wish I were better, but I've forgotten a lot since high school. And I haven't had an authentic Mexican meal in ages." He paused. "We should go to La Vida Feliz for dinner this week."

"W-We?" I sputtered before I could stop myself.

"Hell, yeah. How am I supposed to know the best dishes to order without guidance?" He sent me that knowing, captivating grin again that was pure sexiness. I knew better than to fall for it and, yet, he tempted me.

This was so like Chandler.

Impulsive and charming. Reckless and seductive.

He was too much of everything—not the least of which was too young. I couldn't let myself forget that.

I shook my head. "I don't think that's the best idea. You're going to be so busy with pre-wedding activities and—"

"No." He took a few steps closer until I could feel his body heat radiating toward me. Enough to warm up even this chilly December morning. "Friday night, yes. There's the rehearsal at the church and then the rehearsal dinner. But there's nothing I really have to do tonight or tomorrow. So, which will it be?"

He looked at me so steadily, so suddenly somber that I was forced to make a decision. If I went with him, we'd be out of Mirabelle Harbor at least. It would be less like a date, I reasoned, and more like an outing. With a friend. Right?

Well, sort of.

"Please, Jaleina," he whispered. "I'd really like to spend some time with you. Only with you. *Solamente contigo*. Just catching up."

I felt myself giving in. He was utterly enchanting and persuasive. More so now than he was when I was dating his big brother. Or maybe he'd always been this way and I just hadn't wanted to acknowledge it. "I've got a book club meeting to attend tonight. But tomorrow, I'm free after the bookstore closes," I admitted.

He shot a cursory glance at the store hours posted in white type on the window. "Six p.m. then," he said. "Tomorrow night. I'll pick you up here. And, uh—" He scanned my body, paying special attention to my legs, which, despite my long skirt, burned hotter under his gaze. "You'll want to dress warm and wear slacks. Maybe jeans."

"Why?"

He flashed a smile at me that was disarmingly polite, but the mischievous glint in his eye gave him away. "Just trust me." Then, with a parting wave, he added, "Thanks for saying yes. I'm looking forward to our evening together."

Before I could reply, he was gone.

A customer asked me a question about the latest psychological thriller at the top of this week's *USA Today Bestseller List*, and as I moved to answer her, I saw a motorcycle speed by my bookstore, Chandler riding it.

Ah. Dress warm. Wear slacks. Trust him. I understood now, and I could handle two out of three. But as powerful and alluring as those guys might be, I'd vowed to never fully trust a Michaelsen man again.

Especially not one who looked so dangerously hot in his black leather jacket and jeans.

I had a sneaking suspicion that a ride on his sleek motorcycle wasn't the only kind of ride the clever and ever-charismatic Chandler had in mind.

Sneaky, sexy boy. *Too* sneaky and *too* sexy for his own damn good.

Or for mine.

CHAPTER FOUR

Chandler, Thursday, December 14th

There were things you knew you couldn't do as a member of a family. Not without consequences, anyway. Making a serious play for your brother's former fiancée was probably one of them, even if said brother was happily married to someone else.

So, of course, I didn't tell any of my siblings about my Thursday night dinner date with Jaleina. Not during the endless tuxedo fittings that morning. Not during the lame-ass excuse for a "bachelor party" that Chance had requested yesterday afternoon. (A *healthy luncheon*, for chrissake. The guy was hopeless.) And especially not during the many hours we'd all been hanging out together at Derek and Olivia's house.

Then again, everyone in my family already thought I was a fuck up because of the whole Abby thing, so it wasn't as though their expectations of me were all that high. Still, why rush to make my totally screwed status official?

It took half a century for six o'clock to finally arrive

but, when it did, I parked my bike in front of Between the Pages and watched her from the outside looking in as she finished with her last few customers and locked up. Part of me was sorely tempted to slip inside, pull down the shades, and have my wicked way with her between the stacks. I'd had that particular Jaleina fantasy more than once, and as recently as last night in bed. But before I could act on it, she was standing next to me on the pavement, studying my bike—and me—with an expression I didn't have a damn clue how to read.

"Hey," she said. "You're right on time."

"Of course. Been waiting all day for this." *And the whole last decade and a half, but who's counting?* She looked cute as hell in her black jeans and puffy down jacket—dark gray to match her mittens. I wanted to cuddle her like I would a fluffy bunny. But, instead, I just smiled at her and held out my helmet. "Put this on if you wanna ride to the restaurant on my bike. If you'd rather go by car, I'd understand, though."

She impressed me by reaching for the helmet without hesitation and fastening it to her beautiful head. "It's been too long since I've been on a motorcycle, Chandler. Let's see what you can do with this thing."

Oh, baby. A laugh burst out of my throat. I couldn't even fake being cool after a line like that. This woman was so fucking hot, even when she wasn't trying. "Hop on and I'll show you," I said.

When I felt her thighs hug mine and her arms wrapped around my waist, it was all I could do not to groan aloud with desire. La Vida Feliz was only a few miles from here, but I wished it would've been three states away, just so I could feel her touching and squeezing me for hours and hours.

When she was settled behind me, I kicked the bike into gear and wove us through the streets of Mirabelle Harbor and into Glen Forest with all the smoothness and skill my

Harley and I could maneuver, leaning into the curves and speeding just above the limit, so she could feel the rush. I heard her gasp and laugh in delight as the wind pushed us from the back, accelerating our journey.

And, too soon, we were there. I felt the immediate ache of her absence when she pulled her body away from mine and slid off the bike.

"That was fun," she told me.

Fun? The word I'm thinking of is rapturous, darlin'. But I said, "Glad you liked it." *Oh, I could do so much more for you, if you'd only let me.*

She grinned and—shit. Every single inch of me reacted. I'd have to fight against a killer hard-on all night, just remembering the sensation of her breath on my neck. And her body heat surrounding me. And the warmth of her smile.

Jaleina pointed at the entrance to the restaurant. "Let's go inside."

"Yeah, yeah. Good idea." It was December in Illinois, after all. But, man, I wasn't cold. I was burning up, even as I exhaled a lungful of visible air.

We were seated at a table near the back, at a booth with red vinyl cushions. I flipped through the menu, unseeingly. The waiter could serve us grilled scorpion slathered with salsa verde and sour cream for all I cared. I just wanted to be with her.

"What do you recommend?" I asked Jaleina. "In addition to the *sopapillas*. We should get an order of that for dessert."

She nodded. "The cheesy quesadillas, beef enchiladas, and ultimate nachos are all really good. Not quite as good as my *abuela*'s homemade versions, but that would be practically impossible to top. I've never tried their pork tamales or the cilantro-lime chicken, but I can also recommend their tortilla soup, the avocado-steak burrito bowl, and the Mexican grilled chicken Cobb salad. A friend of mine told me the baked chicken chimichangas were a hit, too. So I don't think you can go wrong." She licked her lips in anticipation of the meal, and it was all I could do to keep my hands and my mouth on my side of the table.

"Let's try one of your old favorites," I suggested, "along with a couple of new dishes, just for fun. I'm open to anything here—" *Anything with you*, I almost added. "And I don't mind sharing plates, if you don't. Just choose what appeals to you."

She glanced up at me with sharp, wary eyes, the brown irises so deep and questioning that I, again, wondered what she must be thinking of me. Of this night so far. Was a dinner date too intimate for her? Was I pushing her beyond the comfort level she'd set for us?

The thing was, I'd be damned if I'd let her friend zone me. I had to make her see me as someone other than the kid brother of her ex, and I knew I needed to do it *tonight* while we were still getting reacquainted, or it'd be too late. She'd distance herself from me. Shrug off the possibility of what might happen between us. Justify blowing me off. Even now, I could almost see her thinking, "He's too young," and trying to dismiss me.

So, I met her gaze and held it steady. I looked across the table at her and, despite the fear of risk or embarrassment, which was sizable, I didn't try to hide from her the desire and appreciation in my heart. If she was going to reject me, she'd better reject the man she saw tonight, not the boy she remembered from more than a dozen years ago.

I saw her swallow before she finally broke eye contact and opened her mouth to reply. "Okay. Um, sure," she murmured, her brow furrowed. And when the waiter appeared a few seconds later, she opted for the burrito bowl, the cilantro-lime chicken, and the tamales for us to share. Plus a pitcher of margaritas, which I suspected was more for her courage than for mine.

For the first time in a long time, I had almost no interest in getting drunk...or even a little buzzed. I needed a totally clear head for this.

Jaleina, by contrast, downed an entire glass before the chips and salsa even arrived. I watched her, amused. She was obviously nervous, but I'd had enough experience with past hookups to recognize when a woman found me attractive. She did—*thank God!*—but it bothered the hell out of her.

That was all right, though. Indifference would've been a big problem. Sexual tension, on the other hand...that I could work with. And I would.

We talked about nothing for the first twenty minutes. The atmosphere of the restaurant. The food. The upcoming holidays. But after she started on her second margarita, she ran her fingertip along the rim of the glass and brought up Derek. Asked about my nephews. Made a show of sounding like a "friend of the family." It was annoyingly deliberate and exactly what I'd expected her to do.

I changed the subject.

But like a persistent moth to a goddamn flame, she brought up my brother's name again, this time along with specific memories from fourteen years ago.

"I loved how Derek used to make sure there were snacks for you and Chance after school," she stated brightly. "You boys were always so ravenous when you got home. All that whining about homework while the two of you scarfed down microwave popcorn and complained about your English essays. It was cute."

Ah, yes. *Cute.* A pointed reminder that I was still a kid, in her eyes, and I needed to stay in my place. *Not gonna happen, sweetheart.*

I crossed my arms and shook my head.

"What?" she blurted when she caught me staring at her. She reached for a tortilla chip and fidgeted with it until it cracked, sending crumbs flying across the table toward me.

I laughed. "You're beautiful, Jaleina. And I sincerely like you, so just relax, okay?"

She exhaled unsteadily. "Look, Chandler, we've known each other a long time, but you're Derek's little brother and—"

"I'm Derek's *younger* brother," I corrected. "I am not *little*."

She waved this off. "Fine, you're not little. You've grown up a lot. I—I, um, can see that."

Even before I'd left on the road with Abby, Jaleina and I had only run into each other a handful of times after she and Derek broke up. These were odd and hasty encounters, mostly on the streets of Mirabelle Harbor. Only once before, about seven years ago, had she even acknowledged that I wasn't the teenager she'd first met. She'd said something very similar to me at the time about my having "grown up a lot." It felt dismissive and wasn't much of a concession then. It was even less so now.

"I'm glad you've officially recognized that. *Bien por ti.*" *Good for you.* My sarcasm was hard to miss.

She looked slightly taken aback, both by my use of another Spanish phrase and by my attitude. I remembered more of the language than I'd admitted to, and I wasn't planning to defend my age all evening. She needed to know that.

I pushed the basket of chips aside and leaned toward her. "Please stop using Derek as a wall between us. He's been out of the picture for a long time, and he has nothing to do with what's going on here tonight."

"But he and I were engaged once."

"Yep. And I thought he was a fucking idiot for letting you go. I love my sister-in-law and all, and I think Derek and Olivia are good together. But I was so damn jealous of him back then because he was with you and I wasn't." I shot her a significant look and willed her to pay attention to the truth of my words. "I get that I was too young for you then. I do. But I'm not gonna hide my interest in you. And I think you know I'm *not* too young for you *now*."

She frowned. "You're not even thirty."

"I will be in less than a month."

"And I'm almost *forty*," she insisted. "We just can't—"

"Like hell we can't. We're adults, Jaleina, and you're nowhere near forty. I *know* your birthday. Forty is a year and a half away for you. And even if you were fifty, it wouldn't matter to me."

"Well, it should," she snapped. "But even if we were the same age, and even if your brother and I hadn't been engaged, you don't live in Mirabelle Harbor anymore. This is just a vacation flirtation for you. It couldn't be anything else anyway."

I didn't know how to answer that, so I did the only thing I could do. I leaned even closer to her—all the way across the table—and I kissed her. For a split second, she resisted and didn't open her lips for me.

Then she did.

And, in an instant, everything between us changed.

No more pretense. No more holding back. No more talk about my oldest brother and all that crap from years and years ago.

For a few beautiful seconds, it was just about us.

Every bloody fantasy I'd ever had felt within reach for the first time in my life. I was floating between the ground and the sky. Dancing on the edge of ecstasy, even though I was touching her with nothing but my mouth. In my imagination, though, I was rubbing her bare skin with my fingertips. Stripping off her—

I heard someone clear his throat, and we broke apart. The waiter with our entrees.

With an inaudible groan and tremendous restraint, I made myself sit back down on the red vinyl cushion. But I cursed the table, the food, and every centimeter of space separating us. At least I had the satisfaction of seeing

Jaleina, her eyes blazing with arousal and surprise, sigh and wet her lips. And I knew it wasn't because of the burrito bowl, the chicken, or the tamales, no matter how authentic they all were.

"Enjoy your meal, *señor e señorita*," the waiter said with a knowing grin, as he placed the steaming platters in front of us.

Jaleina blushed, and I thanked the man without taking my eyes off of her.

As soon as he meandered away, though, I leaned toward her again and reached for her hand. She was trembling.

"Listen to me," I whispered, noting that she was no longer looking at me like I was anything other than a hot-blooded male. Definite progress. "I don't want to hear another word about our ages. I dated someone 'age-appropriate' for years. I started going out with Abby because of *you*, Jaleina. Abby was cute and caring. She and I were in the same grade. And...and I was trying like hell to get you out of my head," I told her, admitting this truth aloud for the first time ever. "But it was never quite right, and it was really unfair to her, especially when a part of me knew from the beginning that I wanted someone like you." I paused. "Well, no. I very specifically wanted *you*."

We barely touched our dinner.

She kept stealing glances at me, and I kept forgetting to eat because—damn. The woman I'd been crazy about for half my life was right in front of me. Spanish rice, queso sauce, and refried beans, no matter how tasty, couldn't compete. Not even the sweet *sopapillas* were tempting enough to turn my attention away from Jaleina's face.

Our waiter finally took pity on us and offered to box up the leftovers.

I paid the bill almost blindly, tipped heavily, and raced out of the restaurant—Jaleina's hand snugly in mine.

Before we even got within a few yards of my

motorcycle, I cupped her face in my palms and kissed her again, pressing my body to hers and letting her feel how much I wanted her. She moaned softly against my mouth, and I was at her mercy.

I don't know how long we stood in that cold parking lot just making out, and I had no freakin' idea how I managed to drive us back to the bookstore. It was by some miraculous combination of steering skills and survival instincts that I even stayed on the road. My thoughts were only on her.

When we got off my bike, I walked her to her car. She was cagier now, more careful, guarded, and watchful, ever since we'd gotten back into Mirabelle Harbor. We both knew how easily we could be spotted by people around town who knew us as individuals or knew members of my family.

She stepped back when I tried to kiss her goodnight. "It's not you," she murmured. "It's being here."

I nodded. "Where do you live?"

"You can't come home with me tonight, Chandler—"

"I'm not. But maybe I could stop by tomorrow. To take a look at your computer."

She raised an eyebrow. "Is that what all the kids are calling it these days?" Even in the darkness, she couldn't disguise her grin. And neither could I.

I chuckled. "Maybe. But it's as good an excuse as any." I waited a moment and thought about what I really wanted her to know. "I'd like to see you again—privately—and I don't care what terms we use or what reasons we give. Will you let me come over tomorrow night? It'll be later. Probably after nine." I had Chance and Nia's rehearsal dinner to get through, not that I needed to mention that. Jaleina already knew the schedule because of her friendship with the bride.

It was an eternity before she finally replied. "All right." She gave me her address.

"Thank you," I said, squeezing her mittened fingers gently before taking a step backward, my heart all but screaming at me not to leave her. Not even for a minute.

But I did. Only because I *had* to. And gossipy town residents be damned, I blew her a kiss from across the parking lot.

Just before I turned away, I saw her reach her hand up in the air and catch it.

Oh, yeah.

My flying heart—more than my bike—sped me back to my brother's house.

CHAPTER FIVE

Chance, The Rehearsal Dinner, Friday, December 15th

Chance was going to be a married man by the end of the day tomorrow, and that fact couldn't have made him happier. But something was definitely going on with his twin, and he wanted to get to the bottom of it.

He exhaled heavily and scanned the room of the rehearsal hall. They'd run through the ceremony step by step at the church. His future mother-in-law, his sister, his sister-in-law, and his soon-to-be wife had the wedding planned down to the nanosecond, which was good. Chance didn't have to do anything more than show up in his tux tomorrow, make sure his bro had the rings, and pledge his love for his gorgeous bride.

That was going to be easy.

Dealing with his siblings during this lengthy weekend, however, would certainly be more of a challenge.

Sharlene was her usual bossy self, but he could handle that—for the most part. His sister had only gotten on his nerves a handful of times, and he knew her excruciating attention to detail was truly out of love. She was trying to step in for their late mother and make the wedding beautiful for him and Nia. Sometimes, though, she took that Mother Hen role too far.

Case in point: In less than twenty-four hours, Chance would be marrying the woman of his dreams. Did Shar really think he gave a fig about what kind of appetizers were served at the reception? Or who sat at which table? Yet, she persisted in questioning him and racing in every direction, ordering people around. She got so hyper last night that Chance even resorted to telling her boyfriend, Declan, to force her to sit somewhere and drink *anything* (even a beverage with high-fructose corn syrup or a potent amount of alcohol, if necessary) just to get her to calm the hell down.

Derek and Olivia were great, as usual, but they were the parents of three squirmy boys. They were doing their best to keep the little guys under control at a long family event, and that had to be exhausting as parents. Still, if he heard Derek bellow, "Peter, please don't touch that!" one more time or witnessed Olivia scolding James and Riley for "unnecessary roughness," Chance just might start yelling at the kids, too. And that was definitely not like him.

Blake's squirminess rivaled that of their nephews. Seriously, his DJ brother was pacing around the room like he was warming up for a breakdance set. Chance caught Blake's girlfriend, Vicky, rolling her eyes at her man, but did she do anything to get him to settle down? That would be a big, fat *nope*.

Clearly, Blake needed at least a shoulder rub or something. If he kept up this behavior, Chance would have to suggest that massage idea to Vicky, which went against the grain. He strove to never interfere when it came to his siblings' relationships. It was like all of them were more nervous about the Big Day than he was.

And worst of all was Chandler.

His twin was a flippin' mess. Ever since the guy had blown back into town, he'd been so distracted that he could barely focus on a conversation—even one happening right in front of him—let alone relax for five minutes during the rehearsal dinner. Chance wanted to order him to go to the gym and run a couple of fast miles on the treadmill. The guy had some energy he desperately needed to burn off.

Chandler was going to be the best man tomorrow, and, yet, Chance wasn't sure he should entrust his twin with the rings until just a few minutes before the ceremony. From the semi-wild expression on his brother's face during dessert, it looked like he'd finally cracked, just like their other siblings predicted he might someday. Especially once he'd broken up with Abby and hidden himself on the East Coast, a thousand miles away from the rest of the family.

But Chance couldn't figure out *why* Chandler was behaving so strangely here and now. What would be the reason for all this angst from his twin when he'd barely been back in Mirabelle Harbor for four days? It didn't make sense.

Derek clapped him on the shoulder, breaking his train of thought. And, honestly, it was a welcome reprieve.

"You got the honeymoon details all squared away?" Derek asked.

"Yep," Chance said, feeling a burst of lightness return to his chest. This was the fun stuff. "Nia's father and her brother helped me with the Grecian cruise line details," he whispered to his brother. They'd all managed to keep the location of the honeymoon a secret from his bride, but Chance was assured by Nia's family that she'd love a ten-day cruise through the Greek Isles. He aimed to please. "All she knows is that she needs to pack for warm weather and to bring her passport," he added, grinning at the thought of her in those cropped summer outfits and skimpy swimwear.

Derek nodded. "You two are going to have an incredible time," he murmured. "And I know Mom and Dad are smiling down on all of us—thrilled for you and pleased to have a lovely lady like Nia joining the family."

"Thanks." He grinned at his brother. "I can almost feel their presence tonight."

"Me, too," Derek agreed.

It was true. Their parents would have been delighted that he'd found true love. And Chance knew the weight of responsibility Derek had taken on as head of the Michaelsen clan after Mom and Dad had died had been a heavy one. This wedding would, hopefully, lighten the load for his big brother, at least a bit. Chance would soon be married, not just a little kid for Derek to worry about. Plus, Shar was finally in a happy romance, and even Blake was in a stable, monogamous relationship. Wonders never ceased.

Of course, their parents would worry like hell if they took a good look at Chandler.

What the devil was going on with him?

Chance studied his brother from two tables away. He looked as solemn as he had at their parents' funerals—and equally as impatient to leave. Thankfully, his twin's jumpiness didn't seem to be caused by alcohol. Almost every time Chance had called him in Atlanta, he'd been wasted, or well on the way to getting there.

But, no.

Tonight, he'd been keeping tabs on his twin, and Chandler hadn't been drinking. Whatever calories he didn't imbibe in liquid form, however, he made up for in junk food. Olivia had insisted on placing large crystal bowls of green, red, and silver wrapped Christmas chocolates on every table, which weren't merely for decoration, as Chance had hoped. Most of the close friends and family in attendance at the rehearsal dinner sampled a few of the candies, but none more than Chandler, who must have devoured close to fifty grams of saturated fat from the chocolate alone in less than two hours.

Chance knew stress eating when he saw it and, this, in conjunction with all of his twin's other odd behaviors, wasn't a good sign.

So, at the first opportunity he had to break away from his own table, he walked over to talk with his brother. "You feeling okay?" he asked Chandler.

"Sure," he said, twisting open the metallic red wrapper of a Hershey's Kiss and popping the candy into his mouth.

"Really?"

"Yeah," his twin insisted. "I'm all right." He glanced at his watch. "Just, you know, excited about...um, tomorrow." He reached for another chocolate—or, rather, three—and systematically began unwrapping them.

Chance stilled his brother's hand. "Look, I know that growing up you used to do most of the talking for both of us. I've had to practice speaking up and sharing my feelings in the years you've been away. I can't tell you how much I missed you." He smiled warmly at Chandler and had the satisfaction of seeing him return the grin. "But I'm still a good listener. If there's anything you want to—"

"Oh, no," Chandler interrupted. "Really. I'm totally fine. And like everyone else who knows and loves you, I'm extremely happy for you and Nia." He tapped his breast pocket. "I've got my best man speech written down, and I'll be ready to toast you and your blushing bride tomorrow afternoon." He stuffed a few wrapped chocolate candies into his pocket, put an unwrapped one into his mouth, and chewed frantically. "I'm just a little...twitchy tonight."

Why?

Before he could ask, Nia came rushing up to them with a platter of baklava—a honey, nut, and phyllo layered Greek dessert that was beyond delicious, but it had an unfathomable amount of sugar, fat grams, and calories.

"Dimitri just brought these over from the bakery," she

said, slightly breathless, offering them each a piece. "I'd forgotten to grab them, but he thoughtfully remembered for me."

Chance took one—because he knew the pastry would taste amazing but, mostly, because he knew his future in-laws were watching him. He'd grown to enjoy even the richer Greek foods since he and Nia had met, but always in moderation.

However, he dearly wished Nia's brother hadn't been quite so "thoughtful" in bringing these treats over from The Gala, especially when his twin said, "Thanks!" and grabbed two generous pieces for himself. After all of that chocolate, too! Chance couldn't imagine what havoc Chandler was wreaking on his blood sugar.

But his brother surprised him by putting both pieces on a napkin and wrapping them up, like he was planning to take them to go. This was perplexing because, although it wasn't exactly early in the evening, no one else around them looked as though they were ready to go home.

Chandler slipped the wrapped pieces in his pocket, and Nia fluttered away to personally offer homemade baklava to everybody in the room, like a beautiful crack dealer. Chance found himself grinning at her enthusiasm, and he took a few bites of his pastry. Definitely worth the calories, albeit in small doses.

He was about to make a second attempt at drawing out Chandler and, hopefully, getting his brother to confide in him, when he was interrupted by another loved one. Blake, this time.

"Okay, Twin One and Twin Two, I've got a hypothetical question for you guys," their brother said, using an old family nickname and motioning for them to follow him to a more secluded corner of the room.

"What's it involve?" Chandler wisely asked, cocking a suspicious brow.

"It's about women," Blake admitted.

Chandler laughed. "Then my input would be worthless. Better stick to advice from the nearly married man here," he said, pointing at Chance and backing away from them both. "I gotta run to the bathroom anyway." And he practically fled from the dining hall.

"What's up with him?" Blake asked.

"I was trying to figure that out when you barged in."

He shrugged. "Sorry, but I need to know something. It's about Vicky and me."

"Hypothetically?"

"Ah, fuck. No, not exactly. Just listen to me for a sec, Chance, and tell me what you think."

"All right."

"All right." He took a deep breath. "She and I are happy. *Really* happy. We've been a couple for over a year, and we've been living together officially since we got back from our France trip this past summer. I just—I just don't want to be separated from her."

"Okay."

"Okay." He took another deep breath, exhaling heavily. "She's a romantic, though. I wasn't really ready to pop the question when we were in Paris, but it's been five months since then, and I can't imagine my life without her."

"Yeah?"

"Well, that's the problem," he hissed. "See?"

Chance shook his head. "Not really, Blake. I'm not sure what the problem is *or* the question. You love her. That's obvious to everybody, including Vicky. And, for some incredibly bizarre reason, she loves you, too. What else do you need to know?"

He groaned. "You just don't get it."

"Exactly. I just don't get it. So explain."

Blake rubbed his temples with the pads of his fingers. "How do I come up with a unique and memorable way to ask her to marry me without it sounding lame? I can't just fly her to Paris again. But I was thinking of, maybe, commissioning Trevor's girlfriend, Tina Marie, to write a personalized love song for her. And to record it somehow, so I could, like, play it on the air at the radio station. Doug and Leonard would totally let me."

Blake's bosses at 102.5 "LOVE" FM would probably let him play a four-hour-long heavy metal set on the air, if he wanted to and gave them a good reason, despite the fact that they owned a radio station entirely devoted to love songs. Blake could talk his way into almost anything. And Tina Marie Moran, an aspiring singer in Nashville, had a gorgeous voice and would make any song she sang sound like a hit record. This could work.

"Or," he continued, "I could memorize a romantic poem in French and recite it to her. Or, you know how she likes classic lit? I was thinking I could write her a Mr. Darcy or Captain Wentworth-esque love letter on parchment paper and everything. With a quill and ink. And a wax seal. She digs Austen."

Chance stared at him, struggling to picture Blake writing anything with a quill pen. The guy was completely and utterly whipped—more than any of their family members had thought, and Shar had a pretty decent imagination. Chance had no doubt there'd be another Michaelsen family wedding. Soon.

"You *really* love her," he concluded.

"Yes! And that's why this is such a big a problem. I wanna make my proposal super special for her. And—"

He held up his hand. "Blake?"

"Yeah?"

"You're over-thinking this. *Way* over-thinking it, actually. You've got a bunch of excellent ideas. You could do any one of them, and I'd bet she'd love it. But I think the most important thing for Vicky is that you share your feelings with her. That you get across to her how much she means to you. And just what you told me before—how you can't imagine your life without her and don't want to be separated from her."

Blake squinted at him like he wasn't being helpful. "That's it?"

Chance shrugged. "In my opinion—and you can take it or leave it—that's the important part. But, maybe, do your explaining in a parchment letter, if you want, or in a song written just for her. I honestly don't think the delivery system is going to be a factor, Blake. Trust me, she'll feel 'super special' just knowing she's the only woman you've ever really loved."

He bit his bottom lip and nodded a couple of times. "Okay. I'll think about it. And thanks." Then he broke into a grin. "Hey, I think this might be the first time you've ever given *me* advice. Dude! You're growing up, little bro."

Chance laughed. "Glad I could be the voice of reason. Now, where did Chandler go?"

Both of them glanced around the room, with Chance wondering if his twin was still stuffing his face with various desserts or if, perhaps, he'd already imploded from dangerous levels of trans fats.

But neither of them spotted their brother.

Chance felt a bolt of worry for his restless twin. And, much as he wished this weren't the case, it looked like Chandler had disappeared for the night.

CHAPTER SIX

Chandler, After the Rehearsal Dinner

I slipped out of the reception hall and into the big lot, where I'd parked my Harley, grabbing my leather jacket from the coat room on the way and praying none of my siblings would question my departure.

Thankfully, I escaped unseen, and I was on Jaleina's doorstep within ten minutes.

"Chandler," she said when she swung open the front door, looking momentarily reluctant to let me in. Reminded me uncomfortably of Abby's reaction when she first saw me at her new place earlier this week. Maybe I should get the message and just leave everybody the hell alone.

But then Jaleina said, "You must be freezing," and she motioned me inside.

"I just really wanted to see you tonight," I told her, my heart beating like I'd been sprinting to her townhouse, rather than riding my motorcycle the whole way. "I was hoping we could talk."

"Talk, huh?" She raised a single eyebrow. "Looks like you could use a little coffee or tea to warm up. How about I make us a cup of something hot?"

She was all the "something hot" I needed. Her lips on my mouth would warm me up plenty fast, but I wasn't about to tell her that and, maybe, get myself shoved back out into the cold.

So, I just smiled at her and said, "Either would be great, thank you. And, oh!" I pulled the wrapped baklava out of my pocket and a handful of chocolate candies. "I brought us a couple of Greek pastries and some Hershey's Kisses. Thought you might like a sweet treat."

I caught her swiping her tongue across her bottom lip at the sight of the honeyed dessert and the chocolates, then glancing between these offerings and my face. I was sure there was no way I was disguising my desire for her. She had to be able to read it in my eyes. Fuck. A fifth grader would be able to tell how much I wanted her. But, again, I didn't say any of what I was thinking.

Not: *Every chocolaty kiss I ate tonight made me think of you.*

Not: *I wanna rub honey on your body and lick it off.*

Not even: *Have you been wondering what it'd feel like if I took you up against the wall? 'Cuz I have. Repeatedly...*

And Jaleina—instead of speaking one of my fantasy lines and saying, *Who needs sweets when I've got you here?*—only said, "Thanks. That was thoughtful."

I forced myself to exhale slowly. There was no damn way my lungs were getting enough air in this room. It was too small, especially with her so close to me at last, and my inhalations were shallow to the point of near panting. I had to try to breathe more deeply.

She walked toward her kitchen, and I trailed after her like a kid, unable to stop staring at the gracefulness of her movements. I watched as she made us some kind of minty herbal tea.

"No caffeine for me this late at night," she explained, handing me a steaming mug.

I wasn't much of a tea guy in general, but I didn't care what we drank tonight. Hell, I'd happily sip carburetor fluid, if that was what she wanted to serve. And when she suggested that we take the tea and baklava into her living room, I followed her there, too.

It was a woman's place. Bookshelves dominated the walls, and they were filled top to bottom with enough novels to rival the number of books in the aisles of her store. In between the literature, there were delicate and girly things, placed just so. Ceramic and porcelain items I didn't dare touch for fear of breaking them. Petite dolls. Fine china teapots. Glass figurines.

A man had obviously never lived here—at least not recently. And I was overwhelmingly grateful for that.

"So, how was the rehearsal?" she asked, motioning for me to sit down on her sofa. I knew she was being polite and probably didn't give a shit about those details—or maybe that was just me—but I tried to answer her truthfully. And briefly.

"There was a lot of excited squealing," I said. "From the women mostly. Hugging family members they hadn't seen in weeks or months. Cooing over how cute the youngsters were in their flower girl or ring bearer duties. And jumping around, plotting last-minute changes to the decorations or whatever. Basically, several hours of exhausting minutiae followed by food and more squealing."

She smiled at that description, which lit up her whole face like a bulb, and the heat of that smile went right to my balls. God, how long did I have to wait to touch her again? To kiss her?

I took a gulp of my tea and burned the back of my throat. Damn.

"Well, tomorrow should go smoothly then," she said. "It sounds like everyone knows what they're supposed to do."

I nodded. "Chance and Nia are gonna be happy

together. For me, that's all I really needed to know."

"Me, too," she murmured.

And then...there was silence.

I scrambled to think of something else to say that wasn't either overtly sexually suggestive or completely out in left field. For half a minute, I drew a blank.

Then, finally, I remembered my original excuse for coming over.

I set my mug down on the end table on top of a Dr. Seuss coaster. The Cat in the Hat himself grinned up at me, as if guessing how absurd I was going to sound when I spoke. But I did it anyway. "So, you mentioned you had a computer issue. Would you like me to take a look?"

She narrowed her eyes at me, ever so slightly, but she stood up and said, "Sure, thanks. It's just down the hall."

In her bedroom? I could only hope.

But, no.

The computer—a decent, standard home brand, geared toward customers who didn't need extra memory for gaming or extensive features for manipulating images— was in a second bedroom that she'd transformed into an office.

She turned on the system for me and explained the issue she'd been having. "Ever since I got the new printer, there's been this glitch," she told me, waving her hand in the direction of the system tray on her desktop and chattering about the "weird spinning" that the icon in the taskbar had been doing.

I fought back a laugh. She was so damn adorable.

The fix was beyond easy. The printer driver just needed to be updated, since there'd been a recent upgrade for the model she was using, and the computer had been trying to notify her of that. It took me all of three minutes to download the new software, install it, and reboot.

Jaleina blinked when I told her it was done. "What? That was it? It won't do that thing anymore?"

"Nope. It won't do that thing."

"Oh, Chandler, thank you." She looked so surprised, I almost felt guilty for fixing it so quickly. But truthfulness and pride wouldn't allow me to pretend it was harder than it was.

"It was no problem, Jaleina. Really. Glad I could help."

She was staring at me strangely, as I typed in a few things to check the security of her firewalls, and adjusted them accordingly. Didn't want her getting a nasty virus. When I paused for a moment to explain what I was doing, something in her expression shifted.

"What?" I asked.

She shook her head.

"Everything okay?"

"Yeah, it's just...um, your hands." She gave me another curious look, along with an embarrassed chuckle. "This is going to sound really dorky, I know, but watching you type so fast—you have really strong, lovely hands." She shrugged. "I'm sure people tell you that all the time."

No, they didn't.

My throat was suddenly so dry, I wished I could drink some more scalding tea. "No," I managed to say. "Not really."

"Well, they should." She turned swiftly away from me and started fussing with a stack of papers on a table nearby.

I could barely stop myself from reaching out to her with the hands she'd just admired. I wanted to trail my fingertips across her skin. Push into her softness. Feel her wetness and warmth. Caress her with my palms.

But I held back. I needed to do this just right.

There were plenty of girly things in her office. But, unlike the living room, there weren't floor-to-ceiling bookshelves. In fact, one wall to our left was almost completely empty, except for a small wooden plaque hanging about seven feet up. It showed a pair of entwined doves with the word "Peace" carved beneath the image.

I pushed myself to standing and removed the carving from its hook on the wall. "This is pretty," I told Jaleina, setting it by the keyboard. "But it needs to be taken down for tonight."

"Why?"

"Because I don't want it falling on your head." And I held out my hand for her, waiting.

After what felt like an infinity of microseconds, she touched her fingertips to my palm and let me close my hand around hers. Then I drew her toward me, turned her so her back was to that empty wall, and positioned her against it very gently.

Her eyes widened, but she didn't object.

I did a quick sweep of the windows in the room, making sure all the blinds were closed, and then stepped up to her, bringing my thumb to the side of her cheek. I traced an imaginary line from her earlobe along her jaw to her chin. Paused. Continued down to the tantalizing hollow of her throat. Then further down to the space between her breasts.

I paused again and met her gaze.

She didn't look afraid or try to pull away, so I let my strong fingers do the next thing they craved—pop the buttons on her burgundy blouse.

"Mi corazón late rápidamente por estar a tu lado," I whispered, telling her of my beating heart, as her shirt fell open. There was only her exquisite, smooth, olive skin showing underneath. And her cream-colored bra. I'd get rid of that next.

But first...first, I'd do what I could no longer wait to do. I bent to kiss the tops of her breasts, and the heat from her skin when my lips touched her flesh was nothing short of scorching.

Jaleina gasped as we burned each other—mouth to chest, chest to mouth.

The flimsy blouse, the cream bra, the dress slacks...they

all had to go. I used both hands to remove, unhook, unzip, and discard, until she was wearing only her pink panties, leaning against the wall, breathing heavily, and letting me kiss freely every inch of her exposed skin.

Holy fuck.

Finally. Finally.

"Chandler," she whispered, as I pressed a row of hot kisses along her neck. My hands, meanwhile, massaged her breasts and rolled each nipple between my thumb and index finger until she moaned.

I was dying to rip off her panties, but I needed to know she craved me at least half as much as I craved her. My mouth found her mouth, and I kissed her so deeply, so completely, that she had my whole soul on the tip of her tongue.

When I felt her arms wrapped around my waist, pulling me closer, urging me onward, I knew it was time.

I pulled one hand away from her breast and slipped it between the pink lacy fabric and her body. My lips never left hers, even as I parted her legs and slid one finger and then two deep inside her wetness. I pulsed against her— slow and steady, then firmly and faster—until her breathing quickened and her moans grew harder and more insistent.

"Oh, God, Chandler," she panted, breaking our kiss only long enough to speak.

I grinned against her lips, tickling the corners of her mouth with my tongue as the rest of her body vibrated in time with my fingers. Longer. Harder. Stronger. Faster. Until she broke against me and the slick sweetness of her sex called me down.

I knelt before her, ditched the panties, and put my lips where the wet pink fabric had been.

"You don't have to—oh!" she cried. "I mean, I don't think—"

"That's okay," I murmured. "Don't think right now. Just feel, Jaleina."

Then I covered her clit with my mouth and let my tongue speak for me.

Again, she cried, "Oh, God! Chandler!" as I probed and explored.

No way would I tell her, even if I was willing to pull my lips away from her beautiful body, how many times I'd fantasized about doing this very thing. For fourteen fucking years. It was like going down on a movie star or Miss July in the *Playboy* calendar.

My Dream Girl.

With my forehead, I pressed her against the wall, while pulling her closer to me with my hands on the backs of her thighs. I could feel the delicious tension increasing inside of her again. Building up. Her hands raked the top of my head, yanking on my hair. And, suddenly, she pushed my shoulders with both hands, forcing me to almost fall back on my ass.

"Chandler," she panted, shaking her head. "I don't want you to keep doing this."

And just like that, my heart crashed to the floor, shattering like porcelain on cement.

I glanced up at her lovely face, so flushed with passion, and I just couldn't wrap my mind around why she'd want me to stop. But I pressed my lips shut and pulled my hands away from her legs, willing to respect her wishes but unable to speak a fucking word aloud.

She must have guessed at my confusion because she said, "No, no, I mean, this is amazing—*you're* amazing—but I've already come once. What about you?"

When the realization of what she meant finally hit my stunned brain, I stood up on shaky limbs and half laughed, half sobbed with relief. I hugged her, my chest heaving. "I'm *fine*, Jaleina. Trust me on this. And you're allowed to come multiple times. I'd encourage it."

A slow smile lit her face. "Well, I want you to be more than *fine*. And, also, I have a bedroom…"

"Lead the way."

She reached for my belt, still attached to my black jeans, and tugged me in the direction of the hallway and the master bedroom.

My cock was so hard, it was gonna be a project getting my pants off, but I'd cut them off with fabric shears if I had to.

Turned out, I didn't have to think about removing my jeans, though. Jaleina did it for me.

When we reached her room, she unlatched my belt and unbuttoned my waistband. With her hands doing all the work of unzipping and wrenching down the denim, I really didn't care how long it took. The journey to disrobing was half the fun.

I almost cried out in pure ecstasy when she'd stripped away my black briefs, too, and encircled my cock with her slim fingers—stroking, rubbing, teasing.

Aw, Jesus.

"Do you have a condom with you?" she whispered. Tentatively. Like I was an adolescent who didn't know better and who might not be prepared.

"Yesss. Of course I do."

"Why, then, are you taking so long to put it on?" She flashed a grin at me and hopped onto the mattress. Entirely naked, except for the saucy expression on her face.

I dug out my wallet from the puddle of clothing on the floor, took care of the condom issue, and joined Jaleina in bed.

Soft. Silky. Warm. Just like her. And I had her beneath me on those satiny sheets within seconds. I was literally a heartbeat away from plunging into her when she sighed and whispered, "This can't possibly be a good idea."

FUCK.

Or *NOT fuck*, as it were.

I gritted my teeth and steadied my body on my elbows, holding myself above her as still as I could manage. My limbs were shaking from the intensity of wanting her, but a man just couldn't make love to someone with a sentence like that hanging between them.

"What do you mean, exactly?" I ground out.

Her fingertips played the harp or something on my bare skin, making my back tingle with her touch. "I mean, this—this is *wonderful*, Chandler. I want you." And she kissed me, which would've meant the satisfying fulfillment of my every fantasy, if I couldn't hear the big BUT that lingered behind her words.

"But...?" I prompted.

"But, Chandler, beyond tonight, there's not really a future for us. You know that, don't you?"

I knew no such goddamn thing.

So I kissed her, long and slow, until I could feel her interest in conversation lessening. Then I pulled away and asked, "Do you like it when I kiss you?"

"Yes," she whispered, leaning up toward me.

"Good." I reached between us and found her clit. I rubbed just the tip of it, circling gently with my thumb, until I could feel her pressing against me and practically humming with desire. I slid my hand away. "Do you like it when I touch your clit?"

She exhaled sharply. "Yes. Why'd you stop?"

I decided not to answer that. Instead, I skimmed my cock, snug in its rubber, against her clit and all around her pussy.

She responded by arching toward me, squeezing my ass like it was in a vise grip, and tugging me closer. But I didn't push myself inside of her, much as it was killing me to hold back.

Jaleina groaned. "Chandler, what are you doing?"

"I'm explaining something," I said to her with exaggerated patience. "Do you think—from the way I've kissed you and touched you tonight—that you'd like it if we had sex?"

"Yes, of course. I *told* you I wanted you."

"You *also* told me this couldn't possibly be a good idea."

"Those beliefs aren't mutually exclusive," she murmured.

"They are to me. Especially when it comes to you."

Even if my face hadn't been a few inches from hers, I would've been able to read the surprise in her eyes when I said this.

"What are you saying?" she asked.

"I'm saying that I don't want to be something you regret. I get the appeal of a one-night stand, and though I'm not thrilled you're thinking of me that way, I could accept it, if it was what you really wanted. What I can't accept is that you aren't willing to own your decision. That you can't admit that what you want tonight is okay, whether or not it lasts. I don't want to be your 'bad idea,' Jaleina. I care about you too much."

She closed her eyes, but not before I saw a flash of pain in her expression.

And then, after a long, lonely second, I felt her arms slide up around my torso and hug me to her. "You *do* care about me, don't you?" she whispered, a ribbon of awe in her voice.

I nodded and let myself sink down against her, our bodies flush from chest to toe. I allowed her to caress me this time—wherever and however she pleased, position me where she wanted me, and kiss me until I was nearly incoherent from lack of oxygen and unadulterated lust.

But I still didn't enter her, and I knew she knew why.

My body was more than willing to fuck her senseless, but my mind and my soul were united in waiting until she not only told me what I needed to hear but, also, did it believably.

She tried a number of arguments on me, all of which I parried like a champion fencer.

"I'm so much older than you," she whined.

"We've already covered this. That's totally irrelevant."

"There's no way, given my history with your brother, that you and I could ever be a couple in the eyes of your family."

"That's absolute bullshit, too. If it's what we both really wanted, they'd deal with it."

"And you live too far away."

Well, all right. That assertion had some merit, but I said, "People make long-distance relationships work all the time, Jaleina."

"Anything beyond this weekend is just really improbable."

"Maybe, but so what?" I shot back. "Since when was anything worthwhile easy?"

I had no idea how long we were in bed like that—debating, kissing, fondling, but not actually screwing. It felt like hours.

Some things, though, were worth the wait.

Finally, she whispered, "Chandler, please make love to me. I need you—*just you*—tonight. *Te necesito esta noche. Sólo tu.* I don't know what's going to happen with us next, but I know for sure that I'll never regret this."

It took her saying all of that, but I did believe her.

I grinned down at her. "Was that really so damned difficult to admit?"

"Yes," she said with a laugh. "It kind of was."

But I kissed her then, this time as passionately and honestly as I could. And I thrust into her as deeply as I was able. And I wished as hard as humanly possible that all of the things that'd been true about me in the past—my restlessness, my late-light drinking binges, my hookups, and my aimless job hopping—could be unraveled like a bad yarn project and woven again into the kind of man Jaleina might approve of and see a future with. Even if I couldn't change things like my age or my family.

Even if I wasn't *her* fantasy the way she'd always been mine.

CHAPTER SEVEN

Chandler, The Wedding, Saturday, December 16th

I got back to Michaelsen Manor late. *Really* late. Not that the evening with Jaleina wasn't fuckingly, undeniably worth it. I didn't give a damn about the consequences tomorrow—or, rather, today.

Checked the time on my phone. Quarter to three.

Shit. I'd be lucky if I got four hours of sleep.

Derek and Olivia made sure years ago that all of us siblings had house keys. I reached for mine and unlocked the back door. Even though I'd texted my brother and told him not to worry about me or wait up, I felt like a naughty teenager again, sneaking into the house. I remembered creeping upstairs with cat-burglar stealth when I was in high school and tech college. Abby and I had spent some steamy nights down by Barrett's Pier. Hard to forget those days and everything that'd happened since.

I made it to within a yard of my old bedroom when I heard a little-boy voice in the darkness. "Uncle Chandler?"

Peter.

I swiveled around to try to locate him and finally did by the bathroom door. "Hey, kiddo. What'cha doing up?"

"I needed to pee."

Made sense. I nodded. "Oh."

"Why aren't you in your pajamas?" he asked me.

"Uh, well, I was just about to change into them. Glad you reminded me."

He pointed to my leather jacket. "You're wearing a coat. Were you outside?"

Damn. Busted by a six-year-old.

"It's cold," I said, not answering directly. Then I mock shivered for effect.

The kid giggled in the dark hallway. Cute, but a bit loud. And I wasn't eager for him to wake up his parents, who I knew wouldn't let me off the hook half as easily.

"We'd better go to bed," I whispered. "We've got a big day ahead."

"Yeah. I've got an important job."

True that. Peter was the ring bearer, even though I'd be the one holding the real wedding bands. "That's why you need your sleep. But I know you'll be great," I told him.

"Thanks, Uncle Chandler." He walked up to me and patted my arm. "You will be, too."

In spite of myself, I laughed. Then I kissed the top of his curly, dark blond head. "G'night, buddy," I murmured, and we both went to our respective beds.

In mine, I closed my eyes and replayed the moments with Jaleina in slow motion—over and over and over again. The feel of her in my arms. The taste of her on my lips. The essence of her in my heart.

No telling when I really fell asleep, but it felt like I'd only gotten about a half hour of shuteye before I heard a rap on my door.

James poked his head into the room. "Mom says you need to get up, Uncle Chandler. She's got brunch for us downstairs. We all need to help do the decorations at the church in an hour. And then there are the pictures..." He let this thought trail off because, even though he was only twelve, he knew what a long, long day we had ahead of us.

"I'm coming," I mumbled, glad that I'd get to see Jaleina again this afternoon, once all the pre-wedding stuff was in place. A *lot* had to happen before then, though.

I managed to eat a bagel with cream cheese and chives, some scrambled eggs, and drink two cups of coffee before flipping a quarter with Riley for the next spot in the shower line. I won—but I let him keep the quarter—and, soon, we were all on our way to the church, rented tuxes and requisite formalwear in tow.

My twin, who'd been an early bird since, practically, the womb, looked bright-eyed and ready to get this ceremony going. My guess was that he'd been up since at least five a.m. Not sure how the guy was going to stay awake for a round or two of wedding-night sex after this day of pomp and fluffy white cake was over but, hey, that was between him and his bride.

I was trying to follow Olivia's instructions to position just perfectly a small flower arrangement on the stand where the wedding speakers would be when Chance cornered me.

"Where'd you disappear to last night?" he demanded.

"Just needed to get some air, bro," I said, which was sort of true.

He squinted at me. "Derek said you didn't get back until nearly three. You didn't go out drinking, did you?"

I rolled my eyes. "No. I did not." At least I could be completely honest about that, but I was surprised Derek knew when I'd gotten back, since neither he nor Olivia had mentioned anything to me this morning. Guess I hadn't been as stealthy as I'd thought last night.

Chance exhaled. "Well, I have the gold wedding bands. I'll give them to you right before the ceremony, and—"

"You don't trust me with them before then, huh?" I interrupted.

My twin didn't immediately answer and, damn, that actually hurt. When he finally spoke, though, he said, "I'd trust you with my life, Chandler. I just can't help but feel that something important has been going on with you, and that it has nothing at all to do with my wedding."

He looked at me so earnestly and kindly, despite his confusion, that I was tempted to come clean with him. But he didn't need to take on the drama of my relationship issues today of all days.

"I'm working through something," I admitted. "And, you're right, I've been kind of distracted, but it's not because I'm doing drugs or getting wasted or anything like that. I'm very excited for you and Nia. I've just been...rethinking a few things. Considering, maybe, a lifestyle change or two."

His eyebrows rose slowly. "A *lifestyle* change?" He paused and lowered his voice. "Chandler, you know you can tell me *anything* and I won't judge you. If there's someone—a woman, or another, uh, man—that you wanna spend time with, you don't have to hide—"

I laughed and clapped him on the back. "Dude, I realize we've been living miles apart for a few years, but I haven't changed *that* much. I'm still straight, okay?"

"Okay, okay. I'm just saying that either way, it's cool."

"I appreciate that," I told him. "And you'll be the first to know if there's an alteration of that magnitude. But, for now, it's about a different sort of lifestyle change. Just thinking through where I'd wanna live once I leave Atlanta."

"Oh." He relaxed a bit. "Any chance it might be closer to Mirabelle Harbor?"

"Maybe." I shrugged. "We'll see."

He studied me silently for a moment. "This isn't about Abby, is it? Because she moved back here? Shar told me that she's living with Rick Zim—"

"Yeah, I'm aware," I said, cutting him off. "I won't deny it irritated me a little when I first found out, but no. She deserves to be happy, and what I'm thinking about doesn't involve her."

I noticed Blake pacing a few yards away, so I grabbed my twin by the shoulders and pointed him in our other brother's direction. Blake looked like he was bursting to ask Chance something but didn't want to interrupt us, which was thoughtful, but this conversation needed to be over, like, yesterday.

"All you've got to think about today is saying your lines, bro. The correct response to anything the minister asks is 'I do.' Don't worry about anybody else, least of all me." And, with that, I steered him over to Blake. "Love ya, man," I whispered in Chance's ear before returning to the flowers and altar decorations.

My twin's expression said, "I love you back," and I was pretty sure he mouthed those words, too, before our DJ brother started hounding him with questions about some private matter I was sure I didn't need or want to know.

The next few hours were a blur of activity.

We decorated. We ate sandwiches and Greek finger food that Nia's family had catered for us. The bride—safely sequestered from the groom until the ceremony—was busy getting her hair and makeup done, but the collection of attendants and the close-knit members of the family and wedding party all lent a hand in the preparations.

When the church was ready and all of us were dressed, the professional photographer showed up to take pictures of the bride and groom separately. There were also various group shots that were taken in advance of the ceremony to help lighten the load of photos that would need to be taken afterward. I couldn't speak for anyone else, but I was antsy as hell for this event to finally get started. And I would've bet every dollar in my bank account that Chance had had more than enough special-occasion foreplay.

"Let's *do* this already," I heard him mutter as he pressed the wedding rings into my hand.

At half past two, guests started to arrive to claim their seats. My heart was hammering half out of my chest as I scanned the pews for Jaleina. I saw Vicky Bernier, Blake's girlfriend, sitting next to Declan Night, Shar's man (since neither of them were in the wedding party but their respective lovers were). I saw a swarm of townspeople, fashionably dressed and chatty. And I saw Abby arriving with Rick. I watched them as they walked down the center aisle and sat near some friends of my sister-in-law's.

"Marianna Gregory and Gil Canton from Sarasota," Olivia informed me, when she caught me staring in their direction.

"Ah," I said. "She looks sorta familiar."

Olivia nodded. "Marianna used to live in Mirabelle Harbor. She moved to Florida about a year and a half ago." She paused and sent me a cautionary look. "She and Abby got to know each other pretty well down there."

"Ah," I said again. In my sister-in-law's world, everybody was connected to everybody.

But despite Olivia's gentleness in mentioning Abby, I was okay. Yeah, I still missed her and our friendship but, especially after last night with Jaleina, I knew my breakup with Abby had been the best outcome for us both. We shouldn't have dragged things out as long as we did. But, hey, live and learn, right?

I kept scoping the crowd and even saw the actor, Dane Tyler, with one of Mirabelle Harbor's own, Julia Crane, and her daughter, Analise. Since Julia was Shar's best friend, I'd figured she'd be here, even without her famous sidekick. Nice to see them together, though.

But Jaleina was nowhere in sight, at least not among the early arrivals.

And for the first time all day I wondered if, maybe, she

wouldn't show. The sense of loss I felt at even the *thought* of not getting to see her again was like a punch to the gut.

Fuck.

I missed her like hell already, and it'd been only twelve hours since I'd been with her in her bed. What would it be like to leave Mirabelle Harbor in a few days and not see her for weeks or even months at a time?

Didn't want to imagine that.

And then, at about five minutes to three o'clock, she slipped into the church.

I was up by the altar, standing right beside Chance, with Derek, Blake, and Nia's brother, Dimitri, rounding out the line of groomsmen. The organist had begun to play and all eyes were on the front door, waiting for the procession to begin.

Jaleina wasn't the focus for the majority of the guests, but she was everything in the world to me. Dressed in a simple wraparound green dress, she looked stunning. And when our gazes locked across the rows and rows of wooden pews and people, I felt a lightning-like current snap between us. I pulled myself up straighter and smiled at her with all the affection I could radiate. And I held my breath, waiting for her reaction.

She flashed a quick grin at me but, just as quickly, turned her head away to look—like everyone else—at the front door.

Moments later, the cute children entered. Peter with the replica rings on a white satin pillow and a couple of Nia's young relatives as flower girls tossing rose petals from little baskets.

Then came Nia's cousin, Irena, followed by my sister, Shar, then my sister-in-law, Olivia, and then the maid of honor, Anastasia, a good friend of the bride's from childhood, who'd flown in from Denver for the occasion. As maid of honor and best man, Anastasia and I would be paired up all day long for pictures and promenading and shit. She was pretty, yes, and she was single, as Nia herself had informed me with a wink. But she wasn't who I wanted to be with.

Finally, the music changed and Nia entered the room on the arm of her father.

I glanced between her and my twin, who seemed enraptured by this first glimpse of his lady love in her wedding dress. But while Chance and the rest of the congregation stayed focused on the beautiful bride and her graceful walk down the aisle to her groom, I kept cutting looks over at Jaleina, whose face drew me like a super magnet.

She'd chosen to sit on the bride's side of the church, which made sense on one hand. She and Nia were close, after all. But, on the other, just seeing that she considered herself a better friend of the Pappayiannis family than of ours when, really, we'd known and loved her first, twisted the insides of me into tight knots.

In my case, I knew and loved her *still.*

But what did that matter, really? What did I have to offer her that a hundred other guys wouldn't be able to give her...and from a lot closer to home?

I saw Jason, one of Nia's male cousins, checking out Jaleina when his eyes should've been fixed on the bride, like the rest of his family. He lived less than ninety minutes away, in a suburb of Milwaukee. He was a few years older than me, good looking in that "I love to bench press" sort of way, currently unattached, a successful Greek restaurateur (he owned Jason's Joint, renowned for their gyros) and, oh, not a member of the Michaelsen clan. I'd hated him instantly.

If I could just convince Jaleina to give a relationship with me a real shot, I'd do anything—*anything*—it took to keep her happy. Even move back to Mirabelle Harbor.

The officiant, an older African-American lady everyone called Aisha, smiled at Nia and Chance, and then she spoke to our wedding party and to everyone in the congregation. "Today is a day of celebration. A celebration of friendship, family, and love. A celebration of two people who have made a commitment to entwine their lives together and share in the journey of the years ahead."

I'd never met Aisha until yesterday's rehearsal. I'd heard that she presided over many of the weddings held here at our town's most popular nondenominational church, though, and that she'd agreed to incorporate a few of the Greek traditions in the ceremony, as well as our family's Protestant favorites.

Since Chance wasn't a member of the Greek Orthodox Church (at least not yet—he was considering converting) and Nia, who was proud of her cultural heritage but not overly religious, didn't want him to rush into anything, they'd been happy with this arrangement. Even Nia's mother, who would have preferred a traditional Greek Orthodox wedding, wasn't complaining too much. As she told just about everyone who'd listen, her daughter was *finally* getting married. And, if she had her way, soon there would be grandchildren.

I stole a glance at the Pappayiannis side of the church. Nia's mom and several of her aunts had tears in their eyes. A few of the little kids were already squirming in their seats. One of the boys had nabbed his dad's cell phone and was concentrating hard on whatever was onscreen. That cousin Jason—damn him—was still shooting looks behind him at Jaleina.

But *she*, thank God, was looking at *me*.

Because of that, I missed about half of what Aisha said next, but whatever it was drew some chuckles from the crowd. I turned to study my brother's face. He was beaming with happiness just looking at his bride. That told me all I needed to know.

Some crowd-pleasing fun followed:

A few spirited readings done by close friends of the

couple.

The exchanging of the vows and the rings, when I finally got to step up and do something useful by handing the golden bands to my brother.

Nia and Chance walking around the altar three times, which was one of the Greek traditions they'd chosen to include.

And another interesting ritual, which involved the blessing of twin crowns by an elderly member of Nia's family—her great uncle Markos, in this case—which signified that the newlyweds were heads of their household and that they should rule it with "wisdom, justice, and integrity."

The Greek members of the congregation radiated with pride, and everyone else watched with fascination, delight, and maybe even a little envy.

I couldn't deny that I was a feeling a bit jealous, too, despite my love and happiness for my twin. No way would I ever want to take away a second of Chance's joy, but I did wish I could experience what he was feeling for myself. Vowing to stay forever connected to the woman I loved. Knowing she loved me in return and was making that same promise. Committing our lives to each other in front of everyone important to us.

Never in my life had I fantasized about *marriage*, but today it was all I could think about—as long as I could imagine Jaleina as my bride.

When Aisha pronounced the couple "husband and wife," a roar of cheering and whistling threatened to raise the roof of the church. Chance and Nia walked down the aisle, side by side and grinning, to more wild clapping and, from the Greek side, some enthusiastic spitting.

Anastasia laughed softly at my obvious surprise, as the two of us linked up and began our walk out of the church behind the newlyweds. "Don't worry," she whispered. "They're not *really* spitting at them. It's dry, and very much a gesture of good luck."

"Glad to hear it," I told her. "Although, I'd personally prefer a shower of four-leaf clovers or some lucky pennies."

Her smile broadened. "That would be some other family's tradition."

I caught Jaleina eyeing the maid of honor and me as we promenaded by, and all I wanted to do was break away from the procession and hug her. Make out with her. Ask her about her family's Mexican traditions for good luck. Beg her, if I had to, to spend the rest of her life with me. Let her plan whatever wedding she wanted for us in whatever setting she'd like. God only knew I'd probably make a lousy Catholic, but I'd become one if it made her happy.

Since it was cold outside, the wedding party squeezed together in the lobby of the church to have the receiving line.

There was an awkward moment when Rick and Abby came by, but we all managed to be polite for the fifteen seconds it took to greet each other. (Although, okay, maybe, I did muscle my handshake with him a little more than necessary...) Rick's expression verged on the stern and serious, but maybe it was just because he was preoccupied calculating the distance between the church and the moon or some shit like that. Abby, at least, smiled warmly at me, but she didn't linger.

By the time Jaleina reached me, my palms were clammy from so many handshakes, and I was a little unsteady from remembering the intimacies she and I had shared last night.

When my fingers touched hers, I didn't want to let go.

"Congratulations to you all," she said faintly.

"Thanks," I said and, unlike the quick shake I'd given everyone else, I refused to release Jaleina's hand. "I'm *very* glad to see you here."

"Um, likewise, Chandler. How are you...today?"

"I'm good. Really, *really* good." And then I stared so deeply into her eyes that I hoped she wouldn't be able to miss just how much I cared about her. "And you?"

"I'm fine." She cleared her throat and, before I had a chance to ask her anything else, she said, "Well, I'd better not hold up the line, huh?" She tugged her hand away. So, reluctantly, I had to let her go.

"Okay. But please don't forget about our dance tonight," I murmured, low enough so I hoped no one else heard me.

She nodded once and then continued down the receiving line.

Even as I went through the motions of greeting the other guests, then doing the last of the pictures in the church, and then heading over to the reception hall for the dinner and the party to follow, my mind never strayed far from Jaleina. The few times it did, it was only because I thought about how much my parents would've loved to have been here for Chance's wedding. They would've enjoyed every second.

I felt the usual jab of pain at the loss. It'd been hell since they died. We'd been close and, damn, I still missed them like crazy.

But I realized something I hadn't wanted to admit to myself before. The hot grief I'd tried to stuff down with booze, one-night stands, and living anywhere but in Mirabelle Harbor...it still blazed inside of me. Being with Jaleina was just about the only thing that tempered that dark fire. The only thing that made me feel optimistic again.

During the dinner, I got to draw on this feeling during my toast to Chance and Nia as their best man, as I wished them well on their new life.

"There are people you have the good fortune to meet," I said in an unscripted addition to my original speech, after sharing a few funny stories about my twin. "People who make you believe anything's possible." I nodded at my brother and his bride, but then I scanned the room for the woman I was *also* talking to tonight. "When you find someone who fills the broken crevices of your heart with joy and who makes you look forward to tomorrow, you never want to let that person go."

I stared at Jaleina, several tables away and sitting with Nia's aunt and uncle from Wisconsin, their two sons— Nick, who'd brought his partner and soon-to-be husband, and Jason (*shit, shit, shit!*), who'd come to the wedding stag. She blushed slightly and looked down.

"That my brother and his lovely bride found each other is an inspiration for the rest of us," I concluded, returning to smile at my twin and his new wife. "And I can only hope that, one day, I'll get to have a celebration filled with as much love and good will as this one. May you both have the happiest future imaginable together." I raised my glass of champagne, and the entire room joined me. "To Chance and Nia."

"To Chance and Nia!" everyone chimed in.

When I lowered my glass and sat back down, my brother reached behind Nia to where I was sitting and nudged me. "Thanks, man," he said.

Nia gave me a side hug and a quick kiss on my cheek. "That was beautiful, Chandler."

Even Blake, from the other side of the long wedding party table, leaned forward and gave me a thumbs up.

But, once the family accolades were over, my gaze returned immediately to Jaleina, who was deep in conversation with the ever-attentive Jason—my new Greek cousin-in-law from hell. And she seemed so interested in whatever the guy was saying. Fuck. I had to get her away from him.

There was the cutting of the cake and the first dance for the bride and groom. Directly after that, Anastasia and I joined the rest of the attendants on the parquet floor for our obligatory wedding-party slow dance.

Derek, the groomsman who was conveniently paired up with Olivia as his bridesmaid dancing partner, grinned at me over his wife's shoulder as I swayed side to side with Nia's good friend. The stories of the best man hooking up with the maid of honor were legendary. Something my brother Blake felt compelled to remind me of constantly. He winked blatantly at me while twirling across the dance floor with Shar and nodded approvingly at the maid of honor whenever her back was turned.

No reflection on the pretty Anastasia, who seemed bizarrely content to keep dancing with me, but I was dying for this portion of the reception to be over so I could finally dance with the woman I'd been waiting all day to hold in my arms again.

Eventually, Chance began dancing with Nia's mom and Nia with her dad. Blake turned our sister over to Declan and then got to shimmy on the dance floor with Vicky, his main squeeze. Derek and Olivia politely danced with other people at first—like Irena, Nia's cousin, and the bride's brother, Dimitri—but they later found their way back to each other.

I, however, didn't want to be a polite little Michaelsen anymore. Once the regular guests began joining the wedding party on the dance floor and, more specifically, I saw Jason lead Jaleina to the center of the dancing space, I knew it was time for me to act.

I deliberately steered the maid of honor near where the other couple was dancing and, okay, maybe this wasn't entirely subtle, but I bumped into Jason's back. Hard.

"Oh, sorry!" I said, stopping cold on the floor and waiting for him to recover his balance. Jaleina narrowed her dark-brown eyes at me.

"That's, uh, okay," Jason said, turning to study me with well-deserved wariness.

"Anastasia, you've met Nia's cousin, Jason, haven't you?" I asked her.

She nodded. "Oh, yes. Just yesterday at the rehearsal dinner. Hi, again."

"Hi, Anastasia," Jason said dutifully. He tried not to show it, but I caught him scanning her up and down, and glancing at her chest in appreciation. "Loved your toast to the happy couple."

"Thank you!" Anastasia enthused, and I noticed her smile broadened. "I meant every word."

I could not recall a single syllable that she'd said during her toast, but I was sure every sentence was very sweet and heartfelt. My mind, though, had been otherwise engaged.

"And this is Jaleina Longoria, a friend of Nia's and—and *mine*." I paused, remembering soul-kissing her as I thrust deeply into her last night. I hadn't meant to sound quite so possessive, but fuck it. That was how I felt. "And all of us, actually," I added. "*Everyone* in Mirabelle Harbor loves Jaleina." Or they should.

She tried to shrug that off. "I think Chandler's exaggerating," she told Anastasia with a soft laugh. "But it's very nice to meet you."

The ladies shook hands, and I used that moment to shoot Jason a warning look that didn't take a genius to understand. *Back the hell off, buddy.* He took a slight step away from my woman.

Hey, I fully intended to steal his dance partner, but I didn't intend to be a *total* dick about it. The maid of honor was hot, and she had a decent rack. He should be thanking me for what I was going to do next.

I nodded at him and turned to Anastasia. "I've been rudely hogging you on the dance floor," I told the lovely maid of honor, then motioned between her and Jason. "Perhaps you two would like to give it a whirl?"

Jason, with an Old World gallantry I had to give him credit for, immediately reached out to Anastasia and asked her for a dance. She agreed, and with only a fleeting look back in our direction, they were off.

Then I faced Jaleina, who'd crossed her arms, raised her eyebrows, and was shaking her head in obvious disapproval. "Seriously?" she said.

"Look, I'm not claiming to be some polished gentleman. And you know damn well how impatiently I've been waiting for this dance with you tonight. Did you really expect me to wait another half hour, lightly tap the bastard on the shoulder, and ask to cut in, like some 19th century British dude?" I reached my palm out toward her.

She slowly placed her fingers in mine and let me pull her closer. "Maybe not, Chandler, but your little bump and switch maneuver called attention to us." She surreptitiously motioned with her head toward Shar and Declan, who weren't dancing and were staring at us curiously.

"I don't fucking care," I whispered. "My sister needs to do something other than meddle in the lives of her brothers."

Jaleina snorted. "At this point, she's not actually meddling. I think she's just speculating. Although, she does look a little peaked."

"Whatever. My point is that I don't care what anybody thinks."

"Easy for you to say. You don't live here anymore."

"Would it make a difference to you if I did?" I asked her.

She cut a sharp look at me. "Why would you do that? Move back home after all this time?"

"I think you know why." I pulled her body flush with mine and let her feel how she affected me.

She gasped softly in my ear, her breath quickening against me as we continued our dance to whatever cheesy love song the band was playing. I wasn't actively trying to scandalize the wedding guests, so I didn't grind my cock against her or grab her ass or French kiss her in the middle of the dance floor—though I wanted to do all three—but I didn't try to restrain my desire for her either.

Jaleina knew what I was feeling. And if I had to guess at her emotions, she was feeling the same way, no matter how controlled she tried to be or how properly she acted.

Thing was, I'd spent all day wanting her in my arms. Now, I still wanted her in my arms—just somewhere private.

~Jaleina~

I hadn't had the easiest day to begin with, and Chandler sure wasn't making it any easier.

After spending last night with him, I'd been unable to take a single thought to completion in my addled brain today. I'd start to reason my way through something important or even kind of mundane, but I'd get distracted remembering his body on mine. His fingers caressing me. His tongue...absolutely everywhere.

And now, here we were again. He had his hands skimming along my upper back—no different, in the eyes of the world, than Jason's had been a few minutes ago. But, trust me, it was an *entirely* different sensation.

Shar and her boyfriend were watching us. And, oh, shit. Derek and his wife, standing on the other side of the dance floor, were taking turns glancing at us strangely, too. Just what I needed. To be a source of gossip for the Mirabelle Harbor rumor mill after my ex-fiancé's kid brother, whom I'd just started sleeping with, hightailed it back to Atlanta.

Yeah. That'd be awesome.

Then again, maybe Chandler wouldn't be leaving after all.

I wasn't sure if I should feel relieved by his desire to stay here—with me, for me—or if a much greater sense of worry was in order.

But I'd been trying too hard to rein in my emotions all

week, especially when it came to Chandler. I couldn't be tasked with letting them out all of a sudden, and then puzzling through the distinctions between them.

My dance partner was silent—or, rather, he wasn't speaking aloud. Nonverbal communication was another story.

As the Rascal Flatts song "Waiting All My Life" ended and made way for the next tune, the band's cover of Michael Jackson's "Human Nature," Chandler held me like I was the only woman in the room. We swayed together to the music, and I was sure that if anyone looked at my face too closely, they'd see in my expression how attracted I was to him. They'd guess that we'd made love. They'd wonder about us and, ultimately, figure out the truth—that I was crazy about a guy I couldn't really have. This reckless, restless younger man. This surprisingly tender and weirdly principled lover, who'd refused to let me regret our passionate night together, even though we had no future.

When the song finally stopped, the band's lead singer started chatting. The group had more good wishes for the bride and groom. They had the lineup of activities for the night—the bouquet and garter tosses were coming up soon. They had hit songs they planned to play.

"Wanna get outta here?" Chandler asked.

"And go where?"

He shrugged. "Anywhere."

So we wandered to the fringes of the dance floor first. "There's, um, wedding cake," I told him. "And platters of Greek pastries. If you haven't had dessert."

"That's not the dessert I want," he said in a low and dangerously suggestive voice.

Yeah. I had to admit, it wasn't the dessert I wanted either.

"I was having this fantasy last night at the rehearsal dinner," he whispered. "It involved you, some especially sticky pieces of baklava, and my mouth." He motioned toward the dessert table. "I could snitch a few pieces and demonstrate, if you'd like."

I laughed. And then felt myself blushing. Everywhere.

We *really* needed to leave the ballroom. If he kept this up, I'd be telegraphing my embarrassing and powerful attraction to him to every single person within a twenty-yard radius.

"Let's, maybe, go for a stroll in the hallway," I suggested. "We could get a glass of wine and—and, I don't know, just wander around for a bit. Away from the crowd."

"I love the way you think, Ms. Longoria. Wine and wandering works for me." And, with that, he cut through the collection of guests like a warm knife through butter, gliding over to the bar, getting us both our beverages, and leading me away from the goldfish bowl that was the wedding dance.

At first, we simply sipped our white wines and chatted about nothing. But the farther we traveled from the reception ballroom, the more I noticed Chandler's eyes darting around, like a hawk scoping for its prey.

"What are you looking for?" I finally asked.

He downed the rest of his drink in one gulp and stopped abruptly in the middle of the hallway. "That," he said, pointing with his empty wine glass to a darkened alcove in the corner ahead.

With one hand, he reached for my half-full drink and set both of our glasses down on a small table with a tasteful ceramic vase on top. With the other hand, he reached for me, and he led me into the delicious veil of shadows just down the hall.

Instant anonymity.

Unless somebody was looking for us specifically, we wouldn't be easy to find or quickly recognizable.

He leaned me against one side of a petite love seat that was nestled into the darkened nook. And though he didn't technically remove any of my clothing, his gaze undressed me. Slowly, he brought his lips to mine, anchoring me in place between the cushions of the love seat and the sidewall.

"I can't wait another second to touch you," he murmured, his fingers slipping under the hem of my dress and inching their way upward. And upward. All the way up to my hip. He chuckled lightly when he reached the thin waistband of my panties and skimmed his palm across my bare behind. "You're wearing a thong," he said between kisses so sensual and tender that my heart and soul melted like the gooey chocolate in a dessert fountain. "You had me going there for a minute. I thought, maybe, you weren't wearing panties at all. Tell me, are they as green as your dress?"

"That's something you'll have to find out for yourself. Later."

His mouth devoured mine and, for the longest time, nothing changed but how wet I was getting and how quickly I was losing my sanity.

"Mmm." He hooked his thumb on my waistband and began tugging downward. "I think there's a way I can figure that out *now*."

I moaned as he rubbed the pads of his fingers against my clit, while he slowly slid the fabric down...down to the tops of my thighs...and further down to—

I heard a sound beside us. A man clearing his throat.

Chandler's hand stilled on my body, under cover of my dress. We broke our kiss and both turned our heads to look at the intruder, who was standing in the light.

Oh, holy crap!

Derek Michaelsen.

CHAPTER EIGHT

Derek, During the Reception

Granted, it'd been an emotional day for Derek long before he took that walk to the dark side of the hallway.

As the eldest of the Michaelsens and the current head of the family, he'd experienced a rollercoaster of feelings throughout the week.

Chance and Chandler—just seeing the twins reunited and side by side at the altar was an extraordinary moment in time. *Chance was married!* God, their parents would've been so proud. And having the pleasure of getting all of the siblings together again for the first time since Mom's funeral...hard to believe how the years had flown by.

There also the fun of observing his three boys playing with Julia's daughter, Analise, at the reception, along with Nia's cousins' kids. They were having a blast.

Derek had been laughing with his new sister-in-law as they watched her brother, Dimitri, flirting with all of the single twenty-something women throughout the afternoon and evening. Nia was a wonderful addition to their family, and he truly liked the Pappayiannis clan.

He'd enjoyed Olivia's excitement in getting to spend some time with one of her best friends, Marianna, and this Gil guy she was in love with from Florida.

Shar had been exhilarated by her involvement in the wedding planning and getting to share today's joy with her boyfriend, Declan, with her best friend, Julia, and even with the famous Dane Tyler. The actor's presence added a dash of celebrity fodder to their otherwise simple event. Not that this mattered to Derek or to any member of his family. He just loved seeing his sister and her friend so happy in each other's company.

And then there was Blake, the brother Derek thought might never, ever settle down. His love and commitment to Vicky blazed apparent, despite their lack of formal vows.

It was even a bit touching to see Abby Solinski again, with her new man, Rick. And then there was Jaleina, who'd come to the wedding alone.

Aw, shit.

His heart always ached when he thought about the end of their relationship. She was beautiful, intelligent, very kind...and, yet, it hadn't been enough. He'd fallen hard for Olivia, knew deep in his bones that they belonged together instead, and even though it'd killed him to have the conversation that ended his engagement with Jaleina, it'd been the right decision.

His parents, who were still alive back then, said they understood.

Shar had been mad at him initially, but she got over it, especially once she got to know Olivia. Those two were practically like real sisters nowadays.

Blake and Chance kept their own counsel when it came to relationships and had just supported him silently.

But when Derek saw Chandler dancing with Jaleina at the wedding reception, he recalled with a rush of memories that his kid brother had been furious with him after the big breakup, and it was an anger that had lingered. Chandler had even spat out to Derek once, "How could you hurt her like that? It's unforgivable."

Although he hadn't had the heart to point out his brother's hypocrisy, Derek thought the way Chandler had strung Abby along for so many years was pretty effing unforgivable, too.

Then again, maybe a man didn't know for sure what he wanted until it was standing right in front of him.

In a green dress, for instance.

Dancing to "Human Nature."

Hmm.

Derek watched, his eyes unblinking, as Chandler pulled Jaleina closer. Interestingly, his ex-fiancée didn't seem to mind the lack of personal space. Derek had loved her as much as he thought was possible back when he was twenty-six—until Olivia waltzed into his life and proved him a damned liar. And in the decade or so since then, he'd always hoped Jaleina would find someone who could make her truly and genuinely happy.

Never in a billion years did he expect that someone might be *Chandler*.

He frowned as a new realization crept into his consciousness and felt his jaw drop.

Olivia sidled up to him and, nodding in the dancing couple's direction, she hissed, "Did I miss something? The two of them look like they're...um..."

"Screwing?" Derek supplied.

"I was going to say 'dating,' but yeah. They seem sort of—oh, what's the right word? *Familiar* with each other."

He scowled at his wife. "In no way do I want to think about that."

She laughed softly. "That would be a fascinating twist, though, huh?"

He knew had no right to dictate who Jaleina dated or slept with, especially not after all of these years. But Chandler? His kid brother was the least settled, the least mature, the most restless, and the most unpredictable member of the entire family. Even six-year-old Peter was more grounded.

Chandler was the opposite of reliable and stable, which were qualities Jaleina had always prized. What were his brother's intentions toward her? He couldn't possibly be serious about pursuing a relationship—could he?

Derek felt oddly protective of his ex and uncharacteristically suspicious of his own younger sibling, much as he loved the guy. And, if truth be told, there was also a deep sense of responsibility he felt toward them both.

The band was yakking on about the activities ahead, but Derek couldn't stop his brain from spinning through a variety of scenarios that had nothing to do with bouquet tosses or garter throws.

Olivia slipped away to talk with some other guests. Chance and Nia were laughing with friends just off the dance floor. It took Derek a few moments to spot Blake. He and Declan were discussing something that apparently required lots of hand gestures to describe. Looked like some sort of sports game wrap-up.

In fact, by the time Derek had successfully located every member of the wedding party, all necessary participants for the events coming up soon, he realized that the best man had disappeared from the dance floor. And so had his lady partner.

He scanned every section of the ballroom. Chandler and Jaleina were nowhere to be seen.

Derek checked his watch. The ladies would do the bouquet toss first, so he had a little time to find his brother. All the guys were supposed to be present for that garter thing, though. In fact, the best man would be the one in charge of blindfolding the groom. Not necessarily an essential duty, in Derek's opinion, but everyone at the reception would wonder where Chandler was if he suddenly went AOWL.

He jogged into the hallway and looked in both directions. No sight of them.

A male guest—someone from Nia's side because Derek didn't recognize him—was just finishing up a call on his cell phone.

"Excuse me," Derek said to the guy. "Any chance you saw a man in a tux and a woman in a green dress walking through here?"

The guy nodded. "Oh, the best man, right?"

"Yes."

"Yep. About two or three minutes ago." He pointed left. "They went that way—" His phone rang again. "Sorry, I need to get this."

"No problem," Derek said, heading in the direction he'd indicated. "Thanks for the help."

He heard his brother and Jaleina before he saw them. There was some murmuring and, to his horror, some moaning, but the people in question weren't visible. For that, at least, he was grateful.

It wasn't until he'd gotten to the very end of the hall that he saw them. Or, really, their silhouettes, kissing in the shadows.

Damn. He did not want to do this. But fuck it. Chandler was *the best man*, and he had a responsibility to his twin.

He cleared his throat, and the couple in front of him stopped cold, frozen in action.

Even though Derek knew what he was interrupting, it was still a shock to witness Chandler with his hand up Jaleina's skirt. And his mouth on her neck. And both pairs of eyes, open wide and staring back at him.

When he could finally move his lips to speak, he said, "Uh, sorry to disturb you two but, Chandler, everyone in the wedding party is gathering for the next two activities. There'll be pictures and stuff that you, um, need to be present for."

Chandler looked between Derek and Jaleina. He

grimaced and began to shake his head.

She spoke instead. "You should be out there," she told him. "It's Chance and Nia's big day. They'd notice if you were missing."

His brother swallowed and sighed. "Will you stay?" he asked her. It felt like such an intimate moment to Derek. He wished the hallway would swallow him up, so he wouldn't have to witness it.

Jaleina didn't look at Chandler when she replied. Her eyes grazed over Derek instead, and he couldn't guess at the full range of what she must be feeling.

"No," she said. "I've been out in public long enough for today." She tried to laugh, but it came out sort of strangled.

Both men watched her in silence as she straightened her clothing, and Derek finally caught an expression of pure embarrassment crossing her face. She'd never been a big PDA person when they'd dated, but she was still sexy as hell. Despite being a happily married man, he could appreciate the rare beauty and sensuality of his ex. A woman who looked even more stunning at thirty-eight than she had at twenty-four.

Honestly, he couldn't blame *any* man for being attracted to her—not even Chandler. But it was the way she seemed to be equally attracted to his kid brother that made him squirm under her gaze. That made him realize just how uncomfortable she must be, especially having *him* be the one to discover them.

He abruptly stepped back.

Chandler, who was obviously struggling to get his emotions (and his lower body) under control, whispered, "Jaleina, don't leave. Please."

Derek couldn't help but notice that his brother's usual tough-guy veneer had been stripped away. The guy cared about her. A lot.

"I need to go home," she was saying. "You've got things to do here, and I'm getting...tired. Especially after being up late last night."

The two of them gazed at each other with a kind of private understanding that Derek was pretty damn sure he didn't want to know the details of tonight. Or any night. Seriously, when were these walls going to sweep him up and make him disappear?

"Just call me tomorrow," Jaleina whispered to Chandler. "We'll talk then, okay?"

"Okay," his brother said, but he was shaking his head the whole time, negating his own words.

Then, with a quick squeeze of Chandler's arm and a nod at Derek, Jaleina slipped out of the darkness and into the lit hallway. Her long legs striding purposefully away from them both, toward the coat check and, then, out of the reception hall.

Chandler, arms crossed, mouth agape, was looking more grim and determined than Derek had ever seen him. He was almost unrecognizable, and it took a moment to figure out why. The expression in his eyes was like that of a world-weary octogenarian, brooding and bleak.

Derek wasn't inclined to be overly chatty and lighthearted himself after what he'd just witnessed but, as he and Chandler plodded back toward the ballroom, he did have one thing to say. "What the hell are you doing, little brother?"

~Sharlene~

Shar made it to the bathroom just in time.

She'd carefully avoided drinking any alcohol—taking just a few fake sips of champagne during the many wedding toasts—but she'd made the mistake of actually trying to eat the baked chicken. Cooked meat smelled revolting to her, and it tasted even worse. And then there were the mashed potatoes, which reeked of garlic. And the texture of the asparagus stalks on her plate, which was the worst thing of all!

Ugh. Food sucked.

She'd done a few required dances and made it through them okay, but then she got tricked into having a bite of cake. When did frosting become so outrageously sugary? Like sweetened paste. It'd never made her vomit before, but now... What. The. Hell.

Shar honestly had no idea how she was going to survive on bottled water, dry cereal, and bananas until July, but she'd do what was necessary to see this pregnancy through to completion.

She emerged from the stall, rinsed, and dried her mouth, only to find her BFF, Julia Crane, standing by the sinks, hands fisted on her hips, and an "O" formed with her mouth.

"I can't believe you didn't tell me," Julia said.

"Oh, girlfriend. I haven't told anyone except for Dec. We just found out last week and were waiting until after the three-month mark to spring it on the family. But I fully intended on telling *you* this weekend in person. If only I could stay in one place for long enough without throwing up."

There were tears in her friend's eyes. "Aw, Shar." She paused to swipe at the wet drops on her lashes. "You're gonna be a mom!"

"I'm gonna be a mom," she repeated, hugging her dear friend. "I'm only eight weeks pregnant, but I want to get this request in early because I know you've got a busy schedule. Will you be the baby's godmother?"

Julia squealed.

"I'll take that as a yes," she said, then she and Julia jumped around and hugged some more.

"So, what made you and Declan decide to become parents? Or was it, um—"

"A surprise?" Shar finished for her.

Her friend nodded.

"It was only a surprise in that it happened so quickly," she told Julia. "Dec and I are both getting older, and we thought that if we ever wanted to be parents, we should, maybe, get a move on. So, we've been kind of lax with the contraception since October. He and I thought it might take months or even a year or more...but, clearly, it didn't." She rubbed her belly. "Determined little swimmer. Bet he's going to be an athlete like his daddy."

"Or *her* daddy."

They laughed.

"Yes," Shar agreed. "Either way is good."

"I know you love him, Shar, but are you ready for this? Is he?"

She bobbed her head. "I can't even tell you all the ways Dec is different than my slimy ex-husband. I know I've tried during our many, many conversations about men, but he's just so cool, Julia. Such a good partner for me."

"You guys are still living in separate places, though. Have you talked about marriage or even just moving in together—at least once the baby's born? You're going to need help during those newborn months."

Shar shuddered. "Not marriage. Please. I'm still not ready to do *that* again. But, to be honest, I can *almost* imagine it happening with Dec someday. As for moving in together, yes. I'd like to finish out the school year, if possible, then we'll see. He asked me to move into his place above The Penalty Box with him, but with a baby, we might need more space, sooner rather than later." She lowered her voice. "Don't tell anyone, but he's kinda started looking at houses."

"What?" Julia was glowing with excitement. "This is serious then."

"It is. I never would've believed it six months ago, but here we are." She paused and leaned against the marble countertop for support. "I know you've been pretty hot and heavy with Dane for the past year and a half. He seems to be keeping you busy with events all over the country."

Julia agreed. "Yeah, his filming schedule has been crazy, and you know how obnoxious the tabloids get whenever he's promoting a new movie..." She let that thought trail off. There was a lot of history Julia wanted to forget when it came to the paparazzi. "But, uh, I've got something to ask you, too."

"Anything, girlfriend."

She lowered her voice. "Remember when I said I'd never consent to getting married without you as my matron of honor?"

"Oh, my God, Julia!" Shar knew immediately what that meant. "You're officially engaged then?"

She nodded. "I'm not wearing the ring because—well, you know, we've got to keep it a secret until afterward. But, yes! Official!"

They both squealed, hugged, and jumped around again. Shar was getting more exercise in the bathroom than she ever got at the gym.

"Just tell me where and when, and I'll be there," she told her friend.

Julia stared at her stomach. "Well, do you think you'll be over your morning sickness by mid-February? Or should I tell Dane we need to postpone until spring break?"

"You guys are planning a Valentine's wedding? Ohhhh, that is so romantic, girlfriend!" Shar shook her head. "No problem. I'll be at four months then, and I should be fine." She hoped so anyway. "Where are we flying to?"

"A little beach on a Caribbean island—details to be disclosed nearer to the event and will be utterly confidential." Julia lowered her voice even more. "This is going to be a very small, very private affair. As in, fewer than ten people, including Dane, Analise, and me. There will be the officiant, who's an old friend of Dane's. A couple members of his family will be there—his brother, who'll be our best man, and his wife. You, of course, and

Declan, if he'd like to come, and if he can keep a secret."

Shar laughed. "I'll make sure of that, don't worry."

"Good. Dane's mother knows about the wedding, but flying is difficult for her at her age, so we'll have a special celebration with her and the rest of his family when we return. And we're definitely not inviting my parents or sister to the island, but we'll host a reception with them after the fact as well."

No surprise to Shar that Julia wasn't inviting her family, particularly that snotty sister of hers. "Okay. You can count on me to keep mum about it. Dec needs to know, of course, but I promise neither of us will tell anyone else. Not even my brothers."

"Thanks," Julia whispered. "After it's all done, we'll announce it everywhere and even have a few parties in L.A. and in Mirabelle Harbor. But an extremely limited number of people will know about the wedding beforehand. We want the ceremony to be truly *ours*—with no one else intruding."

Just then, some other women came into the bathroom, so Julia and Shar left and made a beeline for the reception.

"I can't tell you how glad I am that my family's been so distracted by Chance and Nia's wedding," Shar confided. "That my 'condition' could fly under the radar with them is a near miracle. I expected to get away with it when it came to the guys, at least for a while, but Olivia is usually too observant to fool."

Julia inclined her head in Olivia's direction. "Funny thing, though, from the look on her face, it seems like something's up."

True, Shar had to agree, as they neared the dance floor. Olivia was walking toward Derek but eyeing something on the floor with growing concern. What had she noticed?

Julia went to talk to Dane, and Shar hunted down Declan, while trying not to look as nauseated as she felt when the photographer or one of the guests strolled by.

"Feeling okay?" Dec asked her.

"Yeah, more or less," she said. "Just don't make me eat anything else tonight. And, oh, I told Julia."

He grinned, his pride in his forthcoming fatherhood already evident. "Good."

"She's got some extra-special news, too, which I'll share with you later. When we're alone."

He raised one dark eyebrow. "Does it involve that movie star dude, who all the female wedding guests are swooning over?"

Shar chuckled. "Yeah. But since when do you use the word *swooning*, hmm?"

Dec shrugged and leaned down to kiss the top of her head. "I have a good vocabulary. I like to exercise it."

She was about to say something about what a showoff he could be, when a situation on the dance floor caught her eye. There had been a sort of bumping incident involving Chandler, Anastasia, Jason, and Jaleina. For a second, it looked like something out of a sitcom.

And then, the maid of honor and Nia's hunky cousin were dancing. And so were Chandler and Jaleina. Only, it wasn't quite the same with the latter pair. There was something Shar couldn't quite put her finger on when it came to the way they were moving. If pressed, she'd have to say it was surprisingly...*cozy*.

She and Declan stared at them. Derek and Olivia, who were standing together now, were staring at them, too. Even Nia and Chance, who should've been too busy being playing bride and groom tonight, were glancing over there repeatedly. Huh.

Shar got distracted by a guest and was caught up in a conversation for several minutes. But, sometime after the band had announced that the throwing of the bouquet and the garter would be coming up, Olivia shot Shar a worried look from across the ballroom.

She followed the direction of her sister-in-law's gaze,

which had become fixed on one of the doors. Derek was returning to the room, Chandler by his side. But the expressions on both of the men's faces were unlike anything Shar had seen between them before.

"What's going on with those two?" Shar said, after walking over to Olivia and putting an arm around her. She looked like she needed some sisterly support.

Olivia pursed her lips as the guys neared the dance floor. "All I know for sure is that it has something to do with Jaleina Longoria and your brother."

"You don't mean Jaleina and Derek?" Shar whispered. She remembered the broken engagement from years ago and all the drama that followed. But Derek couldn't be jealous or anything because Chandler had danced with his ex, could he?

Olivia shook her head. "No, no. The other brother. The one who's been sleeping with her."

"WHAT?"

"Shhh." Her sister-in-law exhaled slowly. "C'mon. The photographer wants pictures of all the bridesmaids before the bouquet toss. We've gotta get out there."

"Wait. Olivia—I saw them dancing together, but you don't think they're really—"

"Did you take a look at my husband's face?"

Sure enough, Derek looked mighty odd. Like he'd been trying to put together a jigsaw puzzle with pieces all mixed up from three or four different sets. She thought about what it might mean for the family if this thing between Chandler and Jaleina were true. Yeah, it would be a little weird at first, but the two of them weren't so far apart in age now that it would matter much. And, wow. If it inspired their little brother to finally move closer to Mirabelle Harbor again, or even just spend more time here, what a blessing that would be.

But hooking up with Derek's ex-fiancée? Shar felt for her sister-in-law. Olivia had been so insecure about that relationship in the early days, especially since Derek had broken up with Jaleina to be with *her*. Shar knew it had to bring back all kinds of uncomfortable emotions and memories for everyone involved.

Still! Chandler and Jaleina? Who would've guessed?

"This could get a little awkward," Shar murmured, as she and her sister-in-law reached the dance floor.

Olivia chuckled dryly and actually rolled her eyes. "No shit, Shar."

~*Chandler*~

Jaleina left. Dammit. She'd *left*.

And I had to be dragged back into the reception by my big brother like I was a toddler who'd run off at a neighborhood block party.

"What the hell are you doing, little brother?" Derek asked.

"What's it to you?" I shot back. "You don't still have feelings for her, do you?"

"Of course I have *feelings* for her, you little shit," he hissed at me under his breath. "I *cared* about her a lot. I still do. What game are you playing?"

"I'm not playing a fucking game. You're not the only one who can have *feelings* for her, by the way. Who can *care* about her."

"Since when, though?" Derek turned to glare at me. "You've been away from Mirabelle Harbor for almost six years, Chandler. When the hell did those magical, mysterious feelings for Jaleina develop?"

I glared right back at him. He couldn't make me admit aloud just how long or how strong my feelings for her had been. But, somehow, he must've guessed anyway.

"You were a *kid* when she and I were together," Derek said,

"I wasn't a kid. I was sixteen when the two of you

broke up. Old enough to know she was off limits then. Old enough to have sex with someone else." Not old enough to own up to the fact that my desire for Abby was, in part, a substitute for my longing for Jaleina. I couldn't even confess that to myself until, oh, this week. Still couldn't say anything like that to Derek, whose expression looked like he wanted to wring my neck, right there at the edge of the dance floor.

Which would've been a little disruptive in the middle of my twin's wedding reception and all.

He clapped his hand on the back of my neck and squeezed, none too gently either, but to most of the guests standing near us, it probably looked like a brotherly gesture. Then he leaned closer to me and, with a grimace that vaguely resembled a smile, he whispered, "Don't do anything stupid. We need to talk about this when we're not about to do a fucking garter toss, okay?"

"Fine. We'll talk," I told him, wrenching free of his grip. "Later."

"Soon," my big brother countered. "Before you talk to her again."

I shrugged. Like hell we would. I wasn't waiting for Derek's goddamn permission to speak with Jaleina. And I wasn't going to wait until *tomorrow* to call her either.

God, I missed her already.

And contrary to what my pain-in-the-ass older brother was saying, I wasn't trying to fool with her or do anything that might hurt her. I was in love with her. An undisputable fact that had been steady and true for nearly half my life.

As soon as the obligatory events were over and the photographer had gotten his friggin' pictures, I pulled the cheerful groom aside.

"Hey, Chance, are you good?"

He squinted at me. "Yeah," he said. Not much of a talker, that guy.

"I mean, you got hitched, danced with your bride, took

pictures, even had cake and pastries and champagne. You're in a good place, right?"

"Moderation is the key with the sweets and the alcohol, bro," he said, but he was grinning. Damn. He was *truly* happy, and it was incredible to see him this way. He'd earned it.

"Yep, you're right about that. And, um, I could stay here for longer, if you need me, and do the Bunny Hop or the Chicken Dance or whatever you and your bride might have planned next. But if you don't need me, would you be okay if I went...out? I need to talk with someone."

"Who?"

"It's, uh, kind of a long story."

My twin just raised his eyebrows.

I shook my head. "Can I explain it to you in the morning, maybe?" After Derek's reaction, I didn't want Chance to get all riled up at me, too.

He wrinkled his nose. "We leave on our honeymoon after the brunch, so it'll have to be before noon."

"I can do that. Promise."

"Good. Because I want to hear all about this person who's enticing enough to pull you away from your twin brother's wedding." He paused. "Must be a woman."

I sighed. "Look, I can stay for a little while longer and—"

He laughed at me. "Get going, Chandler. You are my *brother*, and I *love* you. If it's that important, you'd better go talk with her. Now."

"Thank you," I murmured, fighting an outrageous urge to hug the hell out of him.

I was about to turn away, but Chance grabbed my arm. "Oh, and tell her that green is definitely her color. Even Nia said so."

I stared at him. "You knew?"

He glanced heavenward. "Let me repeat. You are my *brother*, and I *love* you. You're also my twin, and we've

193

got a special connection." He motioned between his brain and mine. "Plus, I saw you and Jaleina dancing together and, man, water couldn't separate you two." He nodded toward the exit. "I won't tell on you, okay? But considering the way you guys were looking at each other, a few people may have guessed."

"Well, shit. And here I thought I'd been so discreet."

Chance just grinned at me. He knew I had a sarcastic side, but he chose not to respond in kind. True to his nature, he said instead, "The people who love us, know us...and they *still* love us." Then he winked at me and walked away.

I sent him a mental blessing, slipped out the back door, and headed to Jaleina's.

CHAPTER NINE

Jaleina, After the Wedding

There was a knock on my door and, for the second time this week, I found a shivering Chandler Michaelsen waiting for me on the front step.

I didn't ask if he wanted to come in. I just swung the door open for him.

"Did you ride your motorcycle here from the reception?" I asked. I hadn't heard it and couldn't see it anywhere.

He shook his head. "We'd taken the limo over to the reception hall from the church. I didn't have my bike or a car available, and I didn't want to borrow anyone's. So I just walked."

"You walked? Jeez, Chandler, it's the middle of December!" Even three blocks without a winter coat in this weather... I grabbed his hands in mine. They were like ice cubes.

"Warm me up," he whispered.

So, even though I knew we needed to talk, and despite being determined to put the brakes on whatever the heck this thing was between us—especially after the mortification of Derek coming up on us in the hallway—I couldn't help but hold Chandler right then.

"Fine. But we'll talk tomorrow." I locked the front door, pushed off his tuxedo jacket, unbuttoned his shirt, unfastened his bow tie and belt, and led him into my bedroom.

Although I'd kicked off my heels when I'd gotten home, I hadn't gotten around to changing out of my dress. Chandler didn't mind this, however. He said, "I've been waiting to peel this damn thing off of you for hours."

Then he kissed me like the sun wouldn't rise in the morning. And, ohhh, after the embarrassment I'd endured tonight, I wasn't sure I wanted tomorrow to come anyway.

But I wasn't going to think about that right this second. No.

I was going to live in the moment. A moment that was blissfully free of loneliness when I was in Chandler's arms. And maybe I didn't want to overanalyze why that was so, but it simply was. As my beloved *abuelo* used to say, *"No puedes negar la veridad."* You can't deny the truth.

One other thing I couldn't deny—a different Chandler Michaelsen made love to me that night. The evening before, he'd been flirty and fun, passionate and vigorous, teasing and so very hot. But his youthful energy had left me worried and wondering how long I'd be able to keep pace with him.

Tonight, by contrast, the playfulness and charm was set aside for someone much more serious and intense. He had a weight on his shoulders that had aged him overnight.

Admittedly, this made me feel less like a cougar, which was a good thing, but more like the cause of his pain, which wasn't good at all.

He made me come twice—first with his mouth and, then, with his cock—and, finally, he climaxed himself. But, afterward, he hugged me like he was afraid I'd sneak away in the middle of the night. And, tired as he looked, he wouldn't let himself fall asleep.

"I guess it's after midnight now," I whispered. "So, technically, it's tomorrow. Which means the wedding is over and we need to discuss a few things."

"Yeah," he said, his voice hoarse and filled with emotion. I hadn't expected that. "I'm sorry about Derek. I know it would be a lot easier on you if he and I weren't brothers—"

"It would be," I interrupted. "But it still couldn't make this—*us*—work long term, Chandler."

A shuddering sigh came out of him, like a trembling gust of wind. "Please don't say that." His eyes pleaded with me to take it back, but I couldn't.

"The Michaelsens, collectively, are a formidable bunch. You have a tight family. And they're very protective of you. The way Derek looked at me tonight...I just..." I swallowed. I couldn't even express how humiliated I'd felt.

"No, you got it all wrong, Jaleina. Derek was being protective of *you*. I'm the one he's pissed at. Not you, sweetheart. He was worried I was playing games with your heart. That I might hurt you, which is the last thing I want to do."

I considered this briefly, but then waved it away. "It doesn't matter, even if it's true. You're here for a short time. You might talk of staying in town for a while or moving back eventually, but you know you don't have to. That's not the same for me. I live here, Chandler. I'm staying in Mirabelle Harbor, long into the foreseeable future. My life and my business are here. And I have to face everyone who's still here with me. Like your *entire* family." I looked into his eyes, which were looking back at me so intently—they were like lasers—and his heart was shining through them. There was real adoration in that gaze.

But, as strong as it was, it wasn't enough. Not to make

a relationship last through all the ups and downs. I knew this. I doubted he did.

"I fell in love with you years ago," he told me. "That hasn't changed. And I'd move oceans and mountain ranges to be with you."

The way he said it, I could almost believe him. Chandler had such a rep of being a heartbreaker, but he'd had an undeniable passion, even as a teen. I'd always thought the town gossips had gotten him wrong. He wasn't the "dangerous twin" or the "bad boy." He just wanted to be taken seriously. To be fully and completely loved. Loved as wildly and irrationally, perhaps, as he loved in return.

Chance, only two minutes younger, was so different. He was taken seriously from birth. Too much so, if you asked me. He desperately needed to loosen up and be more childlike. Nia was the perfect complement to him. Thanks to her, Chance was quicker to smile these days. More likely to laugh. And he even ate sweets on occasion.

Chandler, though, had always been regarded as an irresponsible kid, even by his siblings. I remembered how well he responded to me when I recognized the adult within him and treated him accordingly.

So, I didn't try to be gentle with him tonight. I told it to him straight, and exactly as I thought and felt it to be.

"After these past few days, it would be easy for me to fall for you, too. You're a good man, Chandler Michaelsen." I paused, working up the courage to say the rest. "But it's because I really, really like you and because I know I *could* love you back...that I need to let you go. You didn't want to return to Mirabelle Harbor. Not yet, anyway. You weren't ready to be here when you came to town this week. Your brother's wedding forced your hand, and here you are. But, if it weren't for me, you'd leave again in a heartbeat. We both know that. And I need to stay. So, until one of us changes what we want or need, everything else is irrelevant. Our age difference. The history I have with your family. Whether a real relationship between us could work. It's all academic if we're not on the same page with our lives and our goals."

I had to give him credit. He did me the honor of listening to every word I said. Hearing me out, even though it was obvious from his facial expression that he disagreed. Vehemently.

When he finally spoke, it was with the grave, aged tone of a man who'd been battered by elements out of his control. Weathered by storm conditions that just kept coming. "I don't know what to say to that," he told me. "You're right, I guess, but I wish you weren't. I wish you'd dreamed of hopping on the back of my Harley and riding off into the sunset—or into the sunrise—with me."

I smiled at him. "Yeah, that's a nice dream. Although, I remember the last woman you took with you out on the open road. From what I've heard, that didn't turn out so well."

"Ouch." He laughed ruefully and shook his head. "Damn, Jaleina, you're not pulling any punches tonight, are you?" He swiped his hand across his forehead. "Maybe I was an ass, okay? But Abby turned out all right. She's happy now, despite having wasted so many years on me."

"Don't say that. She didn't *waste* those years. And I don't think you did either, for what it's worth. You two just needed to figure out what you each really wanted. I talked to Abby for a little while after the wedding, and I think she has figured it out for herself. But, maybe, you need a little longer—"

He tried to cut me off, but I held up my hand.

"And this part isn't a matter of maturity or age," I added. "It's about making sure you've had enough experiences to know which of your passions have staying power."

"Are you fucking kidding me?" His eyes flashed with

surprise, fury, and more than a little hurt. "You don't think *fourteen years* of me having strong feelings for you proves that my passion has 'staying power'? Jesus, Jaleina."

I sighed. "Okay. Maybe it does. A little. But I still think—"

He succeeded in cutting me off this time. "*No*. I know what I want. All I need to know now is what it's gonna take for you to believe me."

Then he kissed me—an infinite soul kiss that held within it a promise I wasn't yet prepared to accept. He must have realized this, too, because a moment later, he slipped out of my bed, got dressed, and left my home in the middle of the cold night before I had a chance to stop him.

CHAPTER TEN

Chandler, The Morning-After Brunch, Sunday, December 17th

Not that there was anything wrong with the restaurant's buffet brunch, but I didn't give a shit about Eggs Benedict and blueberry muffins this morning.

I poured myself some coffee, poked at a sausage link rolling at the edge of my plate, and tried to ignore the fact that every flippin' member of my family was shooting anxious looks my way. I'd been away from home for so long, I'd almost forgotten what a collective bunch of worriers the Michaelsens were. That was an oversight on my part.

But, hey, it was still my brother's wedding weekend. They needed to idle the hell down and focus their energy on the twin who deserved it most.

The twin in question, however, wasn't going to let me off the hook after the promise I'd made to him last night. He left the side of his bride to come sit next to me at the end of a long, mostly empty table, bringing with him his egg-white-and-veggie omelet and a fresh fruit cup.

"Too many of those things will give you a heart attack," Chance stated, pointing at the sausage.

"No worries. I'm not gonna eat it. I'm having too much fun stabbing it." I gave the link a couple of extra jabs with my knife, just for emphasis.

He grinned. "Okay. What happened last night?"

I shook my head.

"That bad, huh?" he said.

"Yeah."

He lowered his voice. "C'mon, Chandler. Tell me about it. Please. I'm *here* for you."

So, after a deep breath or two, I gave him a summary of all that had gone down since I'd returned to Mirabelle Harbor. And, well, a few of the things that I'd thought and felt about Jaleina long before I'd ever left home.

He took this all in, unblinkingly. Then he said, "If you love someone, don't be afraid—or too proud—to follow your heart and fight for that love. But—" He paused.

"But what?"

"But 'fighting' doesn't always mean debating or trying to talk her into anything before she's ready. There are less obvious methods. And, in certain situations, rethinking the way you approach it is necessary. Trust me on this when I say that sometimes fighting for love means patience."

I knew only a little about the early days of Chance and Nia's courtship but, from what he'd let slip, he'd been ready to marry Nia long before she'd consented. "Patience, you say?"

He nodded. "And, for what it's worth, Nia and I are both pulling for you two. I'd love to see you happy in a relationship, bro."

"Thanks."

We sat in silence for a few minutes, while I drank a few more sips of my coffee and he ate his ultra-healthy breakfast. But before he got up, he said, "I've gotta leave on my honeymoon in a half hour, but we'll talk after I get back, okay?"

"Yeah, okay."

"Good. And, oh, you should ask Blake privately about his proposal plans, if you need an interesting suggestion or two. He had this one letter-writing idea with a quill pen and ink—"

"Proposal plans?" I snorted. "Hell, Chance, I'm still trying to get the woman to agree to date me or even just talk to me on a regular basis."

He raised his brows and smiled. "All I'm saying is that it might come in handy when romancing a book lover. Have a chat with Blake. Seriously." Then he man-hugged me and, soon, he and his bride bid farewell to us all and left for the airport. Destination: Athens.

But, just because they were on their way to the Parthenon, it didn't mean I could escape the brunch. Not quite yet. I was forced into talking about superficial things with a few distant relatives and, when all else failed and I needed a minute alone, I wandered up and down the buffet aisles, glancing at the offerings I didn't want to eat.

Blake cornered me by the make-your-own-waffle station.

"I gotta admit, bro, I didn't see this thing between you and Jaleina coming, and it takes a helluva lot to surprise me. And not that you need my approval or anything, but I think you two work—in a weird but cool way."

I stared at him. "Thank you. I think."

He flashed a grin at me and leaned closer. "Look, I know Jaleina fairly well, and I like her. I visit Between the Pages a *lot*. I buy at least as many books at her store as I do online because she's fun to talk to, a good person, and knowledgeable about literary things. Her extensive reading has made her wise."

"Yeah, about that—Chance was saying I should ask you about letter writing with quills or something. I don't know. He wanted me to talk to you."

Blake nodded and lowered his voice to a whisper. "That was one of my best proposal ideas for Vicky. But I'll give it to you, being that your woman couldn't be a truer book lover." He pulled out his cell phone, typed in a few words, and then held up the screen for me. It was a picture of a Jane Austen novel. *Persuasion.*

"So? What about it?"

"Don't get distracted by the Regency setting or all the dresses and ballroom dances and crap, just focus on the love story and what Captain Wentworth writes in his letter to Anne."

"Captain who?"

Blake rolled his eyes. "Just read the book, Chandler, okay? Or at least watch the full-length movie, and you'll understand what I'm talking about. Women eat this shit up but, in this case, it's actually pretty good."

I could not for the life of me imagine how a two-hundred-year-old novel could possibly be helpful, but why the hell not at least try? Jaleina owned a bookstore, after all, and I remembered her saying she loved Austen and this novel in particular. Maybe Blake was onto something.

So, I thanked him and mentally pocketed the suggestion. I also wished him well on his own relationship, which seemed to be going great guns.

He slapped my back. "If I'm lucky and can do this proposal thing right, maybe you'll have another wedding to come back to in a few months."

"That'd be awesome, man."

Less than a minute, literally, after Blake sauntered away in search of his girlfriend, Shar materialized.

"I want to talk to you," she said.

I squinted at her. "Is that absolutely necessary?"

"Oh, yes." She half dragged me behind some giant floral display, away from the food and people, crossed her wiry little arms, and inhaled. As she exhaled, a stream of words flew out. "I've really only got one thing to say to you, Chandler, but it's a big and important thing, so you'd better be listening to me."

Mutely, I nodded. Wasn't like I had a choice anyway.

"Excellent. Here it is. *Whatever* or *whoever* brings you home more often is a very good thing, in my opinion. I'd welcome Jaleina Longoria—or *any* woman—into the family who managed to achieve that magical feat. You've been missed a ton, little brother, and I just want you closer to us again. Got it?"

"Yep."

"Good." Then she kissed my cheek and squeezed my body so tight that my arms practically went numb.

I'd just begun to regain the feeling in them when I spotted Derek, halfway across the room, eyeing me uneasily.

Shit.

None of my siblings were invested in the outcome of my relationship with Jaleina quite the way Derek was, and we all knew it.

I'd been actively avoiding him all morning but, now that the brunch party was starting to break up, he pulled me aside as well. This time, I was taken clear out of the restaurant's dining area and into the lobby for privacy.

Maybe the caffeine on a mostly empty stomach had started to take effect—or maybe all the emotions and memories were starting to get the better of me—but I was a little shaky even before Derek started speaking. I'd been doing the best I could to hold it together for these past couple of hours. And while it helped to know that Chance, Blake, and Shar were on my side, my confidence was faltering, just replaying Jaleina's words from last night. I was someone she *could* love, she'd said. But she didn't think I was ready to be here with her. Didn't think my passions were strong enough.

Dammit. Her lack of trust in me shredded my heart.

My head had been spinning since I'd left her place, trying to figure out a way to convince her my love for her was true. But standing here, facing Derek and all the doubt I saw in his eyes, it hurt almost as much knowing that my eldest brother had even less faith in me than she did.

He swallowed a few times before he spoke, and I expected nothing less than another accusation that I was being a dick, or worse. Hell, considering Jaleina's opinion of me, maybe I deserved it.

"All right, Chandler. This isn't easy for me to say but, first of all, I'm sorry. I've been thinking a lot about what happened last night at the reception and I—I, um, am pretty sure I overreacted." He paused and looked at me with a contriteness I didn't recall ever seeing on his face.

It took me a few seconds before I actually registered his apology. It was so genuine, though, that I felt my wall of fury and frustration starting to collapse. Made it hard for me to reply, but I managed to shrug and say, "It's okay."

"No. No, it isn't. Granted, you totally blindsided me with this, but neither you nor Jaleina did anything wrong. I was being overbearing and treating you like you were still a teenager, and that was ridiculous and arrogant of me. I'd underestimated you...and her." He laid a hand on my shoulder. "I spent hours talking this through with Olivia late last night because, you know, this is an unusual situation and it kind of affects her."

"Understatement, right?"

He nodded. "Yeah. Any holidays or events when we're all together might be a little awkward for all of us at first, but we're a strong family. We'll get through it. My wife kept reminding me that you're an adult and you deserve the same chance at happiness in love as the rest of us. Besides, after more than a decade, the statute of limitations on dating an ex-fiancée ought to be up. Even between brothers." He chuckled lightly. "So, you go get her, Chandler. Jaleina's always welcome in our home and with our family."

And, with that, the rest of my resistance crumbled, and so did I. "Well, damn, Derek," I murmured. "I'm glad you're all so good with this, but it doesn't mean shit if she doesn't want to be with me."

Weeping like a little kid was fucking embarrassing and it'd been years since it'd happened, but I couldn't control it now. The lobby was swimming in front of my eyes and I was shaking too hard to stop.

"Hey—" He stared at me. "Hey, it's okay." And he pulled me close to him like the protective big brother he'd always been. The one who brushed me off when I fell on the playground. The one who had my back when the neighborhood bullies picked on me and my twin. The one who stood strong for us all during our parents' funerals.

I fought like hell to not completely lose it in public, and I could tell Derek was trying to shield me from anyone else's view until I could pull myself together. I'd love him forever just for that. But I had plenty of other reasons, too.

"Um, sorry, Derek," I said, when I could finally step back and speak. I swiped viciously at the wetness on my face until all evidence was gone. Hopefully. And here he'd just been telling me how I was such a grownup. Yeah, right.

"Don't be sorry," he whispered. "You *love* her. I get that now. I see it."

I shrugged. It was true. What could I say?

"And what you were telling me about her not wanting to be with you—" He paused, but then shook his head. "I don't know what she told you to make you think that, but I, uh, I knew her pretty well at one time. And, Chandler, the woman I saw kissing you last night is crazy about you."

"But she said—"

"I don't need to know what she said or what she was trying to make you believe. Women have reasons for saying things that don't always make a lot of sense to me."

He grinned. "But what I saw on her face and in her body language was *clear*. I understand that your feelings for her aren't new, but hers might not go back quite so far," he said gently. "My guess is that her mind is probably trying to catch up to where her heart is, and her history with our family complicates things. She's a private person, who's always kept her own counsel. She might just need a little more time and a little less pressure for everything to finally balance out for her."

I nodded. This made sense. All of it. I'd been fantasizing about Jaleina and picturing the two of us together for so long that I kept forgetting that, in her mind, we'd barely been together for a week. But I could be—as Chance and Derek had both suggested—patient.

"Thanks for the insight," I told him. "I'm gonna give it my best shot."

"I'm glad, little brother. Really. And for what it's worth, we're all going to do everything we can to make her feel like part of the Michaelsen clan, just as soon as we get your go ahead." He grimaced slightly and then added, "Although, knowing your sister, I wouldn't be surprised if she barged into Jaleina's bookstore and flat out said, 'Chandler loves you and I always thought you'd make a great sister-in-law, so will you hurry up and marry him?' Or something like that."

I snorted. "I *can* actually see Shar doing that. Unfortunately. If I go back to Atlanta, please stop her."

He cracked a smile. "I'll try, but I make no promises. You and I both know she's a force beyond either of our control." Then he asked, "When would you need to leave, if you do go back?"

I sighed. "I'm planning to see Jaleina this afternoon. Depending on what she says, I'll head back to Georgia either tomorrow...or never."

He took this in and, for a minute, said nothing. Finally, he gave me a nod. "Okay. But just know that, whatever happens, we'll support you."

I hugged my big brother. Hard. "I know." And, truly, I did.

It wasn't until around four p.m. that I worked up the nerve to call her and ask if I could stop by. She agreed.

As I pulled my bike into her driveway, I took note of the atmosphere surrounding me and tried not to think of it as foreboding. But it was nearing the shortest day in the year, so the sun was already low in the sky, and I could feel the darkness approaching.

"Thanks for letting me come over," I told her, once we were both inside together.

"Of course," she said graciously, but she looked exhausted today. Worn out from her own emotions, perhaps, and certainly from lack of sleep. And, well, both of these were my fault, even if she was too kind and too polite to say so. "You know how much I've enjoyed spending time with you," she added.

Enjoyed. Past tense. Shit.

"Do you want me to stay?" I asked her point blank. "It only takes a word from you, and I will."

She hesitated, and I knew before she said anything else that the answer would be no. But I waited and let her explain it in the way she wanted to, even though my heart was in fucking pieces on her hardwood floor.

"I can't. I can't say yes to that, Chandler. I can't tell you to rearrange your life for me when, as you know, I think you're still longing to be out there, somewhere." She motioned toward the road, the lake, the world beyond Mirabelle Harbor.

"I'm longing to be where *you* are, Jaleina," I insisted, but I could see that her beliefs from last night were unchanged. She felt the same damn way. That this was happening too soon. That my feelings for her weren't strong enough. That I'd get restless in no time and want to leave again. Or that I'd resent her if she tried to make me stay. All that bullshit.

I knew it'd be near impossible to change her mind *today*, so I needed another plan. And I had one...kind of. At least the beginnings of it.

"I want you to know that I'm going back to Atlanta in the morning, then. But only to prove a point to you. You don't believe my love for you is true or that it'll stay constant. It is and it will. But I'm prepared to wait it out until you can see that for yourself. And I don't care how fucking long it takes. You *will* see it."

"Chandler, you don't have to prove anything to me. You want what you want. And it's okay to be a wanderer. To love adventure. To not want to settle down or—"

I frowned. "I'm not as afraid of settling down as you seem to think. No place I've ever been has held me for long, that's true, but only because you weren't there with me." I could feel the utter truth of what I was saying down to my bone marrow. Getting her to understand this might take some time, but *nothing* would change what I knew. It was pure fact. "I told you I'd tried for years to find someone like you, but you aren't replaceable, Jaleina. I could ride my Harley through every fucking city in North America or fly to every continent, and it wouldn't matter. Because you're *here*, not out there."

I pulled her into my arms and kissed her. It was the longest goodbye-for-now kiss that I could manage. I felt her responding. Felt her melting into me. And I poured my heart into our embrace, hoping she could feel everything I was trying to tell her. I wanted to make love to her again right this second and plead with her to reconsider—but that wasn't how patience worked, was it?

So, finally, I let her go, smiled at her sweet face, and

whispered, "I love you. *Te amo, dulzura.* I've spent half my life loving you. But you don't have to take my word for it today." I walked to the door and opened it. "Just give me a little time, and I'll show you."

EPILOGUE

Chandler, Mirabelle Harbor, Three and a Half Months Later

The smell of springtime in the Midwest assaulted my senses as I wound my Harley through downtown Mirabelle Harbor and stopped at the Cherry Avenue and Main Street intersection. Freaky déjà vu being here again so soon— only with newly blossoming flowers this time, rather than the threat of snowflakes.

I'd promised my sister that I'd head directly to her condo when I got back into town and, well, I had my reasons for not stopping at the bookstore first, so I went straight to Shar's. Inside, there were packing boxes everywhere.

More freaky déjà vu, in this case because it reminded me of visiting Abby in December, when she was first moving into her new place in Chicago.

My sister, however, wasn't moving in. She was moving out. And her boyfriend, Declan Night—also the father of her soon-to-be-born baby—was joining her. They'd just bought a house across town, in the same neighborhood as Shar's best friend, Julia Crane. Or, rather, Julia Crane Tyler.

I hugged Sharlene, who was on spring break from teaching at the junior high but no less of a busybody than usual. Even at nearly six months pregnant, she still moved quickly and with purpose, and she was still nosy as hell.

"So?" she demanded. "What's going on with you and Jaleina?"

"How about you catch me up on everything I missed here first?" I said. "I've been riding my bike for hours without a break. I need something cool to drink and time to stretch my legs."

She rolled her eyes at me, tossed me a cold bottled water from her fridge, and started recounting the latest news—some I knew, some I didn't.

"Chance and Nia had a fabulous time in Greece, and their honeymoon pictures are *beautiful*," Shar gushed.

I nodded. "Yeah, they emailed me a few of them. Looked like they loved their cruise."

"They want to go back as soon as they can save up for it, and I've added it to my must-visit locations. But it'll probably be a while before I get to go anywhere." She rubbed her expanding tummy. "Anyway, Dec and I did, at least, get to travel somewhere tropical in the middle of February. Julia and Dane eloped on the island of Martinique, and I was her matron of honor."

"No kidding. You think I didn't hear about that, sis? It was covered by *Entertainment Tonight, Access Hollywood, TMZ,* and every late-night talk show host." Dane Tyler was one popular dude. And it didn't hurt that he'd just signed on to play the lead in some upcoming psychological thriller franchise—a movie trilogy based on a blockbuster book series. "You all looked great in those tabloid photos."

She huffed out some air. "I still can't believe that slimy hotel concierge ratted us out to the paparazzi. What an ass!

But at least it wasn't until the last day. Julia and Dane got their private romantic wedding on the beach, and we only needed to put up with those invasive pseudo journalists on the flight home. I don't know how Julia deals with that crap." Shar sighed. "She's resigning from the school district in June, and she and Analise are officially relocating to L.A. to be with Dane full time then. But they're still keeping the house here, and Dec and I will live just a block away. So, when they're all in town, it'll be easy for us to get together."

"That'll be cool."

"Yeah. I'll miss seeing her every day, though. Oh! But my BFF isn't the only one to get married. Did you hear that Olivia and Derek will be flying to Sarasota in May for Marianna and Gil's wedding?"

I shook my head. Who the fuck could keep up with all of these people? Apparently, Shar and Olivia could...but c'mon.

My sister was rattling off wedding-related details as if they were her own. Gil and Marianna got engaged on New Year's Eve. Olivia, who'd already been planning to visit Florida to spend time with her friend, now had a good reason to book the trip. She was going to be an attendant in the wedding. Marianna's sister, Ellen, was the matron of honor. Marianna's daughter, Kathryn, was also involved somehow, and on and on. I could feel myself starting to tune out the chatter, until Shar said, "And Abby's gonna be a bridesmaid, too."

"Really?"

"Oh, yeah. She and Marianna are good friends, remember?"

I shrugged. What I mostly remembered about seeing Abby a few months ago was how much she was in love with Rick Zimmerman. Everything else sort of faded into the background.

"Rick and Derek already have plans to hang out

together and go golfing down there while the women are doing the pre-wedding things."

"Glad our big brother will have a, um, *buddy* in Florida." I managed to say.

She snorted. "Keep working on that line, Chandler. Maybe, with practice, you can get it to sound almost sincere."

We laughed.

"Maybe," I said. "So, who's watching the kids while Derek and Olivia are away?"

"Blake and Vicky. Can you believe it? They're going to stay with James, Riley, and Peter for four days at the big house. And Winston's going to go wild. He *loves* it there." Blake's mutt, Winston, was pretty crazy about squirrels, and Michaelsen Manor had a ton of them. "Plus," Shar added, "our brother owes that dog a vacation. The pup's been busy!"

This was one bit of news I actually knew all the details about and was even able to keep the story straight. Blake had been trying all winter to come up with a creative way to propose to Vicky, but his dog took matters into his own hands. Or mouth, as it were.

At the beginning of March, Blake bought a diamond engagement ring for Vicky and stashed it in the back of his sock drawer. But he made the mistake of not closing it all the way. Winston, ever fond of retrieving things, poked his nose in the drawer and trotted out to the living room with the blue ring box between his teeth, like a favorite toy.

"What are you chewing on, Winston?" Vicky had asked, confused at first.

Blake gasped and then laughed when his dog dropped the ring box at Vicky's feet.

"This wasn't exactly how I'd planned to ask you," he told her. "But, maybe, Winston had the best idea of all." And then Blake got down on one knee and formally proposed—in both English and in French.

Vicky said yes and *oui*, respectively. And after the two of them "celebrated privately," which I was pretty sure was code for "had wild sex on the living room floor," the couple called all of us siblings, one at a time, to share the happy news.

They were planning an August wedding and, yeah, I was gonna need to wear a tux again and stand up as a groomsman in that one. Though not as the best man. That honor was going to Derek, who'd chosen Blake as *his* best man when Derek and Olivia got married. If I ever got married, I'd return the favor and ask Chance to be mine, but I knew all of my brothers would be there at the altar for me as well.

Maybe someday I'd get to experience that. Knock on wood.

"As for me and Declan," Shar said, waddling around the room, picking up some knickknack she wanted to pack, and wrapping it up in newspaper, "we're doing fine. But obviously, I'm as big as a house already. And I've got some secret news I wasn't going to tell the rest of the family until you got here."

"Oooh! I never get to hear the secrets first," I said. "Hit me with it."

She grinned. "We had another ultrasound a few days ago, and the results are in." She did a mock drum roll on one of the cardboard boxes. "It's a boy!"

"Aw." I walked over to her and kissed her cheek. "Congrats, sis. He's gonna be a lucky little baby to have you as his mom. Can't wait to meet my newest nephew. Mid-July, right?"

"Yep. The eleventh, if he's on schedule. And since I'm a big believer in promptness, I'm expecting my son to be on time."

"Ha. Well, I'm sure he will be, if he knows what's good for him."

Shar laughed. "Okay, now you've had more than

enough time to recover from your long ride, and I've exhausted all the family and friend gossip. So, spill, little brother. What's happening with you and Jaleina?"

There was no way to quickly tell this story, but my sister loved nothing more than relationship details about people she loved. (And, hell, even those she didn't.) Anyway, she'd been nothing but supportive, cheering me on from the sidelines for months. She'd earned getting to hear the full scoop, even if I couldn't give her the final verdict yet.

"All right," I said. "A lot's happened since Chance and Nia's wedding. How much do you know already about the letters?"

"Not nearly enough," Shar declared. "Start at the beginning."

So, I took a deep breath and began the tale...

I had to hand it to Blake, the guy knew literature.

When I returned to Atlanta, I spent the first few nights, admittedly, getting drunk in my apartment and feeling very sorry for myself because, shit, it hurt.

But I was also trying to pull together a plan, and my siblings were fucking relentless about calling and texting and emailing and reminding me constantly that I needed to get over my initial disappointment and move forward.

"Remember what I told you," Blake advised, quoting some lame-ass line from *Persuasion* that he kept insisting would help. It was a line that meant nothing to me initially, since I wasn't familiar with the story, but I was desperate to try anything that might get Jaleina to understand the depth of my love for her.

So, I gave Blake's suggestion a shot and watched the film.

Then I watched it again.

Then I downloaded the study guide and pored over the plot summary, character analysis, themes, motifs, and symbols. It was like lit class all over again—only this time I was motivated to pay attention.

Finally, I gave in and just bought a copy of the Austen novel, so I'd have Captain Wentworth's letter to Anne Elliot, the woman he'd been in love with for ages, right in front of me as I started to write one of my own.

There was something about the opening lines of his letter that spoke to me:

> *"I can listen no longer in silence. I*
> *must speak to you by such means as*
> *are within my reach. You pierce my*
> *soul. I am half agony, half hope."*

That "half agony, half hope" part just slayed me, as my brother seemed to know it would. Damn Blake for being so insightful, but if this worked, I'd owe him. Big time.

In spite of myself, and despite the difference in situations between the characters' love lives and my relationship with Jaleina, I got what the good Captain was saying. I felt what he was feeling. And when he went on to write, *"I have loved none but you,"* I was exactly where he'd been, wanting to convince a woman of his devotion to her when he knew for sure she doubted his commitment.

I'd been looking for a way to reach Jaleina's heart. And, since she'd said *Persuasion* was her favorite of the Austen stories, I figured she'd be quick to guess where I got my inspiration when she read my letter.

Dear Jaleina, I began, setting actual pen to paper for the first time in, like, a decade. Who used envelopes and stamps anymore when we had email, social media sites, and texting?

Well, me, as it turned out.

"You pierce my soul," I quoted just underneath her name. But then I went on to write some original thoughts.

I hadn't ridden my bike five miles out of Mirabelle Harbor before I wanted to turn around and come back to you. But I'm trying to honor your wishes. To not rush the relationship that I hope is growing between us. To give you a chance to get to know me in a way that might be more comfortable and natural for you—by reading my words on a page.

Think of this letter as Chapter One in The Book of Chandler Michaelsen. See if you like the main character. If he's somebody you'd enjoy getting to know better outside of the narrative.

If not, you've lost nothing but a little time reading a bad book.

But if so, maybe this unlikely protagonist—this guy who seems so unsuitable at the beginning of the story—can, eventually, turn into a hero you'll care about and trust.

I'll let the booklover in you be the judge.

And then I went on to describe what had been happening in life back in Georgia. My job. The techie friends I'd made at work. The makeshift Christmas decorations I'd put up in my crummy little apartment. Random thoughts I'd had about what was going on in the world. Feelings and observations. And, of course, anything that made me think of her.

The letter was seven pages long before I finally stopped, figuring this would probably bore the hell out of her before she got to my signature at the end.

I'd signed off, *"Yours, C.M."* And I mailed it to her the following day.

Then, the next night, I wrote to her again.

And the next night.

And the night after that.

It got to where my sort of shitty penmanship was actually starting to improve. I'd alternate sending the letters to her home or to the bookstore, figuring she might like receiving them at both locations. I'd try to surprise her by stuffing an interesting item or two into the envelopes sometimes, like a few pressed flower petals or a funny cartoon I'd ripped from a magazine left in a café booth. I even bought a wax seal with the letter "C" on it that I found at a novelty shop in downtown Atlanta. It came with a box of wax sticks, so I used them to the seal the back of the envelopes. Looked antiquated as hell, but so fucking cool. I knew she'd get a kick out of that.

And she did.

Jaleina didn't write me nearly as often as I wrote her— at least not at first—but she'd emailed me in delight after she'd received my first few letters. And then, after a couple of weeks, she wrote a handwritten note to me on this really pretty paper, scented with her perfume. I kept it on the nightstand next to my pillow for practically a month, so I could inhale her scent whenever I wanted. Which was about every twenty seconds.

A few weeks later, after I'd sent her a dozen more letters, she mailed me a Valentine's Day card, and she'd kissed the back of the envelope with her lipstick.

Sealed with a kiss.

Oh, yeah, baby. I could work with that—until I could collect a kiss for real.

And though it was killing me to be patient some days, I found there were rewards to biding my time. I noticed she was letting down her guard more when we spoke on the phone. We still texted and emailed fairly often, but our phone conversations were getting longer, deeper, and more frequent as the weeks went on.

Even so, I still kept penning handwritten letters to her, mailing her one almost every day. I even tried to write one with a quill pen dipped in ink, but that was some messy shit. Once was enough with that.

But my ballpoint pens got a real workout.

This month, right after Blake and Vicky announced their engagement, I wrote to Jaleina, letting her know the big news and that I'd for sure be back in Mirabelle Harbor in August for their wedding.

She wrote back almost immediately this time, and she said, "It'll be *that long* before I see you again?"

I grinned, whispered a prayer of thanks to the literary gods, and wrote back, "I might be able to make it sooner..." Then I set about dismantling the life I no longer wanted in hopes of getting the one I desired most.

I gave my boss two weeks' notice, started job hunting online for openings in the Chicago suburbs, and began shedding my possessions in Atlanta like unwanted skin. The few items I chose to keep, I shipped to my siblings' homes in Mirabelle Harbor, with their blessing. And, when I was ready to leave, I turned in the keys to my apartment.

The last thing I did before jumping on my Harley and heading for home was to send Jaleina one more handwritten letter—this one by FedEx Priority Overnight to ensure its timely delivery. In it, I told her of my plans and paraphrased the final lines of Captain Wentworth's letter, which I'd long since memorized. I wrote, *"I must go, uncertain of my fate; but I shall come to see you as soon as possible. A word, a look, will be enough to decide whether I enter your bookstore tomorrow evening, or never."*

"And now I'm here," I explained to Shar. "I'm going over to Between the Pages to see Jaleina at six o'clock. Closing time. And I'm hoping for the best."

My hard-ass sister was staring at me, her eyes glistening. Tears were streaming down her face and she sniffled before she spoke. "Okay, okay, I'm hormonal and everything but, damn, Chandler. That was good."

"God, I just hope it was good enough." I checked the time: 5:24 p.m. "You'll wish me luck tonight?"

She reached for a tissue and shook her head. "You don't need luck."

"Why the hell not?"

"Because you have something better. Quiet conviction. It's kind of irresistible to a woman, especially when she loves a man." Shar wiped her eyes, kissed me on both cheeks, and pointed me toward the door. "Go early. I know she's waiting for you."

"I hope you're right, sis."

Shar exhaled in a show of exasperation and looked heavenward. "When will my brothers learn? Chandler, I'm *always* right."

I parked my bike in an open spot just across the street from Jaleina's bookstore. Then I stood on the sidewalk, watching her from the opposite side of the road and through the window of her shop as she helped her customers.

Even after all of these weeks—after the entire season that'd gone by since I'd last seen her—my memory of her was razor sharp. Her posture. Her movements. And I knew, once I got closer, the sound of her voice. Her pattern of breathing. And, hopefully, her smile, welcoming me in.

My mind, my heart, and my soul told me this was a worthy risk. That Jaleina's feelings for me had strengthened since December. That she now saw and felt my love and loyalty toward her.

My fears were another story, though. They still whistled through my brain. What if, after everything, she still said no to us? What if she liked the man from the letters well enough, but she shied away from me once we were together in person? What if she got caught up again in those old issues about my age or my family or my wanderlust past?

I sighed. Dammit. I'd come a thousand miles—and

through half a lifetime—just to be with her. I wasn't gonna turn back now.

A few cars zipped by before I could cross the street, but I'd just stepped onto the curb when Jaleina glanced out of her window and saw me approaching. I stopped to a dead halt on the pavement, my eyes fixed on her. The line *"A word, a look will be enough to decide whether I enter..."* ran through my head as I gazed at her, waiting, waiting, waiting for her response.

It seemed like an eternity before I got one, but when I did—man, it was worth every fucking moment of misery.

Her face broke into a smile so beautiful, it was like sunshine bursting onto a field of spring flowers. She said something to the customer at the counter, but left her place behind the register at once, rushed outside, and met me in the middle of the sidewalk.

"Chandler!" she cried, flying into my arms. "You're back."

There were curious customers inside the bookstore staring at us. There were curious townspeople lingering nearby staring at us. There were curious drivers slowing down and staring at us. I sensed a theme.

But Jaleina didn't seem to be paying attention to any of the onlookers. Her arms encircled my waist and she immediately brought her lips up to mine, claiming me as her own—right there in front of everybody in Mirabelle Harbor who might be watching us—with a passionate, joyful kiss that held nothing back.

Ah. Patience.

That was exactly what I'd been waiting for. If Jaleina believed in us, anything in the whole wide world was possible.

"Sí, mi amor," I told her, when I could finally catch my breath. "I'm home."

~End~

Up Next: If you love handsome, motorcycle-riding heroes and would enjoy reading a contemporary romance with a dash of suspense & international intrigue, keep an eye out for Marilyn's next novel—*The Secret Life of Maggie Blake*—coming soon!

STORY EXCERPTS

TAKE A CHANCE ON ME (MIRABELLE HARBOR, BOOK 1) – OUT NOW!

Welcome to Mirabelle Harbor! In this scenic suburb on Chicago's North Shore, overlooking the sparkling waters of Lake Michigan, the Michaelsen family has made their home for generations. Although their parents and grandparents are now gone, siblings Derek, Blake, Sharlene, and the twins—Chandler and Chance—all have fond memories of growing up in town, and most still live there.

Chance Michaelsen, the youngest member of the family (by two minutes) and the quietest (by far), is a dedicated twenty-eight-year-old personal trainer at the local gym. While he might not say much, Chance has made it clear that he's not a fan of toxic people, unhealthy habits, or sharing too many of his emotions. With anybody.

Enter Antonia "Nia" Pappayiannis—the prettiest member of the loudest and most overly demonstrative family in town. They're also the owners of The Gala, a Greek restaurant and bakery known for its decadent pastries and located just a few steps from Chance's gym. He considers their entire family business to be the enemy of good health, but he can't quite shake his attraction to Nia, who doesn't seem nearly as impressed with him or his sculpted physique as most of the women around Mirabelle Harbor.

Unfortunately, between her doctor's orders and the

interfering ways of Chance's crazy-making ex-girlfriend, who just happens to be one of Nia's long-time friends, Chance gets assigned to be Nia's fitness coach for the month. Pure torture. And if his ex weren't already causing enough problems, he also has to deal with Nia's current boyfriend—some hotshot Chicago CEO who talks big but, in Chance's opinion, is as fake as a Styrofoam barbell.

The road to romance is going to be a rocky one, and though Nia has her doubts about getting involved, Chance has a well-developed competitive streak and might just be willing to give it a shot…if he can convince her to do the same.

In matters of the heart, would you risk it all? TAKE A CHANCE ON ME, a Mirabelle Harbor story.

From the Novel:

I couldn't dismiss Chance's gaze. He was watching my every movement, noticing each inch of exposed skin, which wasn't much on my side, really. The white towels gave comprehensive coverage. They were jumbo sized, so only my shoulders, arms, lower thighs, calves, and feet were visible.

But Chance took in every bit, and I squirmed under that level of scrutiny.

We sat in silence for a long time.

Finally, he cleared his throat. "So, Nia, is Grant Jordan still your boyfriend?"

I shook my head. I hadn't said any official breakup words to Grant, which would really be more like, "Hey, I don't think we should hang out for a few hours during the weekend anymore." Our relationship had hardly been the stuff of soulmates. But, after tonight, I knew I didn't want to go back to Grant's large but lonely mansion.

"My parents liked him a lot, though," I explained to Chance. "They'll be disappointed."

He narrowed his eyes. "Are *you* disappointed?"

"No."

He abruptly stood up and walked over to me. With no shirt fabric as a shield, there was nothing that could camouflage his incredibly buff upper body. Bet he did more than torso twists to get that six pack, huh? Even more than wanting to touch him, though, I wanted to know what he was thinking. My attention kept getting drawn back to his face. To his inquisitive hazel eyes.

He stood in front of me and pulled me to standing. "Turn around," he whispered.

"Why?" I murmured, glancing at the door. There was an oval sliver of a window where people walking by could peek in on us, if they were so inclined.

"I'm going to rub your shoulders," he said simply. "Don't worry. I'll stop anytime you want, but now's the best time to loosen those tight muscles. You can lean against the wall for balance."

There was almost nothing in the world I wanted more than to feel Chance's hands on my skin. Between his nearness to me, my anticipation of his touch, and the blazing temperature of the sauna, I could only take quick, shallow breaths but, nevertheless, I turned around.

From the very second his fingertips connected with the top of my shoulders, it was all I could do not to gasp or moan. He had magic hands, that man. A grip that was strong, firm, but not pinching. My neck and shoulders had never felt better.

I could only imagine what he could do to my back if I were to throw the towel on the floor and let him rub whatever he wanted, or wherever he wanted. Aunt Helen would be evoking all kinds of prayers to the blessed Virgin if she knew what I was thinking.

"You really missed your calling," I managed to say.

Chance made that low chuckling sound that sent a bolt of desire from my ears to my toenails. "I have some background in deep tissue and Swedish massage," he told me. "Board certified, actually. But I'm very selective in choosing my clientele for that service."

The air in the sauna must have hit about three thousand degrees when he spoke. I was burning up. But he continued to rub only above the towel line. Nothing remotely inappropriate. And his self-control made me want to scream, "Go lower! Push the towel down, Chance. Tell me you want me half as much as I want you."

Instead, I just sighed, and his fingers stilled. *No!*

He very gently turned me around to face him, lowered his head until his lips were millimeters from mine, and whispered, "Number 127 Arpeggio Avenue. Apartment 3."

"What?" I asked. There was steam all around us and, more than that, my brain was in a fog.

"That's my address. Just two blocks south of here." He paused. "It's your choice, Nia. But remember your question when we were texting tonight? When you asked if I was propositioning you?"

I nodded. Oh, yes. I remembered. *If I were propositioning you, I'd say to meet me at my apartment...*

"So," he said slowly, "if you would like, meet me at my apartment." Then Chance smiled, stepped away from me, and walked out of the sauna.

❀❁❀

THE ONE THAT I WANT (BOOK 2) – OUT NOW!

The summer after her beloved husband died in a car accident, Julia Meriwether Crane is still picking up the pieces of her life in Mirabelle Harbor and trying to help her ten-year-old daughter adjust to this difficult new reality.

After her best friend Sharlene—one of the well-connected Michaelsen siblings—talks her into finally going out on the town again, Julia finds herself stunned to be the object of interest of several different men: The boy who'd broken her heart back in high school. The college ex she'd left behind. And most surprising of all, the movie actor she'd always fantasized about but had never met in person...until now. Can one woman have more than one "great love" in the same lifetime? And, if so, how can she be sure which man that'll be?

Sometimes the person you think will be best for you isn't the one you really want. THE ONE THAT I WANT, a Mirabelle Harbor story.

<u>From the Novel:</u>

With the exception of my best friend Sharlene, the others in the wine bar had gone back to their conversations so, thankfully, I didn't have too many people witnessing my fumbles with setting up a (sort-of) date for the first time in twelve years. It was awkward, but I agreed to coffee with my old high-school boyfriend and gave Kristopher my phone number, which he dutifully punched into his cell so we could arrange a time and day to meet later.

Shar nudged me when he wasn't looking and whispered, "See? Not so hard, is it?"

I made a face at her and shrugged.

Finally, the party at The Lounge was beginning to break up. I was mentally congratulating myself on making it through the evening when the very sweet, well-dressed woman—Elsie was her name—wolf whistled. "Wait, people!"

Everyone halted.

"I've been wanting to tell you this good news all night." She paused for effect. "You know my friend Rosemary, the one who works at the Knightsbridge Theater in the city, right?"

Most of the group nodded, seeming to have met Elsie's friend or, at least, heard about her.

"There's a dress rehearsal for their upcoming summer production, 'The Bachelor Pad,' this Thursday at six-thirty in the evening, in advance of next Friday's Opening Night," Elsie said. "And Rosemary reserved a block of seats for us."

Despite the noise in the wine bar, an audible spike in sound came on the heels of those words, and a couple of the women actually squealed.

I squinted at them. I mean, tickets to a play were always nice, but wasn't this taking theatrical enthusiasm a bit far?

"But that's not all," Elsie continued enthusiastically. "Rosemary also got us passes to meet the cast, just as she did for that steampunk musical last year—"

"Steampunk musical?" I hissed in Shar's ear.

She nodded. "It was bizarre. Tell you more about it later."

I grinned and brought my glass of wine to my lips, draining it of its final swallow.

"—including a special Q&A session with the director, Zachary Leeward," Elsie added, "and with the star of the show, Dane Tyler."

I choked on the last drops of merlot, coughing so hard that Bill reached across the table to hand me a fresh glass of ice water, Shar patted me on the back, and everyone else stared at me worriedly. Except for Kristopher. He shot me a knowing look.

Yeah, of course he'd remember *that*.

"Are you okay?" Elsie asked me.

I gulped down half the water. *Oh, God. Of all the actors on the planet—Dane Tyler. Here? REALLY?*

My teen world had just materialized out of thin air, like that freaky phantom ship that came from absolutely nowhere in *Pirates of the Caribbean*. My gut twisted weirdly, and I could barely breathe. "P-Please go on," I managed to whisper.

She smiled. "So, if any of you want to go to the performance, and I know you do, let me know now, and I'll email the list of names to Rosemary in the morning."

Elsie was right. With the exception of one accountant guy, who had an out-of-town business trip next week, and a very disappointed single mom, whose kid was playing in a baseball tournament Thursday night, everyone else signed up to go.

Including *me,* at Shar's insistence. And including Kristopher.

My old high-school boyfriend leaned over the table and said with a laugh, "Well, isn't that something? Maybe, if you ask him real nice, he'll recite your favorite lines from your favorite movie to you."

"Ha," I said weakly.

"Which lines? Which movie?" Shar asked.

Before I could reply, Elise jumped in and pointed to Shar and then me. "You two want to ride down with me?"

Shar answered for both of us. "Oh, yeah!"

Although I managed to stop tripping over my own tongue and was able to thank the kind woman, I didn't succeed in making more than a few last bits of small talk. All I could do was blush furiously and think to myself, in the fevered squeaking of an adolescent schoolgirl, *OMG, I'm finally going to see Dane Tyler in person! Maybe even talk to him!*

In just one evening, three distinct memories of men from my past played out like a warped summertime version of *A Christmas Carol* in my mind. Haunting memories of relationships that I'd had or had lost or had wanted— sometimes simultaneously and always more powerfully than I'd expected—were reeling through my brain on a continuous loop, braiding my emotions with the mental film footage.

Before my best friend could ask me any more questions I didn't want to answer, I hugged her goodnight and raced into the evening, forgetting until my feet hit the pavement and I collapsed into the driver's seat of my car that I wasn't, in fact, lost in time.

That I wasn't living out some high-school fantasy.

That I wasn't a vulnerable young woman, helpless in the face of fate.

I started the engine, replayed those last three thoughts again, and shook my head.

Like hell I wasn't.

✿❀✿

YOU GIVE LOVE A BAD NAME (BOOK 3) – OUT NOW!

"Nothing but love, 24/7" is the slogan of Mirabelle Harbor's only radio station, 102.5 "LOVE" FM. On the verge of turning thirty-five, local DJ Blake Michaelsen is well-known for several reasons: his very sexy on-air voice, his omnipresent family, his eligible bachelor status, and his reputation as one of the most impulsive men in Chicago's northern suburbs.

High-school French teacher and lifelong romantic Vicky Bernier is not at all wild about people who exhibit reckless conduct. (Blake.) Or men who have gigantic egos. (Blake.) Or grownups who still act like teenagers. (Blake, again.) She deals with enough adolescent behavior during the school day. Unfortunately, she's the staff advisor to the Homecoming Committee, and they've chosen him as their DJ for the big fall dance.

What happens when a man whose job it is to play love songs for a living is forced to admit his deepest secret—that he doesn't believe in true love—only to discover that the one woman who might capture his heart is the same woman who distrusts him the most?

No matter what you call it, with love there's an exception to every rule. YOU GIVE LOVE A BAD NAME, a Mirabelle Harbor story.

<u>From the Novel:</u>

We settled our bill and stepped outside of The Lounge just as a ruckus was getting started next door at Max's Pub.

"You asshole!" this dopey, burly, drunk guy screamed, ineffectively swinging at another drunk guy.

"You witless dickhead!" slurred the second guy. But that didn't mask his identity. As soon as he spoke, I knew who it was. Everyone did.

"Vicky, isn't that Blake Michaelsen?" Janet whispered.

"Yep," I whispered back. I'd only seen him in person once before—at a big event at the radio station this summer—and it was, literally, across a crowded room. But Blake's voice on 102.5 LOVE FM was one of the sexiest I'd ever heard. I listened to him on the radio all the time. And he was my friend Sharlene's older brother, so I knew a few additional facts about him than I might have otherwise.

Like that he was impulsive.

And loud.

And kind of a manwhore.

Then again, he had a rep in town, so most women knew these things, too. It was just that Shar had actually confirmed them for me.

Blake landed a decent punch and sent the other guy stumbling. But Dopey Dude got back up.

Oh, boy.

Shar was going to be *so* pissed when she heard about this. And she would. Probably within three minutes or less. Gossip traveled at the speed of sound in Mirabelle Harbor.

There was more yelling between the men, along with a

bunch of shouts from the sports-bar crowd surrounding them. It reminded me of the stupid hall fights I'd had the misfortune to have to try to break up at the high school. Dumb boy behavior at its finest. Guys who fought each other because they couldn't rationally reason their way through a discussion. So foolish and immature. And, worse, so painful to the people who actually cared about these cretins.

Dopey Dude landed a crushing blow to Blake's abdomen. He doubled over and fell to the pavement. Then the other guy started to seriously pummel Blake while the crowd alternately jeered, taunted, and screamed their encouragement.

I winced. Blake's dark hair was matted against his forehead with sweat and, also, with some fresh blood. He had a gash across his cheekbones, dirt on his face and neck, and more blood dripping from the corner of his mouth.

And he was devastatingly handsome, even then.

Although, with the angry eyes and the snarl on his lips, he looked like the poster child for one the French revolutionary insurgents in *Les Misérables*. If he decided to build a barricade, storm the Bastille, or lead the crowd in the first verse of "Do You Hear the People Sing?" I wouldn't dare to stand in his way.

The fact that I couldn't guess whether he'd be more like a hero or a terrorist in any uprising made me immediately uncomfortable, though. I hadn't known he'd be like this. His sister could get a little fiery sometimes, but Shar had a marshmallow heart. Blake, by contrast, looked both self-destructive and vicious. Like he could quite effectively kill someone.

Finally, an officer came on the scene and broke up the fight. He ordered us all to leave, but I was rooted to the spot. I couldn't take my eyes off Blake's cut-up face. So many bruises, and he was even spitting blood.

Lisa nudged me. "Let's go, Vicky."

Before I could make my feet move, Blake looked up at me and our gazes collided. I kept imagining the shock Shar would feel if she saw her brother in this horribly battered, sweaty, and drunken state. She was very protective of her family. But nothing was going to protect Blake from the wrath of one massive hangover and the need for some serious first aid.

His eyes turned even darker and they narrowed dangerously as he continued to stare at me.

Christine tugged me away.

"They were like a couple of wasted jocks after a football game," she observed on the drive home.

"I know. I was thinking the same thing. Like those boys that get into fights in the school cafeteria. With them, it's all crazy levels of testosterone and impaired judgment, leading to damage of property and reckless endangerment of themselves and others. Imagine someone acting that way after being out of high school for fifteen years? It's like they never got all the way through adolescence."

Christine nodded. "Although I can't say being a mature grownup all the time is a barrel of laughs."

I smiled. "True. But anything is better than being forever seventeen."

I remembered myself at seventeen and suppressed a shudder. That was one time of my life I'd *never* want to relive, and I had daily witness as to why in my classroom.

Though, if forced to be completely honest with myself, one of the main reasons I'd been drawn to teaching was to see if I could make high school a better experience for kids like me. For those quirky, quiet, culture-loving, rule-following bookworms who really wanted to learn. Not that I was so different now, really. It was just that, back then, I'd felt so alone. I hadn't realized there might be others like me out there.

At least I had good female friends. But it was too bad my male counterpart didn't seem to exist. At least not in large enough quantities to keep searching for him. There were probably only fifty straight, single, American men who'd fit my criteria for dating. And chances were high that they were spread randomly across the United States. I'd be lucky to find even one or two anywhere in Illinois. My ideal, most compatible love match was probably living in a remote town in northern New Mexico or something.

I said goodnight to Christine, went inside my apartment, and leaned against the door with a deep sigh. I should go to sleep, but I just couldn't. All I'd be able to see behind my closed eyes would be Blake Michaelsen's bloodied, infuriated face.

✿❀✿

STRANGER ON THE SHORE (BOOK 4) – OUT NOW!

On the verge of turning forty and having just lost her job, Marianna Gregory flees Mirabelle Harbor for the summer with little more than a suitcase, her beat-up car, and the blessings of her good friend Olivia Michaelsen. Her ex-husband is living a new life in California. Her college-aged daughter is spending her vacation with her boyfriend in Michigan. And the house Marianna once called her own finally sold, so she has nowhere to live in Illinois now anyway.

However, her wealthy sister Ellen owns an empty bungalow on the beach in Sarasota, Florida, so Marianna turns to the sea for a chance to go shelling, regroup, and figure out what to do with this new chapter in her life. She doesn't bargain on having to face down several family crises while she's away, nor does she count on meeting a handsome beachcomber who bears a striking resemblance to Elvis. Just as surprising is the craft project she gets roped into volunteering for and the new group of friends who might just change the way she views the world and her future.

The most unexpected gifts can be found where the land meets the sea. STRANGER ON THE SHORE, a Mirabelle Harbor story.

From the Novel:

A mix of cerulean with teal for the furthest watery depths.

A dabbling of silvery sunlight, whiting out patches of sea and sand like a spotlight.

Gil Canton studied the shoreline with the practiced eye of an artist. Which was what he was, he reminded himself. Never mind the low, deep voice from decades' past that told him otherwise. That told him he should be using his powers of observation on "a worthier, more lucrative cause."

Bullshit.

A faint blend of burnt umber and goldenrod in a subtle line underscoring the crisp cottony tufts of rolling waves.

A flash of gray and green as the sunfish tangled with the seaweed just below the surface.

Anyone with a heart knew the creatures of the ocean were as *worthy* as anything out in the world. That the Gulf was not only a visual feast for a painter, but it was a composer's symphony, a poet's playground.

Anyone with a heart...ahh. But that was the problem, wasn't it?

Gil grimaced. Calf-deep in the warm water and strolling languidly along the Siesta Key shoreline, he picked up his stride to outrace that old, familiar voice. It didn't work. It never the hell worked. But he turned his attention to the passersby in hopes of a distraction.

Shades of skin color in a palette of creams, tans,

bronzes, chocolates and, sometimes, sunburned reds.

The fascinating discordance of fabric hues and textures and patterns, draping the wearer in a manner that left no question as to whether the individual wanted to be noticed...or wanted to blend into the seascape.

He knew he looked at the beach differently than he had when he'd first moved here twenty-six years ago. And, unlike the appreciative but unobservant gazes of the bikini-clad tourists, he needed to distinguish between the various ranges of blues and greens, the buffet of multicolored accessory images and the differing degrees of whiteness from the sand to the bungalows—for the sake of his passion. His paintings.

Why was it so easy, so natural for him to be both loving and discerning in one area of his life but not in another?

With a canvas, he could step back and assess it. If he saw he'd done something wrong or, more frequently, had neglected to do something completely right, he would be able to see the problem area with the help of a few feet of distance and, then, correct it.

With relationships—parental, romantic, professional or otherwise—it was never that simple. Stepping back was harder for the other person to accept. And it tended to create more damage, even when the objective was to do just the opposite. To achieve a fresh perspective. Clarity.

Art and life? Not so much the same.

He kicked lightly at a broken conch with the tip of his water shoe. Even with a chunk of its shell missing, it was still beautiful. There was almost heartbreaking beauty on this shore.

Seagulls squawking above and around him in a flying dance of circles and landings.

Children splashing and frolicking, often with a battalion of siblings and water toys.

An old woman dressed all in white, someone he'd seen many times, stood several yards from him, chatting with an attractive younger lady—an obvious newcomer. He couldn't help but check out the new woman. She was a tad overdressed in her pinkish t-shirt and navy shorts. Untanned and pensive. Awed by the Gulf setting in that mystified tourist sort of way. The coast was full of visitors like that. Nothing wrong with them, he supposed. His business depended on them, after all. But it was hard to get to know many people well in such a transient environment.

With a shrug, he returned his focus to the water—the rhythmic breaking of the waves trying their darnedest to drown out his father's voice once and for all until, a few minutes later, a sound he couldn't ignore pierced his concentration.

ONE NIGHT LOVE AFFAIR (BOOK 5) – OUT NOW!

After her first marriage ended in a divorce that left her heart in tiny shreds, Sharlene Michaelsen Boyd vowed to keep her distance from men, at least emotionally. An occasional one-night stand wasn't out of the question, though, and with her closest friends hooking up with new loves, she finds herself in the mood for a little male company... Being the only sister with four brothers, not to mention the glue holding the Michaelsen family together after the death of their parents, Shar is used to being strong and in control. She's a junior-high English teacher who's persuasive, personable, and who knows just about everyone in the center of Mirabelle Harbor society, including her brother Blake's super-sexy buddy, Declan Night.

As a former pro hockey player turned sportswriter and businessman, Dec has had his share of relationships, mostly meaningless, short-term flings. He always thought

Blake's little sister was a hottie, but he knew she was off limits—until one Friday night when the stars aligned and the opportunity to hook up presented itself. Shar's intentions couldn't have been clearer: This was for One Night Only. But, for the first time in his life, Dec wonders if, maybe, there isn't something to be said for sticking with just one woman. Especially if that woman knows how to fulfill his every sensual fantasy.

Could one sizzling night turn into a love that has a shot at lasting forever? ONE NIGHT LOVE AFFAIR, a Mirabelle Harbor story.

From the Novel:

Shar ordered a strawberry margarita from Gina, one of the regular bartenders, and glanced around the crowded room. Damn. There was no one who caught her eye. No one who was hot enough to raise the tiny hairs on her forearms. No one who could make her believe in the fantasy of a good man—not even until morning.

But, hey, the music was decent (Fall Out Boy was blaring through the speakers overhead, and she liked them), the margarita was strong, and at the other end of the bar, almost hidden in shadow, sat one of her brother Blake's longtime pals, Declan Night.

Shar took back her thoughts about no one in the bar being hot.

Dec qualified. Big time.

From a purely objective standpoint, the man was a pleasure to look at. She'd always thought so. From the top of his dark head to the tip of his sneaker toe, he was all muscle, intensity, and faded denim. But he might as well have been a monk who'd made a vow of celibacy for all Shar cared.

First and foremost, he was a friend of her brother's, and that put him squarely into the No Touch Zone.

And, secondly, the former hockey player turned sportswriter and business owner was a bigger manwhore than even Blake used to be. And he was a *jock*, heaven forbid. Not that she didn't like sports or that she thought he was totally witless or anything, but she was a self-respecting English teacher and didn't want to talk about slapshots or new draft picks all evening.

Then again, it was summer vacation. She didn't want to discuss *Silas Marner* or *Lord of the Flies* either. Maybe a little hockey talk would distract her.

She picked up her drink and strolled over to where he was sitting, sliding into the stool next to his. Declan Night, a man who usually gave off the air of being King of the World, was staring deeply into his golden whiskey, like he was a fortuneteller and the glass was his crystal ball.

"Hey, Dec. How are you doing?"

He glanced at her and shrugged. "Life sucks, Shar."

Yeah, well, she wasn't going to argue with him on that. "I know."

He lifted his whiskey and she raised her margarita and they clinked. Then he swallowed every drop of his drink and waved Gina over.

He pointed to Shar's half-empty margarita glass. "Want another of those or you want to try a grown-up beverage?"

Shar studied the ice chips left at the bottom of his whiskey glass. "Your grown-up drink sounds good to me, but I want the happy syrup in mine, instead of whatever she added to yours."

This earned her a lazy half grin from Dec and a laugh from Gina.

"Two whiskey sours," he said to Gina. "But give Shar all of my maraschino cherries and maybe a little extra cherry juice, okay? She wants *happy* syrup."

"Sure thing," the bartender said, smiling. She brought over the drinks immediately, and Dec handed her a large bill.

"Oh, here," Shar said, opening her purse. "Let me give you—"

"Nah, it's on me," he told her. "You already cheered me up a bit. I'm grateful."

"So, what's wrong in your world?" Shar asked once Gina had moved out of earshot. "Why does life suck? Not that I don't have my own reasons for believing that, too..."

He raised a dark eyebrow. "I'll share if you'll share."

She nodded.

✿❀✿

GOING FOR IT (BONUS CROSSOVER NOVELLA) - OUT NOW!

Mirabelle Harbor meets Sapphire Falls...

Journalist Trevor Cayne is working on the biggest feature story of his career, and he's on a road trip from his home in the lakeside Chicago suburb of Mirabelle Harbor to Colorado Springs to get the final details. But a quick stop to see his grandmother in Sapphire Falls threatens to derail his carefully constructed plans. Between Gram and her friends, the weather whims of Mother Nature, and the most stunning redhead he's ever laid eyes on in his life, he may not make it further than the western edge of Nebraska.

Aspiring singer-songwriter Tina Marie Moran has vowed to leave Sapphire Falls for Nashville after this week's big fireworks—she's not even waiting for the Annual Town Festival to come to an end. She's put her music dreams on hold for long enough and has no intention of postponing her plans yet again, least of all for another potentially untrustworthy man. But between her loving but meddlesome relatives and friends, a broken heart that's in desperate need of mending, and a handsome stranger who can play her body like a virtuoso lead guitarist, she may find herself engulfed in a new passion that's as strong as her love of music.

When it comes to their creative lives, both Trevor and Tina Marie know all about GOING FOR IT—but are they willing to put that same drive into what just might be the love of a lifetime?

From the Novel:

Trevor was biding his time.

Thankfully, the motel Tina Marie spotted had available rooms for tonight, and they were able to get two with an adjoining door. But, however clearly he might remember her passionate kiss from yesterday, he knew better than to make a move on a woman who was determined to be "just friends." She'd have to come to him first. Which meant he had to be so damn appealing that she couldn't resist. How to ensure that?

Obviously, he needed expert advice. And he knew just where to get it.

When Tina was getting settled into her motel room, he used the time to unpack, change into a dry shirt, brush his teeth and gargle (a guy's breath could never be too fresh), and text his buddy, Blake Michaelsen.

"Got a sec to answer a few questions?" he typed.

Less than fifteen seconds later, his phone buzzed. "Yeah, shoot," came his friend's reply.

Blake was a popular DJ back home in Mirabelle Harbor. He worked at 102.5 "LOVE" FM and spent most of his days—and occasionally some nights—spinning romantic hits for the masses. Let's just say, Blake hadn't been a big believer in love. At least not until he got his heart all tangled up with Vicky, the high-school French teacher. Now he was singing a different tune.

"Okay. So, there's this woman I met. She's gorgeous.

Sweet. We've got amazing chemistry, and we're at a hotel tonight," Trevor began, sending this first part to Blake.

Before he could write out his question, his friend texted back, "If you're in a hotel with her, what the hell are you doing texting me? Priorities, man."

"She and I live in different cities, Blake. She says she wants to be just friends, which I hate but understand. No way could this be anything but a fling... Still, I want her. Even if it's just for tonight. How do I get her to want to stay with me while being honest about it?"

This time there was a longer pause. Finally, his buddy replied. "One word: Foreplay."

Trevor groaned. "Yeah, no shit, Blake. I'm not 14. I mean, what's the fastest, most effective kind?"

"Dancing, or any excuse you have to touch her in a socially acceptable fashion. Food, as in feeding it to her. Attentive listening, which I suck at, but Vicky tells me that's an aphrodisiac for a lot of women."

Trevor grinned. Yeah, Blake was more of a talker than a listener.

"Oh!" Blake added. "You might try a movie. Action thrillers boost adrenaline and can be a turn-on for both sexes. Just read a nonfiction bestseller about that. Check the TV listings."

There was a knock on Trevor's interior door. Tina Marie.

"Good ideas, man," he texted Blake back. "Thanks. Gotta go." Then he opened the connecting door for her and caught his breath at the sight.

Gone was the thin summer dress with the yellow translucent fabric, and in its place was a hip-hugging pair of blue jeans and a long-sleeved baby-blue shirt that caressed her chest and clung to every curve. He wanted to pull her into his arms and strip off both items, along with anything she might have on underneath. But, first, he had to convince her to say yes...

Learn more about the Mirabelle Harbor books on Marilyn's website page for the series:

www.marilynbrant.com/books/the-mirabelle-harbor-series/

<u>A Note to Readers on the Chronology</u>: The entire Mirabelle Harbor series takes place over roughly a two-year time frame. Each book in the following list can be read as a standalone story.

Year One:
Take a Chance on Me (Chance & Nia) - April/May
The One That I Want (Julia & Dane) - June/July/August
Stranger on the Shore (Marianna & Gil) - June/July/August
You Give Love a Bad Name (Blake & Vicky) -
September/October

Year Two:
Going for It/Kindle World Bonus Story (Trevor & Tina
Marie) - June
One Night Love Affair (Sharlene & Declan) - July
Rocket Man/Coming Home (Abby & Rick) - October
Someone Like You/Coming Home (Chandler & Jaleina) -
December

ABOUT THE AUTHOR

Marilyn Brant has been told she writes with honesty, liveliness and wit (descriptors she's grown terribly fond of) about complex, intelligent women—like her friends—and their significant personal relationships. Although her favorite pursuits undoubtedly involve books, she proves she's not just a literary snob by confessing her lifelong fascination (read: obsession) with popular music, especially from the '70s and '80s, most flavors of ice cream, and a variety of sensuous body lotions/oils.

As a former teacher, library staff member, freelance magazine writer, and national book reviewer, Marilyn has spent much of her life lost in literature. She is the *New York Times* and *USA Today* bestselling and award-winning author of twenty novels and novellas to date, and a lifetime member of the Jane Austen Society of North America. The Illinois Association of Teachers of English (IATE) selected her as their 2013 Author of the Year.

Her debut coming-of-age novel, *ACCORDING TO JANE* (Kensington, 2009), featuring the ghost of Jane Austen giving a young woman dating advice, won the Romance Writers of America's prestigious Golden Heart Award and the Booksellers' Best, and it was named one of the "Top 100 Romance Novels of All Time" by Buzzle.com. Her second novel, *FRIDAY MORNINGS AT NINE* (Kensington, 2010), was a Doubleday and Book-of-the-Month Club pick in women's fiction. *A SUMMER IN EUROPE* (Kensington, 2011) was featured in the Literary Guild and BOMC2, and it became a Top 20 Bestseller in Fiction and Literature for the Rhapsody Book Club. The Polish translation of the novel was released in June 2013.

She's also a #1 Kindle & #1 Nook bestseller, who writes fun and flirty romantic comedies, like her stories in *THE SWEET TEMPTATIONS COLLECTION*, that involve sweet treats, unexpected love, and large doses of humor. *THE ROAD TO YOU*—a coming-of-age romantic mystery—was selected as one of the Top 20 Best Books of the Year (December 2013) by The Reading Frenzy. She just finished work on the "Mirabelle Harbor" romances. Look for the completed series: *TAKE A CHANCE ON ME, THE ONE THAT I WANT, YOU GIVE LOVE A BAD NAME, STRANGER ON THE SHORE, ONE NIGHT LOVE AFFAIR, COMING HOME,* and the bonus Kindle Worlds crossover novella, *GOING FOR IT!* Also, be sure to check out her short story, "When Life Imitates Art," in RWA's upcoming romantic anthology, *SECOND CHANCES.*

Marilyn currently lives in the Chicago suburbs with her family. When she isn't reading her friends' books or watching old movies, she's working on her next novel, eating chocolate indiscriminately, and hiding from the laundry.

Please visit her website: www.MarilynBrant.com.